ACCIDE... SERIES:

"With its sharp, witty writing and unique characters, Angie Fox's contemporary paranormal debut is fabulously fun."
—*Chicago Tribune*

"This rollicking paranormal comedy will appeal to fans of Dakota Cassidy, MaryJanice Davidson, and Tate Hallaway."
—*Booklist*

"A new talent just hit the urban fantasy genre, and she has a genuine gift for creating dangerously hilarious drama."
—*RT Book Reviews*

If you're looking for a funny paranormal romp with a little heat and lots of action, this book is for you.
—*Fresh Fiction*

"Filled with humor, fans will enjoy Angie Fox's lighthearted frolic."
—*Midwest Book Review*

"This book is a pleasure to read. It is fun, humorous, and reminiscent of Charlaine Harris or Kim Harrison's books."
—*Sacramento Book Review*

D1014307

My *Big Fat* Demon Slayer Wedding

Angie Fox

NEW YORK TIMES BESTSELLING AUTHOR

MORE BOOKS FROM ANGIE FOX

The Accidental Demon Slayer series
The Accidental Demon Slayer
The Dangerous Book for Demon Slayers
A Tale of Two Demon Slayers
The Last of the Demon Slayers
My Big, Fat Demon Slayer Wedding

The Monster MASH trilogy
Immortally Yours
Immortally Embraced
Immortally Ever After

Short Stories
Gentlemen Prefer Voodoo
(from the My Zombie Valentine anthology)
Murder on Mysteria Lane
(from The Real Werewives of Vampire County
anthology)
What Slays in Vegas
(from the So I Married a Demon Slayer anthology)

To learn more about upcoming releases, sign up for
Angie's quarterly newsletter at www.angiefox.com

To my daughter, Maddie, who was just named "best writer" by her third grade class. I am so proud of you, sweetie.

Acknowledgements

Special thanks to Alexx Miller and Sherrie Hill for early reads.

CHAPTER ONE

My biker witch grandma shut down her Harley and pulled off her helmet, letting loose a tangle of long, gray hair. "You need help, Lizzie Brown," she said, as if I were the one sporting a flaming skull do-rag, rhinestone-studded riding glasses, and a brand new *Ride It Like You Stole It* tattoo.

I snorted. "I'm not the one making us late." I pried off my riding gloves as she blithely hitched her leg over her motorcycle. Shaking my head, I watched her amble toward a bohemian farmers market set up on the side of a country road. It was as if it sprang from the earth between two California strawberry fields.

There was nothing to the place—a stretch of sandy soil in front of a half-dozen or so colorful tents. A mishmash of tables held everything from broccoli to kiwi, mixed in with dozens of kinds of jams, a healthy display of pottery, and a few more specialized booths.

"This better be important," I said, finding my sunglasses in my back pocket.

Not that I objected to the woman selling erotic redwood carvings or the guy peddling bongs made from hollowed-out pineapples and carrots, but we had a bridal tea party in about an hour, and seeing that I was the bride, I'd rather not be late.

Grandma waited for me to catch up, her eyes narrowing. "This is vital resource gathering," she said, which had been her excuse for leaving the main road in the first place. "And if you want to know why we stopped here, take a look at your necklace."

I glanced down. When we'd first met, my fiancé had given me an emerald pendant that held ancient protective magic. Only it had been cold and unresponsive ever since our run in with the Earl of Hell. Now the large, teardrop shaped stone glowed against my bare skin. "Why?" I asked, touching it, feeling the warmth radiate from it.

Grandma shook her head. "Impossible to say. I'll feel better after I grab some goodies to juice my protective wards."

This entire stop made me nervous. "Let's make it quick," I said, heading for the market.

Grandma snorted as she fell in next to me.

Yes, well, we'd just sent twenty-four biker witches, plus my dog, to my mother's party before us.

Maybe I was glad I wouldn't be around for that part.

I hadn't even seen my mother since I'd become a demon slayer. And now, in true Hillary Brown style, she'd flown in from Atlanta, rented a historic house, and was throwing a week's worth of parties before my wedding. I'd run into many fearsome creatures, but nothing like my mom in full hostess mode.

I sighed as Grandma shook the road dust from her fringed black leather pants.

The two sides had to meet sooner or later. Still, *Better Homes & Gardens* was my mom's bible, and the biker witches only knew the difference between lilac and mint because they used both in the spell jars they liked to hurl at people who wanted to kill us.

"What are we looking for?" I asked, as she headed for the fruit stand.

"Kiwis, apples, and grave dirt," she said, nodding to

the guy behind the table. "The fresher the better."

I shrugged. "At least with the fruit."

She merely rolled her eyes.

Grandma didn't like staying in new places without casting a spell to see what was already in the neighborhood. I was all for it, in theory, but in this case, I wished we could have skipped it.

I leaned up against a tent pole while she struck up a lively conversation with the vendor about male versus female fruit. *Because that makes a difference in spell casting.*

Hells bells, it probably did.

Meanwhile the too-skinny, hippie-looking bong seller kept trying to make eye contact with me. Please. I'd tried real cigarettes only once. On a dare. After a particularly strong amaretto sour. I hadn't been much of a risk taker before I'd learned I was a demon slayer and hooked up with the biker witches. I was still getting used to it.

I gazed out over the strawberry fields.

Wouldn't you know it—there was a small family graveyard near the edge, partially shaded by a copse of trees. It was old, with an iron gate that leaned drunkenly to one side.

Nothing like one stop shopping.

I was half way there when the emerald at my neck began to hum. I stopped.

This was the necklace that had morphed into body armor when I needed it, tied me to a tree when I didn't, and fainted dead away at the sight of the Earl of Hell. I supposed everything had its limits.

I held my breath as the bronze chain went liquid, reforming into a heavier looped chain. The warm metal poured over and around the emerald. It hardened around the stone, transforming the pendant into an ornate bronze locket with the emerald at the center.

Okay. I had to think about this one.

I'd never had my jewelry transform into…jewelry.

A change in the necklace usually meant I was about to face a confrontation, or that I needed protection. In this case, I had a stylish accessory.

I blew out a breath. The more I learned about demon slaying, the more I needed to figure out.

Grandma was busy inspecting an apple as if she could see through it. No help there. I didn't feel as if I were in immediate danger. Of course, that usually meant I was about to get ambushed.

The new pendant felt heavy around my neck, ominous. I approached the cemetery a little slower than before. Beyond it lay the ruins of an old Victorian farmhouse. No telling how long ago the family had abandoned this place, and their dead.

A warm breeze blew in from the south as I pushed open the gate. It creaked from time and neglect. There were only three graves that I could see. Scraggly grass and weeds clung to the sandy soil around them.

Two of the graves were marked with standard, rounded headstones. The last one, on the far right, was shaped like an obelisk. It must have been grand at one time. It had softened at the edges with age and black discoloration had washed over the stone. The battered inscription read: Elizabeth 1893.

I bent in front of it and gathered a palm full of dirt. Where I was going to put it was another question.

"Help me," a voice whispered.

I spun and drew a switch star from my belt. Switch stars were the weapon of the slayers. It was round-shaped like a Chinese throwing star, only with jagged edges that twirled like saw blades when I threw it.

But there was no one behind me to fight. I turned in a small circle. A trickle of sweat slicked the back of my neck. I could have sworn I heard a voice. It was urgent, desperate.

"Hello?" I asked, fingers digging into the grips on the star.

A breeze rustled through the trees.

"Help me."

"Who are you?" I demanded.

There was no response.

I waited, opening up my demon slayer senses and searching for anything, good or evil, that could have made that request.

There was nothing.

Grandma ambled up from the market, a produce bag in hand.

"What are you doing?" She eased through the gate I'd left half open. "You say you're in a hurry and I catch you farting around in the cemetery."

I sheathed my switch star. "I heard a voice," I said, scanning the cemetery, half expecting to hear it again.

She stood next to me, listening, her hands on her hips, the bag dangling from her left wrist. After a little while, she shrugged. "I doubt it's anybody we know. You get the dirt?"

"I'm working on it." I'd been a little distracted.

She pulled a Ziploc from her pocket and bent to grab some from the grave at my feet. The one where I'd heard...something.

"Take it from the middle one instead," I told her.

She shrugged and did as I asked.

I touched my necklace, which was now a locket.

Now or never.

Maybe I hadn't even heard a voice, but I was pretty sure that I had. I couldn't get it out of my head.

There was no telling who it belonged to, or why it had spoken to me. But it didn't feel threatening or evil.

I couldn't walk away, not without trying to make a difference.

Besides, my necklace had always looked out for me in the past, protected me. And it had given me a way to take some of the grave dirt with me.

I bent and pinched two fingers full from the base of the obelisk. Grandma raised her brows, but didn't say anything as I opened my locket and stashed it inside.

CHAPTER TWO

We gunned our engines and made it back to the Pacific Coast Highway in record speed. It was a gorgeous, cliff-hugging thrill ride.

I felt good. *Alive.*

Yes, my biker witch family was about to meet my society family. And yes, we were also going to be adding my fiancé's Greek relatives into the mix. But I was also about to marry the most gorgeous, sexy, strong, and wonderful man on the planet.

End of story. I hoped.

It was pretty remote this far south of Monterey. We passed Hearst Castle, with its spires jutting out to the impossibly blue sky. There was almost no shoulder on the right of the road, only a sharp drop to the ocean. To the left were hills lush with spiky wild grasses and dotted with blue oaks, their knotted trunks twisted like bohemian art.

I could see why turn-of-the-century timber barons and railroad tycoons built their getaways out here among the cliffs and the wilderness. It felt like another world, one where I could easily lose myself.

In fact, I almost missed the turn off, a lonely paved road mostly hidden by a large cypress. An iron spike jutted from the ground near the tree, and it had white and silver balloons tied around it. My wedding colors.

My front tire skidded sideways as I turned a little too fast. Grandma was right behind; but her rubber burn was deliberate.

"You should have gone with black and silver," she hollered over the noise of the engines.

"So you don't have to buy a new outfit? I don't like you that much," I said, noticing the mini champagne glasses dangling from the balloon ties. Leave it to my mother.

Grandma let out a guffaw as I gunned my engine past the gate and up the drive. Frankly, I'd get married in a garden shed if it meant saying 'yes' to Dimitri. We'd been through so much together, and there had been times when I wondered if my life, *if being with me*, was too much for him. Not everyone is cut out to marry a demon slayer.

He loved me. He really did. And I would never take that for granted.

The drive wound up a hill, with cypress planted in neat rows on either side, interspersed with—I slowed my bike to get a better look—stone gargoyles. I was used to seeing them on buildings, not as yard art. Someone had interesting taste.

At the top of the hill, the path opened up to a large, flat lawn with artfully trimmed hedges, a fountain and one of the most bizarre looking old mansions I'd ever seen.

It was made entirely of black stone, with ominous looking sculptures anchored to the swooping gray slate roof. They looked like werewolves, only stockier, with sharp spines on their backs and mouths full of angry black teeth.

It was enough to make me pull up short. "What are those?" I squinted to get a better look. "And what's with the pitch of the roof?" You could build a ski jump up there.

Grandma shielded her eyes with her hand. "Oh, the shock of it. A millionaire with more money than taste." She unstrapped her helmet. "You should see the crazy looking spikes on the roof of the Winchester Mystery House."

"I'll put that on the list." I hadn't traveled much, at least until I'd gotten mixed up with Grandma and her gang. We'd been too busy fighting minions of the underworld to do much sight seeing.

Still, I could see the recruitment posters now: *Be a demon slayer and see the world!*

So far, I'd been to Las Vegas, California, the Greek islands—not to mention, purgatory, hell and a psycho demon's laboratory. Come to think of it, a recruiter would need more than a poster.

I hitched a leg over my bike and almost stepped into one of the elaborately trimmed bushes. It sported inch-long thorns and red berries that were probably poisonous.

Never mind. Unless it grew fangs and tried to eat me, I wasn't going to let a creepy shrub ruin my day.

I dug in my saddlebags for my overnight backpack.

We had a week. One week. And I was going to enjoy it, even if my mom had rented some crazy gothic house in the middle of nowhere.

Hades. I slung my bag over my shoulder.

The sprawling main building had a tower on each side. It looked like there might even be a stone walkway above the second floor, below the roof. The windows were opulent, pointed at the top and decorated with stone carvings of vines and crazy beasts.

It was untamed, fantastical even. I shook my head. I couldn't escape the fact. "This is so unlike Hillary."

"To be fair, you sprang an entire summer wedding on her," Grandma said, drawing a few spell jars out of her saddlebag. "She was probably lucky to find this place."

"Are you expecting trouble?" I asked as she handed me a Mind Wiper. Inside, a living spell hovered. It was sticky sweet pink and reminded me of a gob of silly putty. The spell refashioned itself at will—flattening, lengthening, and twirling. It saw me watching and did a somersault before thunking up flat against the glass. "Hello to you, too."

Grandma grinned, her eyes crinkling at the corners. "That's Rose." She held up her own jar. "I've got Blanche and Dorothy, you know, in case things get out of hand." She shrugged a shoulder. "Like usual."

"Yes, well let's hope the Golden Girls can take a break." I balanced the jar against my hip as I veered toward the side of the house. "I want to try and go in the back way," I said when she hesitated.

Grandma frowned. "You sense something bad? If something's after us, Lizzie, it's going to attack no matter what."

"Who said anything about attacking?" I asked, skirting around a box hedge. "I'm trying to avoid my mother. At least until I change out of these leather pants." Not to mention my midriff-baring purple bustier. Hillary would blow a gasket if she saw me in this get-up.

Grandma caught up to me. "Let me get this straight," she drawled. "You're willing to face off against the Earl of Hell, but you don't want your mamma to see you in leather pants?"

"That's about right." And I wasn't going to apologize for it, either.

I ignored her chuckling and opened up my slayer powers. Just in case.

We passed a crowd of bikes parked next to several trellises of purple roses.

"This place is buck wild," I said, looking twice at a fountain along the side of the house. The laughing centaur at the center looked like he could eat my face. *Relax.* He was made of iron. Completely decorative. Maybe we could give him a little flower necklace or something.

Now I was thinking like Hillary.

But truly, even if this place was creepy, and the result of a lack of time—or options—mom had unwittingly found the perfect location to stash biker witches, griffins, my pet dragon and anyone else who might be a little noticeable at a more traditional wedding. Not to mention my mentor, the necromancer.

Grandma seemed to be thinking the same thing. "I got to tell you, I haven't been anywhere this nice since your uncle's funeral in Vegas."

I didn't remind her that she'd been to Dimitri's villa in Santorini. The biker witches had definitely left their mark.

"This may look imposing, but I really am keeping the wedding simple," I said, rounding the corner.

Out back was a huge garden, with stone-lined paths and all kinds of plants and flowers done up in triangular patterns. Silver pots filled with purple prairie flowers and tied with a white ribbon lined the walk up to a large, stone porch.

Yes, Hillary was in charge. Obviously. But I wasn't having any bridesmaids, I ordered my dress from the Ann Taylor online store and we were keeping this as straightforward as possible. And I loved my dress, by the way. It was simple, classic, like I'd always wanted.

Grandma stopped as she eyed the obnoxiously large white tulip and magnolia wreath on the back door. "Does your mom know you're a demon slayer yet?"

"I want to tell her in person," I said, as if I hadn't been avoiding the entire conversation.

She snarfed. "Did you tell her we're witches?"

This whole thing was making me uncomfortable. "I wasn't exactly sure how to phrase that."

She gave me a sidelong glance. "You did mention that the groom is a mythical shape-shifting griffin."

"No," I snapped. I'd tell Hillary in my own good time. Preferably before Dimitri or any of his relatives landed in the back yard. "First, we're going to get through the tea party this afternoon."

There had to be a downstairs bathroom where I could ditch the leather outfit, the shiny black boots, my Harley branded headband, my spell jar. I didn't want to forget my studded leather bracelets, either.

Then I'd stash my switch stars in a straw purse. I'd trade the rest of it for a flowered sundress, wedge sandals and a large hat because, well, my hair was a permanent lavender color thanks to a spell gone wrong.

I took the porch steps two at a time. At least my hair had grown out a bit in the last few months. It was maybe an inch off my shoulders. I dug my fingers through it, trying to put it up in a French twist under the hat. No such luck.

"This garden is great," Grandma said, heading the opposite direction. "She's got mint and chamomile, white sage and sweet grass. And look! Diviner's sage! Right there!" Grandma pointed as if it was the find of the century, as if my mother had somehow planted it all. "You've got to see this."

"Don't pick any plants," I told her. The garden was pretty. Gorgeous, in fact. "I might get married right there."

"On the back porch?" Grandma asked, rooting through the plants. "If that's the case, I'd have dragged you in front of a minister in Las Vegas. At least there you could have gotten married by Elvis."

"No," I said, as she picked some white sage. "I'm going to have a classic wedding."

With biker witches.

I tried not to cringe. Or care that she was stuffing lavender springs into her belt.

Focus on things you can control. Like getting changed before my mom saw me.

Out of habit, my right hand wandered down to my switch stars as I opened the iron and stained glass back door.

So far, so good.

I eased my way inside and found myself in a Spanish kitchen as big as my old house.

The original floor and fixtures looked to be at least one hundred years old, with intricate mosaic designs and large racks of copper pots and pans hanging from the ceiling. The appliances were new, gleaming stainless steel. The countertops and cabinets were dark and imposing, as was a large, wooden table that could seat at least twenty.

A narrow hall led toward the front of the house. There had to be a bathroom somewhere nearby.

"Lizzie?" I heard my mom's voice from only a few rooms away.

Cripes.

Yes, I was a big, bad demon slayer, but for a moment, I really considered ducking behind the massive kitchen island.

The sharp clack of Hillary's kitten heels on the tile sounded like nails in my coffin.

"I heard you pull up," she called. "Next time, try the front door. I know it looks heavy, but it opens fine."

I froze. My mind swirled with panic as my mother rounded the corner. And stopped.

She brought a French manicured hand up to her mouth to stifle a gasp.

Hillary Brown wore an immaculately tailored, white button down dress, along with a pink pearl necklace and matching earrings. Her straight, pale, blond hair curled perfectly at her ears and shoulders. Her skin was unnaturally smooth for her age, as if someone had taken a sand blaster too it. Or more accurately, a scalpel. I'd never seen Hillary when she hadn't been polished to within an inch of her life.

And I looked like a biker witch.

She stared at me for one long moment.

My heart thumped against my chest. I clutched the jar with Grandma's Mind Wiper spell and briefly considered using it.

Instead, I pasted on my best good-daughter smile. "Hi, mom!" I said, trying for cheerful and sounding more like a drunken cheerleader.

She tried to respond but her face had frozen into a pasted-on smile-of-horror. "What on Earth...*happened* to you?"

CHAPTER THREE

My face heated and I began to sweat. Buckets. I pulled up my bustier, even though it was in no danger of falling down. "Funny thing. I was just getting ready to change."

Good God. The last time I'd seen my mom, I was wearing khaki pants and a yellow sweater, along with sensible Oxford shoes. I drove a Saturn. I went to bed at ten o'clock. I worked as a preschool teacher, and I didn't even kill spiders, much less soul-sucking demons.

Had I wiped off my Sinfully Red lipstick? I didn't think so.

She closed the distance between us, as if I was a wild animal and she was afraid to move too fast. "It's good to see you," she said, drawing me into an awkward hug. She smelled like clean cotton and orange blossoms, like always.

Hillary gave a hard exhale and pulled me tighter. It felt nice. She didn't like to touch people. She didn't always express her emotions and, "oof," all of the air left my lungs as she tightened her grip even more.

I managed to pull back. "Thanks for coming." She hated when I called her Hillary.

"It's your wedding," she said, as if it were the most obvious thing in the world. She held me at arm's length. Her brows pinched. "Besides, you need me. I swore I'd never be *that* mom, but in heaven's name, Lizzie, what are you doing to yourself?"

"This?" I said, as if I'd noticed it for the first time. "This is nothing. I have a nice sundress in my bag." As if that would make her go easy on me now.

She looked at me like I'd stripped down naked right there in the kitchen. "Your hair is purple."

Ah. "That was actually a mistake." I'd gotten hit with a biker witch spell that made my hair go prematurely gray. We'd tried to fix it with a counter-spell, but I'd left that on too long because my long-lost biological father had shown up in a tower of flame.

But I didn't think my adoptive mom wanted to hear that.

From the way she kept opening and closing her mouth, she'd had about as much as she could handle already. She paused, straightened her already squared shoulders. "Is this type of style…" she waved a hand over me, "appealing to you? You look like a hooligan."

I let out a sigh. "Try biker."

She glanced past me, toward the back door, as if she knew Grandma was out there rooting around in the garden. "I'm glad you found your biological Grandmother, but you don't have to dress like her. You have so many nice clothes, Lizzie."

Yes, but it wasn't up to her to dictate where and when I wore them. "I can't ride a Harley in white Capri pants." If there were a way, I would have figured it out a long time ago.

She crossed her arms over her chest. "Is there some kind of rule that you can't look nice?"

"Mom," I glanced out over the kitchen, "I haven't been here for five minutes."

She looked so truly pained that I almost felt sorry for her.

Until she gave me the death glare. "Are you rebelling against the way you were raised? Is this my fault?"

As if I, who I was, was somehow bad or unacceptable or wrong.

"They're only clothes." What I needed on the road. To do my job. And I was damned good at it, thank-you-very-much.

Her eyes trained on the switch stars at my waist. "That belt could *cut* you."

It had actually saved my life. Many times over.

At least she couldn't see the actual stars. Those were only visible to magical people. No, she was talking about the spikes that one of the biker witches had added between the oversized pockets on my utility belt. Sure, they were a little over the top, but I liked them. They made me feel badass.

She walked to the refrigerator and removed a bottle of white wine from the top shelf. "Has your fiancé seen this side of you?" She retrieved two glasses from above a large wine rack built in under the counter. "You'd better give up this lifestyle fast, because I don't see any respectable young man from a good family willing to put up with it."

Hmm…Dimitri had ripped off my leather pants before, but it wasn't out of disapproval. My blood heated at the thought of what that man could do to me.

She watched me carefully as she poured two glasses of Sauvignon Blanc.

Yes, life had changed since I'd last seen her. Still, "Deep down, I'm the same person."

Mostly.

Don't think about it.

I took a sip. The wine was tart, crisp and sharp. Very Hillary. "It's not like I can keep up with

Grandma while wearing heirloom pearls and driving an electric car."

Hillary hadn't touched her wine. She ran her manicured finger up and down the stem. "I want to support you, honey. But I worry. With the clothes and the hair and that awful belt...and what are you holding?"

I looked down to the recycled Smuckers jar in my hand, with the Mind Wiper spell plastered up against it like a lovesick puppy.

"This?" I had to think. "Ask Grandma."   ·

Her eyes widened.

"Or better yet, don't." She'd tell mom the truth. I stuffed the Mind Wiper in my bag. "For the record, I hate having purple hair."

She took a small sip of wine. "It's true things don't always turn out like we plan," she ventured.

"Like with this house?" I liked it, but it was so not Hillary.

She gave a small smile. A real one this time. "Most of the pictures they sent were of the gardens," she said, touching a wine droplet at the rim of her glass. "But you know me. I can make anything work."

"You can." It was the God's honest truth. Hillary was a master at planning and organizing. If I'd given her more time, it would have been frightening to see what she could do.

"Follow me," she said, placing her wine on the counter. "I'll show you where you can change."

The hallway was lined with oil paintings of nighttime landscapes and long-dead Victorians posing in uncomfortable clothes. We passed a formal dining room and a sitting room on the left, before we entered a spacious foyer.

Large red and silver patterned rugs decorated the

floor and tapestries hung from the carved wood walls. A classic staircase wound up to a second floor landing that boasted an impressive collection of medieval weapons, all within reach.

Those could come in handy. If I wasn't on vacation, which I was. Crimeny. Maybe my demon slayer lifestyle really had warped my brain.

"The bathroom is right through there," Hillary said, pointing to a door near the foot of the staircase.

"Thanks." I wrapped my hand on the faceted crystal handle and paused. I looked at her over my shoulder. "I know this house isn't something you'd normally choose, but I like it."

Hillary's gaze traveled over the room, as if cataloging everything she'd like to change. "I honestly can't figure out why I picked it," she said, sounding a little lost.

"Well, hey," I said, opening the door on a bathroom with gold plastered walls and an antique sink, "adventure is good." Most of the time. It certainly kept things from getting boring.

Her heels clacked on the tiled foyer and stopped. "I'd like to help you," she said. "With the hair at least."

Heaven above, I'd love it if she could return my hair to its normal dark, dark brown. I'd even settle for light brown, or blonde. I'd take Dolly Parton hair— anything but this unnatural, blaring shade of platinum purple. Still, I didn't want to get my hopes up.

"I've tried everything." I warned her. Sure, Hillary prided herself on her ruthless devotion to style, but, "This is one fashion faux pas I don't think you'll be able to fix."

She perked up at that. "Is that a challenge?"

Oh, no. I'd unwittingly matched an impossible job up against sheer Southern determination.

Hillary reached for my lavender bob. "You'd be surprised at what I've learned over the years." She ran her fingers through my hair, testing its weight, "Hmmm..." she clucked. "Interesting."

"What?" I asked, turning with her as she studied my situation.

She lifted a section and took a long look at my roots. "Do you trust your mother?"

"With my life," I said, wary of her satisfied grin.

"Then leave it to me."

CHAPTER FOUR

One makeover later, I was in danger of being late for the Celebration Tea.

No matter what I did, I couldn't pry myself away from the bathroom mirror. It wasn't the pink seersucker dress, or the diamond studs in my ears. I was wearing my natural hair color. I'd almost forgotten what it felt like to look utterly and blessedly normal.

What was truly disturbing was that I didn't know if I liked it or not.

Now that I had my own hair again, I couldn't stop looking at it, touching it. Hillary, with much more glee than necessary, had treated me with her own special blend of organic herbs and colorants. And it worked. She'd brought me back. I couldn't get over it.

She stood behind me, smiling as I ran my hands through my hair yet again.

Her fingertips dusted my shoulder. "I'll mix a blend for you to use whenever you need." She'd even given me a trim so that my dark hair fell in stylish layers around my face.

"I still don't know how you did it." She'd defied biker witch magic.

Hillary made her own adjustments to her impossibly perfect hair. "Never under-estimate your mother." She patted me on the shoulder. "Time to go. The caterers are ready with tea."

"Right," I said, playing with my hair the entire way as she led me to toward the large sitting room off the foyer. I remembered seeing it when I came in.

A black stone fireplace dominated the room, with an aged wooden shield mounted over it. A coat of arms was carved into the shield, with painted chalices and red pansies. I pitied the knight who had to go into battle with wine glasses and flowers on his shield.

A round, wrought-iron chandelier hung from the ceiling. Under it, Grandma and her biker witch buddies crowded onto the dark red and black leather couches and overflowed onto spare chairs from the dining room. I stifled a gasp. They'd changed as much as I had.

Grandma sat in a straight-backed medieval-looking chair wearing a loud, colorful flowered dress that looked like it had come from a psychotic Hawaiian Mumu enthusiast or more likely, a Goodwill reject box. She'd styled her hair into an honest-to-god bun and had tied a yellow ribbon around it.

Next to her, Frieda had wrapped herself in a tweed suit with a pink silk shirt that tied at the neck into the biggest bow I'd ever seen. She'd tamed her blonde hair from its usual bouffant style and had wound it into a helmet-head bun that had been hair sprayed to within an inch of its life—as if that was what people wore to tea parties.

Buns.

They must have seen it in a magazine.

Creely the engineering witch had gone for the *Little House on the Prairie* look, but had neglected to remove the mini silver deer skulls that dangled from her ears. Or perhaps she figured it completed the look.

My dog, Pirate, was nowhere in sight. However, his pet dragon, Flappy, had his large, nose pressed up against the bay window. Flappy snorted, fogging the glass around his pink and ivory mottled snout. I pretended not to notice.

I still didn't know why my dog needed a pet. The white, snaggle-toothed beast was the size of an SUV, and still growing. At least non-magical people couldn't see him.

Hillary was having enough of a shock as it was. True to form, she kept it all inside. Still, I couldn't help noticing how she stared at the witch who was displaying ample cleavage above a corseted, medieval gown. Two Date Tessa actually looked good. As for the rest of them?

There was no leather, no denim, no doo-rags. Only fashion mistakes as far as the eye could see.

Hillary and I exchanged a glance.

"Welcome to the Celebration Tea!" she chirped, clearly determined to forge ahead, blithely ignoring the biker witch to her left, who was studying a dainty porcelain cup like it was a moon rock. Mom painted a smile on her face. "This is the first event in a week of friendship, family, and joy that will lead us to Lizzie and Dimitri's big day."

I'd happily skip right to the wedding.

She gestured at two catering assistants, who entered from the arched doorway off the dining room. They held gleaming silver serving pots.

"Simply turn over your cups," Hillary instructed as the biker witches eyed the delicate painted tea sets in front of them. "And tell Tina or Gina which of our *seventeen* specialty teas you'd prefer. Each one of them is organic and caffeine free!"

Grandma turned over her teacup like she expected a bug to crawl out from under it.

My assigned chair was across from the couch that held Grandma, Ant Eater and Frieda. At least, I thought the spot was mine. It had a white and silver bow attached. Let's hope I wouldn't have to strangle anyone with it. So far, the witches were remarkably well behaved.

I turned over the pink teacup in front of me, recognizing it from mom's display case back home. She really did go all out. These antique serving sets were from her special collection. I couldn't help but feel touched, and a little worried.

Ant Eater, grandma's second in command, stared at me from behind a green and gold painted fan, as if she needed some kind of spiritual protection from what was taking place. It was clear Grandma had dressed her—and done her hair. The biker witch slowly lowered the barrier, her good tooth glinting in the sunlight streaming through the window. "What happened to your hair?"

"My mom fixed it," I said, refusing to feel embarrassed for looking like myself.

Her eyes traveled over my Malibu Barbie outfit. Okay. So I wasn't exactly the seersucker sundress type anymore, but I didn't think Ant Eater had suddenly taken to giraffe patterned Mumu's, so she could cut me some slack.

I was about to tell her that when Gina, the caterer, popped up on my left faster than Pirate on a pork chop. She wore black pants, a white shirt and a permanent smile. "Hi!" she said, holding out a basket with tea bags in organized slots. "We are so excited about our tea selection today. We have Green Mountain Flower, Pomegranate Black, Welsh Morning, Jasmine, Sweet Ginger Green—"

"Black tea would be fine," I said, as Ant Eater's eyes began to cross.

"Sure," Gina said, "Would that be Tibetan, Darjeeling, Assam—"

"You choose," I said, and then added, "Assam," when Gina seemed confused.

Across from me, Grandma kept eyeing the door and Frieda had gone a bit green.

"I'll have what she's having," Ant Eater said.

I tried to smile, but found I felt as ridiculous as the biker witches looked. It was as if we were all trying to be something we weren't.

Gina slipped a bag of Assam into Ant Eater's cup and poured steaming water over it.

She should like strong tea. "It's got a nice kick," I assured the wary biker witch.

"Like Jack Daniels nice?" Ant Eater asked.

Not quite.

But at least they were trying. I appreciated that. Even if Frieda's sleeve had already gotten into the clotted cream. She swirled her blueberry scone in the cream once more.

Somebody should tell her it wasn't a dipping sauce.

Then again, at least Frieda had sleeves. Yes, Grandma had wrapped several stretchy bangles around the phoenix tattoo on her upper right arm, but they didn't exactly hide anything.

My mother slipped into the chair next to me, teacup in hand.

"This is great, mom. Thanks." It really was nice to have everyone together, safe and happy; to know that the room was still standing after five minutes...

Mom smiled, reaching for a scone until she saw what Frieda was doing to the clotted cream. Hillary cleared her throat and selected a finger sandwich instead.

Maybe this would work out after all.

"So, my daughter tells me that you like motorcycles," Hillary said to Grandma.

Grandma nodded, actually taking care to finish chewing before she responded. "Yes. My," she searched for a word, absently drawing circles in the air with her sandwich, "colleagues and I...of the motorcycle persuasion...have been riding together for several years."

"Fascinating," Hillary said, taking a dainty bite of her cucumber sandwich.

"What she means," Frieda said, warming up as she took a stack of jam sandwiches cut into the shape of hearts. "Is that we had to run like shit from a goose from a fifth level demon before Lizzie here—"

"Frieda!" Grandma closed her hand over Frieda's arm and the blonde witch scattered sandwiches across the table. "The Fifth Level Demons," she said quickly, "are a—"

"Rock band," Ant Eater interjected, pointing her sandwich at Hillary.

Mom had that plastered smile on her face again. Not good.

I took a sip of tea, letting it scald all the way down to my stomach. It didn't help. I considered taking an English shortbread cookie, if only to have something to do. Creely solved that problem by walking past in her long skirt and knocking most of them onto the floor.

Two witches joined her in picking them up, eating as they went.

I willed Hillary not to look at them, and saw that she was too busy watching Frieda, Grandma and Ant Eater, as if she couldn't figure out exactly why they were at her party—or in my life.

Relax. I could do this. It's not like I'd expected them to become best friends. Still, with everyone trying, it would be nice if we could find some sort of common ground.

"I'll see to some more refreshments," Hillary said, standing too quickly. She practically sprinted from the room.

Once I was sure she was gone completely, I leaned forward and fought the urge to throttle Frieda. "What are you doing, telling her about demons?" I hissed.

She was wide-eyed. "It's common knowledge!" She whispered, too loudly for my taste. "Besides," she said, rubbing at her middle, smearing clotted cream as she did, "I can barely keep down my lunch. My girdle is about to cut me in half."

Oh, come on. "Then take it off.""Here?" She brightened.

"No." I snapped. "Grandma?" She'd side with me on this.

Grandma rolled her eyes. "She's got you there, Frieda. This isn't an underwear on the chandelier party." I smirked, until Grandma gave me a stern look. "Still, it's not Frieda's fault you're lying to Hillary."

Okay, so maybe I wasn't telling Hillary the whole truth, but, "What am I supposed to say to the woman? Hello, I'm sorry I haven't seen you in close to a year, but you should know that I'm now a demon slayer, I ride with biker witches, the Earl of Hell has it out for me, and by the way—there's a dragon outside your window."

Frieda shrugged. "It's a start."

Grandma leaned close, elbows on her knees. "Try to be honest with her," she said, glancing at a frowning Ant Eater, "she might surprise you."

I doubted it.

"In the mean time," Ant Eater said, stealing a finger swipe of the clotted cream from along the side of the bowl, "we'll do our part and try to get along with spider monkey."

Hells bells. "What are you talking about now?" They'd better not have brought any monkeys.

"That's our nickname for your mom," Ant Eater said, sliding the five remaining finger sandwiches off the platter and onto her lap. She resisted my death glare. "What? She said she's bringing more."

"Do *not* call my mom a spider monkey," I said. "She's a nice person." She was. It was a matter of getting to know her.

"Twitchy," Ant Eater said between bites.

"Skinny as all get out," Frieda added, stealing a sandwich off Ant Eater's lap.

As if she was one to talk.

Grandma nodded. "Screeches like a banshee when she gets mad."

"What did you do to upset her?" It couldn't have been worse than what I did.

Grandma shared a glance with Ant Eater. "There was a little trouble with our stuff when we got here. We sorted it out."

"Hey, at least we're all getting to know each other, right?" Creely said. I looked up to find the engineering witch, of all people, pouring more water into my cup. She gave everyone refills.

I tried to see past her full-on Laura Ingalls Wilder dress. "What happened to the caterer?"

Creely grinned. "Out in the garden having a giggle fit."

I caught her by her frilly, laced wrist, feeling the biker bracelets underneath. "You said you'd behave."

Creely shrugged. "Those kids needed a laugh. Besides, I can do her job even better."

Grandma took a sip of her tea and grinned. "Yes,

you can!"

I didn't like it. "What did you do?" I reached for my cup and about choked on a sip of pure Jack Daniels. "You spiked the water?" I hissed as Hillary entered the room, tray in hand.

"It's got a tea bag," Frieda reasoned.

I reached for the pot and lifted the lid. It looked like water. It smelled like water. But a little green spell floated on top. I reached for it, the hot water stinging my fingers as the spell skirted away.

"Lizzie!" My mother scolded. She'd stopped and was holding the tray of sandwiches, watching me like I'd gone off my rocker.

It wasn't hard to do around here.

"I was trying to get something out of the pot," I said, as Frieda began to giggle. "Stop it." I pointed to her. There was nothing funny about this.

Hillary placed a new plate of sandwiches as far away from Ant Eater as she could manage. Then I watched helplessly as mom refreshed her tea.

"You might not want to drink that," I told her.

"Nonsense," Hillary said. She raised the cup to her lips. "Where are my caterers?"

"On break," Frieda said as Hillary took a sip of her tea.

Mom jerked back, and then took another sip. "Champagne?"

"Say what?" I asked, watching, waiting for the inevitable shriek.

"Gina must have added even more specialty blends than I thought," Hillary said, voice warming. She broke into an incredulous smile. "My tea tastes like Dom Perignon Rose."

"Takes the edge off, right?" Creely said, slapping her on the back.

Frieda slammed a second cup. "Mine tastes like a Shamrock Shake, spiked with Baileys." She leaned forward on her elbows, legs spread as wide as her tapered suit skirt would allow. "Now how come McDonalds only makes Shamrock Shakes in March?"

"You're going to scald yourself," I warned as my mom drank her whole cup.

"It's actually the perfect temperature," she said, holding her cup out for a refill.

Ant Eater chuckled and even my mom started giggling.

"How fast does this stuff work?" I asked Creely, as my mom started downing a second helping. "Hey. Whoa." I tried to get a hand on mom's cup.

"It's just tea," Hillary said, maneuvering out of my reach, gripping it like a three-year-old with a toy.

Evidently Creely's spell worked very fast. Hillary was grinning like a mad woman. I'd never even seen my mom buzzed and now—

"Down the hatch," Ant Eater declared as everyone did a shot of tea.

"Fix this," I pleaded with Grandma, who at least had the decency to look guilty—as she poured another cup.

"At least everybody's having fun now," she said to me under her breath.

"Because you're getting them drunk," I said, as an impromptu game of *Up and Down the River* broke out at the next table.

Meanwhile, my mom had squeezed in next to Frieda on an already crowded couch. She had her legs crossed toward the witches and was leaning in like a co-conspirator. "So," she said, gesturing with her teacup, "you like it here, right? I was worried you wouldn't like it here. But I said, 'I can do this.' I said,

'Hillary, you don't need this whole shebang to be perfect. You only need it to *look* perfect.'"

Frieda nodded, her expression solemn. "I say the same thing when I make squirrel soup."

"Want to play a fun game?" Ant Eater asked, leaning over Frieda. "Drink every time Lizzie gives us that bug-eyed look. See?"

They all three swiveled at me, and burst into giggles, raised their cups and drank.

"I've got a better one," Frieda said, pouring more water into her cup. "You guys want to play *I Never?*"

Hillary leaned forward, fascinated. "What's that?"

Oh, no. I put my teacup down. "We do not need to be teaching her any drinking games."

Frieda wrapped an arm around my mom's shoulders. "*I Never* is a fun way for everybody to get to know each other."

My mom clasped her hands together. "I love games! What are the rules?"

She didn't like games. She never played games.

"It's easy," Frieda drawled. "When it's your turn, say something you've never done. Anyone who *has* done it has to take a sip of tea."

"Stop," I ordered them.

"Me first," Hillary said. "I Never…" She rubbed her hands together. "…visited Oklahoma!"

She giggled as all the biker witches drank.

Oh, come on. "That was so not…" You know what? Good. I was glad Hillary didn't know how to play. Maybe Frieda and company would get bored and stop.

Grandma piped in. "I never lied about my age."

Hillary paused, confusion flickering across her features as Frieda drank heartily. The biker witch wiped her mouth on her sleeve. "Remember. You drink if you've done it," she said, patting my mom on the leg. Hillary broke into a wide grin and drank.

"Let's talk about something else," I said. "Who wants to admit they're a biker witch?"

"I never skinny dipped," Ant Eater declared.

"We don't need to know that," I said, as everyone drank, except for my mom and me. Of course.

Frieda raised her cup, a mischievous grin tickling her lips. "I never had sex on the kitchen table."

My mom clinked her teacup against Frieda's and drank.

"Awww..." I used to have breakfast at that table. "M-o-m," I protested in a voice I swear I hadn't used since high school.

An hour with her and I'd already reverted back two decades.

Hillary wiped a dribble of tea off her bottom lip. "What honey? I'm a woman with needs. Thank goodness your father has never been shy—"

"Enough!" I'd pry the teacups from their hands if I had to.

Doggie claws scrambled across the hardwood. "Lizzie!"

Pirate, my Jack Russell Terrier, bolted into the sitting room like he was on fire. He was mostly white, with a dollop of brown on his back that wound up his neck and over one eye.

Ever since I became a demon slayer, I could talk to my dog. In real sentences. He thought it was the greatest thing on earth. For me, it depended on the day.

He skidded on the rug at the entrance and nearly thwacked into a plant stand before rushing headlong for me.

"Not now, Pirate" I said, as he leapt up into my arms. I awkwardly adjusted my cup on the table so it wouldn't get hit with a flailing dog leg.

"Oh, hell yes, now." Pirate squirmed, digging dirty

paws against my dress. "I can't believe you're in here clinking tea cups when we got problems."

Okay, well it was a good thing non-magical people, like Hillary, couldn't understand him. I managed to get my cup on the table. Barely. I then held my dog up and away from my dress. His knobby little legs dangled uselessly. "What's wrong?"

Pirate looked at my mom. "Let's just keep her away from the windows."

Yeah, well I had a feeling an entire marching band could parade by and my mom wouldn't notice.

Still, when I glanced at the big picture window, I didn't see anything. Not even a dragon.

Hillary wrinkled her nose. "I forgot what yappy dog you have."

"Oh, geez. He interrupted your game? I'm sorry." Not.

"What's he got?" Grandma asked, with a notable slur to her voice. She could understand Pirate, too. Most magical people could.

"I'll say it to you plain." Pirate struggled to get down. "I understand you have sandwiches. I am a big believer in food. But you need to see the creepy looking crazy bomb I found in the garden."

I stood. "I need to take Pirate out." He had a nose for trouble. And the will to find it. I buried my nose against the wiry fur at his neck. "You're going to show me and only me."

It's not like I could count on the biker witches' discretion at the moment.

Or their sobriety.

But before I left, I asked, "Can I borrow a quarter?"

Creely found one in her pocket. She handed it to me and I slammed it on the table.

"It's my wedding party," I announced, "and I say no more *I Never*. You can play *Quarters* instead."

"Strip quarters?" Frieda asked, hopefully.

"Regular quarters," I told her.

"Who knew she'd be such a bridezilla?" Frieda muttered to my mom.

I tucked Pirate under my arm and headed out.

Chapter Five

On the way out, I grabbed my switch star belt off the hall table. I never should have walked in there without it. Damn fashion. It wasn't just the weapons. The belt had pouches for various crystals, powders and any other concoctions the biker witches invented for me. Around here, it seemed I was going to need all the help I could get.

Pirate dashed ahead, his nails clicking against the slate tile. "It all started when I was digging in the rose garden."

"Pirate," I warned, slipping the belt around my waist.

That back garden was the only bright, non-Adams-Family spot in the house. I hoped.

I really didn't want to have my wedding in the gothic sitting room.

He tilted his head. "Well, I wasn't exactly digging. I simply happened to be there."

The dog did not know how to lie.

His tail was up, his legs going a mile a minute. "But I have to warn you, there may be a few holes. You gotta remember it's my instinct. It's not anything personal."

"Stick to the facts," I said, as he stopped at the back door.

He turned in a circle and sat. "Okay. I smelled something good. I followed it. Then I saw the creepy shit."

Good enough for me.

I opened the heavy wood door and Pirate led the way out into the garden. The late summer sun felt good on my face and arms. It was a relief to be outside where I had a chance to breathe, to think.

My utility belt was chilly around my waist. It was always ten degrees cooler than everything around it, which was a blessing in this case because I was sweating like a fiend.

We passed a sculpture of a crying mermaid as I followed my dog down a gray stone path through a series of low flowerbeds. The garden was laid out in a series of triangular plantings with paths criss-crossing them every so often.

In fact, we had to switch paths several times as we zigzagged deeper and deeper into the foliage. The constant hum of insects grew louder as the garden grew taller. Flowering wolf eye trees, their leaves streaked with red, hung heavy over us. They blocked the direct sun, making my skin chill.

Thorny rose bushes climbed to the left and right, their branches twisted, their foliage overlapping. Somebody needed to take a pair of pruning sheers out here. I had no doubt my mother would take care of it. Once she sobered up.

It could still be pretty. Bright.

"What exactly did you see?" I asked, as thorns reached out for my dress and arms.

"I'm getting to that." Pirate stopped. "Over there," he said, tilting his knobby little head to the left. "That's where I heard the noise." He growled low in his throat. "Sounded exactly like something that needed to be chased."

Definitely not a squirrel. Pirate was terrified of them. I eyed the thick tangle of foliage. There was no telling what could be in there.

He took off through the mass of rose bushes. "Well, I heard it, and you know we can't let that go."

"Not when you're obsessed with the mail man, delivery trucks, the neighbors walking by..." I followed. Barely.

"Do you see any of that around here?" he called through the bushes.

No. This place was downright macabre. Weren't gardens supposed to be open, cheerful places?

He was hard to see through all the foliage, and he was definitely moving faster than me. Thorns tore at my skin, and I raised my arms to keep them away from my face.

"So right here. *This* is where I was when I heard the noise," Pirate said, invisible in the tangle.

"Great." I had to get out of here.

"And this is where I went."

I heard a rustle up ahead and prayed it wasn't too far because, darn it, I was not a camping type of girl and this? Well, it kind of counted. "Pirate, where are you?"

"Here!" He said, as I cleared one last bush that tried to snag my eye. When I emerged from the mess, my entire body itching, I found him next to a large, ornate garden gate.

It was designed to look like a spider web, with intricate iron bars spread from the center. It was beautiful, really, if you discounted the squik factor. I wasn't a fan of spiders.

My necklace warmed against my throat.

Tall stone walls stretched out on either side. We'd somehow lost the path. Only a cleared patch of dirt led into this isolated part of the estate.

And then, briefly, I caught a glimpse of her—a pale woman among the trees.

"Pirate, look!" I hissed.

I didn't know if she was a ghost. She certainly wasn't a wedding guest.

"Where?" Pirate asked, wriggling through a hole in the gate.

"Right in front of you!"

She paused, watching us and a chill went up my spine.

"I don't see anything," Pirate said, dashing right toward her.

"Watch out!" I yelled as he ran right *through* her.

"What?" he asked, spinning around, scattering leaves.

In the blink of an eye, the woman vanished.

Pirate could always see ghosts. He made buddies with them. A ghost had taught him how to play Scrabble for goodness sake.

My breath caught in my throat. "You never saw her." It was more of a statement than a question, but holy h-e-double-hockey-sticks. What did it mean that I was the only person who could?

I wanted nothing more than to leave the way I came. Instead, I tugged at the latch on the gate. It was stiff, locked. Until it loosened under my fingers and clicked open. I tried to ignore the ominous creak as I stepped through. The garden was dense back here, almost jungle-like. I scanned the thick vegetation for another glimpse of the woman.

The afternoon was warm, but I felt chilled to the bone.

"This way," Pirate said, leading me toward the grouping of trees where I'd seen the woman. Thorny vines climbed the thick trunks, their branches brushing my head as I passed underneath.

"Hello?" I called.

Insects screeched and the air felt thick and heavy.

Pirate snerfed. "Ain't no one out here but us."

"Don't be so sure about that."

He picked up his pace. "I'd been guarding this spot. I sent Flappy to find you."

So that's why we'd had a dragon at the window. Too bad Flappy couldn't talk.

I double-checked my switch stars, keeping a hand on them for good measure. But I didn't see the woman again. I wondered if she saw me.

A few moments later, we came to an old tower, made from the same black stone as the house. It reminded me of a misplaced castle turret. There was a wooden door at the bottom and narrow windows on the first two levels. Rusted metal spikes jabbed from the windowsills and from the tower itself.

"I like to get into the mind of my prey," Pirate explained, wriggling into a space near the bottom of the door. "And if I was running from me, this is where I'd go."

"Be careful." He was going to get stuck.

In the second it took me to think that, he was already inside. "I was sniffing around on the first floor," he said, his voice muffled, "Cause, you know, I'm good at that, when I realized whatever I had was gone. Not my fault. Sometimes I like to let them off the hook."

I glanced around, to make sure we were truly alone. It was hard to tell with the thickness of the trees, and the shadows they cast over the garden.

"It's in here," Pirate said from inside.

I yanked on the door.

It wouldn't budge. I pushed harder to make sure.

Nothing.

"Is there another way in?" I asked, keeping an eye out as I made a lap around the structure. It was slow going what with the underbrush and the vines snaking across the ground and up the tower.

"Come *on*, Lizzie," he prodded, as if his doggie time were valuable.

"Chill out, Rapunzel." I didn't find any other doors or breaks in the stone. "And what you wanted to show me... You see it inside, right?" No use killing myself getting in if Pirate was leading me on a wild goose chase.

"It's right *here*," he said, as if I were purposely holding things up.

"Come on out." I didn't like him being alone with something that could be evil.

"No."

Cripes. "Hold on a sec." I was tempted to hit the door with a switch star, but there had to be another way. The lock was antique, valuable. The same probably went for the door itself.

I'd have to levitate, which I hated. I hadn't done it much, and I wasn't all that good. Still, I was a demon slayer, and I wasn't about to wuss out. I closed my eyes and focused on the power I held inside. I felt its intensity, touched the white-hot spark of it, and willed myself off the ground.

My wedge sandals barely left the black soil.

What the heck?

Sure, I'd only been a demon slayer for a year. And I've mostly, okay always, used that power to break my falls. But if I couldn't muster enough spark to lift off the ground, I was in trouble.

Pirate wriggled his head back out of the tower. "What's the matter? Did you gain weight?"

"No," I snapped. At least I didn't think so. And it

shouldn't make a difference anyway. Sure, I was enjoying California cuisine as much as the next person, but, "go back inside. Stop watching me."

I focused again, clearing my head of everything but the searing light of my power, my innate strength, my goodness, my ability to rise up off the ground.

Now.

This time, I didn't even get a fizzle.

Holy Mother.

A sliver of dread ran down my spine. Something was wrong with me.

I braced my hands on my hips. I was compromised. But I couldn't imagine what had happened or how it had started. We hadn't needed my powers much in the last month.

My limbs felt light, the warm garden air, suffocating. I stared up at the top of the tower. Way, way up.

Get it together. I took one deep breath, then another, when strange tickling sensation settled on the back of my neck. It was almost as if someone—or some *thing*—was watching me. I drew a switch star and spun around.

"Ha!"

There was only a shadowy garden.

Right.

I scrubbed a hand over my jaw. I didn't know what to think, but I had to believe I could at least count on my demon slayer senses.

"Anybody there?" As if they'd reveal themselves now.

I waited a moment, trying to detect something—anything unusual. I couldn't escape the idea that there was more than I was seeing. But when I searched, I came up with...I didn't know.

There was no harsh grasp of evil, no terrifying chill of imps or the possessed. Just trees, more trees, and a little niggling in the back of my head.

Sweat trickled down my neck and between my breasts. It could have to do with this house, or even an entity following us from our last adventure. Still, I'd always counted on my demon slayer danger detector, and it wasn't going off. Yet.

I was uneasy all the same.

My emerald necklace felt heavy around my neck. It wasn't morphing, which was both good and bad.

"Hello!" Pirate's head popped over the edge of the roof, nearly giving me a heart attack. Then I saw his front legs and his shoulders. There wasn't much more to him.

"Get away from that edge," I ordered. If he didn't watch it, he was going to fall right off.

I felt a cold, wet nose on my shoulder and about jumped two feet. I turned, ready to do battle, and found Flappy, who simply lowered his head and peered up at me, all innocent-like.

He knew what he was doing.

"I thought dragon noses were supposed to be warm," I said, rubbing some heat back into my shoulder. I don't know why I'd assumed that. Maybe because of the fire belching.

Flappy nudged me again, this time on the knee, effectively shoving me into a thorny vine. "Ow. Quit it!" I didn't have time to pet him or talk to him or do whatever the creature wanted right now.

I looked back up to Pirate, who had retreated a bit from the edge. Thank goodness.

Flappy caught me in the back of the neck with his wet snout, sending a chill straight down to my toes. "That's it!" I spun around to shoo him away.

"You don't have to levitate," Pirate called down, like an impatient teacher, "you only have to climb onto a dragon."

Sure. Piece of cake. Riding on dragon back was like strapping on to one of those mechanical bull rides at a country bar—gut wrenching and uncomfortable, with a good chance of ending up on the ground.

Maybe I didn't care so much what Pirate had found.

The dragon lowered his head, hope shining in his big, green eyes.

"Oh, for heaven's sake." I grabbed hold of the nubby spikes on the beast's neck and hoisted a leg over his back.

These two were going to be the death of me.

"Fly slow," I said, as if I actually expected him to listen. "No clowning around."

I'd barely settled in when Flappy took off like a shot. My stomach settled in somewhere around my knees as I held on for my life.

He bucked and thrust with every beat of his wings. It was like riding a spastic Tasmanian Devil. He was going to throw me. Flat onto the ground. I knew it.

He gave one last lurch, and I said a prayer of thanks when Flappy landed hard on the stone roof of the tower. I half slid, half fell off, my body shaking. I bent over, hands on my knees as I tried to recover.

"Great job, Flappy!" Pirate leapt past me, as the dragon snorted and whipped his head. He shoved his snout against my hip and I nearly fell over.

"Yes. Well done. You didn't kill me." This time.

I waited for my stomach to settle and my head to clear. I looked over the edge, trying to see where we were, but the trees were still too tall.

Funny. I turned, trying to figure out exactly where this place was. That's when I realized this was no tower at all. It was an old observatory. I looked up to the blue sky then back down to the copper dome fastened to the center of the roof. It lay closed, bleeding green patina onto the stone, but I could see where it opened to the night sky.

There was a yawning trap door next to it that Pirate had obviously used. "Lead the way, Kemosabe."

He didn't need to be asked twice. Pirate scrambled down a set of spiraling wrought-iron stairs with me close behind.

The smell of old brick and dust assaulted me as we pounded down to a landing that housed a gorgeous bronze telescope. Holy tomatoes. Yes, it was dusty. And sure, it was old, but the thing was in perfect condition and still pointed at the sky. Or in this case, the copper dome above.

A sturdy iron crank was attached to the workings of the dome. I was tempted to try to open it, but with my luck, I wouldn't get it closed again. It would be a shame to ruin such a fine instrument with rain or weather.

"That's not what I came to show you," Pirate said, still at the steps.

"Right." I found it fascinating all the same.

Below the observatory floor, the tower consisted of a circular room with a staircase. We wound down two more levels. With every step, the air became more stuffy and warm.

The shadows lengthened, as the light from the upper windows grew scarcer. At last, we came to the ground floor with the door.

I stopped a few steps short of the bottom.

Hooded statues lined the walls, their robes, their fingers, carefully detailed. Except their faces were blank stone. Some of the statues gripped daggers. Others clutched bowls, which held the ashes of incense.

It was strangely silent inside. Everything was shrouded in shades of gray. Pirate breathed heavily next to me, and I could barely hear the birds outside.

In the center of the floor, was a thick stone medallion. Scrolled with...my breath caught in my throat...it looked like the dark mark.

"See?" Pirate said next to me. "It was on your hand. The devil's mark. And now it's here on the floor."

Almost. Certainly too close for comfort.

"Let's not panic," I said to Pirate, and myself.

I glanced behind me. Habit. Before crouching to take a closer look. I ran my fingers over six identical swirls and in the middle of what looked to be a burst of fire.

The dark mark that had been etched into my skin had been emblazoned with three swirls. See? Different. I hoped. Also, these marks were not as tight. Each line on this mark ended with the curved, planetary symbol.

I traced my finger over one. "See this? It's the symbol for Pluto, the planet of death and rebirth."

"Pluto's not a planet," my dog said.

"It was when I was a kid," I said, standing. "Certainly when this place was built." I paused, trying to think of what it could mean. Pluto was also god of the underworld. It was also the symbol of hidden power and obsession. Transformation. Pirate followed the path of my fingers with his nose. "Don't sniff it," I murmured.

He jerked his head up. "Why? This is research."

"Yes, but we don't know what this is." I touched the emerald at my neck. It was warm, yet strangely lifeless at my touch.

"We need to show Grandma." And Dimitri, when he arrived tonight.

In the mean time, I took a few pictures with my phone.

Pirate sneezed every time my flash went off.

"Don't mention this to anyone else," I told him.

He nodded. "You know I don't like to share our business." He tilted his head. I could almost see the wheels spinning. "I'll have Flappy stand guard."

Right. "Because a dragon standing outside a tower isn't at all suspicious."

He didn't get the irony.

Still, Flappy was the best we had. He was loyal, good at guarding things, and he wasn't drinking my mom's tea. All three were plusses in my book.

I tried to open the door on the ground floor level, but there was no way to unlock it from the inside.

"As soon as Grandma sobers up, we'll get her out here," I said as we climbed the stairs. Lord knew how we'd get her inside.

Pirate missed a step. "You mean she's not watching her sandwiches?"

"Focus," I told my dog.

Flappy managed to get us down from the tower, with my dog whooping the whole way. He was on cloud nine. I was less so as we headed back to the house.

I didn't know what we'd found, but I didn't like it. I needed things to be normal—well as normal as they could be—for one week. Was that too much to ask?

Apparently so.

When we got back to the house, we found Sidecar Bob at the Steinway, belting out *Only The Good Die Young* like he was at a piano bar.

He'd slapped a few new stickers onto his wheelchair and had crammed a pint of Southern Comfort into the cup holder. His long gray hair stuck out in tufts from his ponytail.

"I thought boys didn't come to tea parties," I said, tugging on his ponytail.

"I crashed," he said, grinning.

He had five cups lined up on the piano. I was glad to see at least one was filled with nickels, pennies, and quarters.

Meanwhile, my wedding tea party attendees had pushed the couches, chairs, and tables to the side of the room. Some witches were actually napping on them. Mom was dancing in a motley circle with at least a dozen Red Skulls. She'd taken off her shoes, wedding reception style, and was wearing Grandma's yellow bow in her hair.

I stopped for a second. It was truly a sight to see. I couldn't help but grin. If this was how my reception turned out, I'd be glad.

Or maybe I was just high on life after almost falling off a dragon. Twice.

I backed up toward Bob, who was blowing kisses at the end of his song.

"Hey," I said, before he started in on another one, "have you guys warded for demons?"

He tisked. "It's the first thing we do. Now go act like a bride. Have fun. You know what fun is, right?"

I gave him a saucy smile. "Yes, but Dimitri isn't here yet."

He responded with a cheery rendition of AC/DC's *You Shook Me All Night Long.*

Ah, well, it's always good to have crazy musicians rooting for you.

In the meantime, Mom spotted me and waved for me to join in.

I walked on over and gave her a hug instead. She smelled like a case of champagne. "I'm beat," I said into her ear, hoping she could hear me. "But thank you so much for the tea party with my friends. It was magic." Literally.

She tried to turn the hug into a dance, but I kissed her on the cheek and headed for the stairs. After a few steps, I stopped. I didn't know where my room was.

My mom seemed to realize it at that exact moment as well because she broke away from the group and took my hand, dragging me out into the foyer like we were school kids.

At least it wasn't as loud out here.

She couldn't stop giggling.

"Hey Mom, have you been out in the garden?" I asked, in the loaded question of the century.

"Of course," she trilled. "I made diagrams. I was thinking of trimming down the rose garden and having the wedding out there. It's so pretty." She held up a finger. "Unless we use the huge, huge grand arch near the back. But we'd have to edit the fountain out of the pictures because I don't want unicorns with penises in the shot."

I didn't even know my mom knew that word.

And I was going to have to see that fountain.

I slipped an arm through hers as we took the stairs. "What do you know about the tower near the rose garden?"

"You can't get close," she said, leaning heavily against me. "The gate's locked."

"Not anymore," I told her.

If she heard me, she didn't let on.

"Here's your room," she said, stopping in front of the second door on the left.

It held an antique four-poster bed with a rich ivory spread and pillows embroidered with birds. The dresser, nightstand, and mirror were all rich, dark wood and very old.

"My room is next door," she said. "You don't even need to go out into the hall to reach me. We connect.

Like this." She walked over to a door by my dresser and opened it to reveal a similar suite, done in Oakwood and yellow. "Dimitri's room is across the hall."

I don't know what passed across my face, but my mom's good mood disappeared. "I know how you kids are these days and *that* won't be happening under my roof."

"This is a rental," I said, hoping for a loophole. Counting on it.

"All the same." Drawing her shoulders back, losing the drunk walk. "You tell him no monkey business because I'm not comfortable talking about sexual things with men I've barely met."

Oh, geez. "You didn't say that to him, did you?"

"No. He's not here yet."

That was strange. He'd had to run a quick errand for his clan, but he should have been here by now. I hoped he was okay.

Her face pinched. "You tell him. If he is going to marry my daughter, he needs to keep his Johnson in his drawers."

Suddenly I wished the house were cursed so the floor could swallow me whole.

"Don't get too worked up until you meet him. Okay?"

She nodded one too many times. "When he gets here. When is he going to get here?"

"Soon." I hoped.

I didn't know what had happened to the groom.

CHAPTER SIX

Dimitri should have arrived by nightfall. He wasn't answering his phone, or my multiple texts.

Something had to be wrong.

But there was nowhere to go. Nothing I could do about it. And so I sat out on the front porch, waiting.

It was the curse of being a demon slayer. I didn't worry about traffic jams or the chance that he'd lost his cell phone or gotten it wet. My mind was filled with…other things.

The cool evening air cut through the thin fabric of my dress, and I rubbed at my chilly arms. What I'd give for a sweater. Or for my fiancé to appear from around the curve in the long driveway.

Laughter and general mayhem from the tea-turned-karaoke party filtered out into the night. I didn't even want to think about what else they might be doing in there. The Darjeeling was certainly flowing.

I stood and immediately regretted it as the chilly air blew straight up my dress. I paced to keep warm.

It didn't help.

I was checking my phone—again—when there was a rustling in the bushes to my left. I turned quickly and relaxed as a knobby head appeared.

"Lizzie!" My dog went from zero to sixty as he clambered out of the bushes and up the front steps. "I was looking for you!"

I reached out and scratched the wiry fur on his back. "You thought I might be hanging out in the hedges?"

Pirate mulled that over for a second. "Nah. I just smelled something. You know I had to check that out. Now I don't want to alarm you, but we have to get inside. I smell bacon, cheese, shrimp, and more cheese!"

I drew him into my arms. "I can't, bub. Too worried." I sat back down on the steps and cradled the dog in my arms. He was toasty warm from all his running around. It felt good.

Maybe it was ridiculous. I mean, Dimitri was strong, fearless. Even if he ran into something terrible out there, he was a good fighter. He could take care of himself.

But I loved him.

I stared out into the black night, trying to see, to anticipate, to imagine the slightest light at the end of the dark driveway.

"Why can't I relax anymore?" I asked Pirate.

"You and me both, sister," he said, rolling over so I could rub his tummy.

Technically, that party in there was for me. My mom had come in all the way from Atlanta. Until today, I hadn't seen her in a year. And the biker witches? Sure, we saw each other all the time, but that didn't mean I should be ignoring them. "They're living it up and I'm sitting out here. Alone."

Pirate nosed my elbow. "Excuse me?"

Okay. So I was sitting outside with a dog.

Had my position as a demon slayer robbed my ability to simply be with the people I loved, to have fun? Had it stolen my life from me?

Pirate wriggled off my lap and curled up next to me on the porch. He rested his head on my leg and exhaled, his warm doggie breath tickling my wrist. "I'd rather be inside eating snacks."

I scratched him on the soft spot behind his ears. "Me, too, bub. Me, too."

After midnight, when my back was stiff and my head ached from worrying, Pirate and I made the climb up to my room. I closed my door, blocking most of the party noise from the first floor, and slipped off my shoes. I rested my phone next to my head and let my doggie curl up next to me.

"I'm sure he's fine," Pirate said on a yawn. "He's tough."

"I hope you're right," I said, as we cuddled in the dark together. Waiting.

†††

I woke to the smell of bacon and eggs. Sunlight filtered through the lace curtains and I realized it had to be at least eight o'clock in the morning. And I hadn't heard from Dimitri.

The thought sat like a rock in my stomach as I pushed past the still-warm, dog-sized spot on the bed covers.

I didn't bother changing, or finding my shoes. I was halfway through brushing my teeth before I even realized I was doing it. Call it force of habit. My mind really wasn't all there. My head still ached and my body felt like I'd slept on the porch.

His room was empty. The hallway was deserted, but at the bottom of the stairs, well, I should have expected this. It looked like a geriatric slumber party gone horribly wrong. Frieda was curled up by the main banister, her pink suit shirt tied like Daisy Duke and her head resting on the bottom step. Ant Eater snored, open mouthed, as she leaned against the front door.

Someone had drawn a moustache and goatee on her face with a black Sharpie.

I thought she had a shiner. That is, until I made my way down the stairs, stepped over Frieda and saw it wasn't a black eye, but a crudely drawn eye patch. Ah, swell. Ant Eater was a pirate.

There were three more witches crashed out in the foyer. At least a dozen on couches in the sitting room.

I stepped over my Grandmother as she snored away in the hallway to the kitchen.

If I were a good granddaughter, like I was before I became the exalted Demon Slayer of Dalea and was forced to deal with all this nonsense, I would have woken Grandma up and escorted her to bed. But she looked so peaceful curled up, her head resting on a potato chip bag. And really, I'd given up trying to tell the biker witches what to do. It wasn't the first time they'd all woken up on the floor, and it certainly wouldn't be the last.

Still, guilt compelled me to grab a couch cushion from the sitting room and trade it for the Lay's Salt & Vinegar.

See? I was nice. "There you go," I said, depositing the chips on a hall table. She mumbled something unintelligible.

Maybe she'd wake up sober. I could always hope.

I could use Grandma and a few of her friends to help me search for Dimitri. If only I knew where to look.

At least my mom wasn't among the snoring drunks. Thank heaven. She might have had the energy to make it up the stairs. More likely, she was the one cooking. Nothing kept Hillary down. She'd keep to her schedule even if it killed her.

Given what transpired yesterday, it just might.

The gray slate floors were chilly against my feet as I nudged Sidecar Bob's wheelchair out of the way and rounded the corner into the kitchen.

Dimitri stood by the massive stove, turning a large skillet full of bacon.

He looked gorgeous in a green, button down shirt that matched his eyes and accented his broad shoulders. Over it, he wore an apron that said *Dude with the Food*.

I let out a small shriek and launched myself straight for him. He caught me by the waist and pulled me close.

"I expected that reaction from Pirate," he smiled, his angled features softening. "Of course, he only cares about the bacon." The sound of his voice, the crisp Greek accent, the relief, made me want to grab him and never let go.

"I wouldn't mind a taste of your bacon," I said, more interested in him than in any kind of banter. I breathed a sigh of relief and hugged him again, grateful for the solid warmth of his chest against my cheek. "Where were you?"

"I got in late. I didn't want to wake you up." He curled his free hand around me and brushed a kiss over my forehead. "What's the matter?"

"Not a thing." Not now.

I needed to relax. Be a bride.

Still, I promised myself a long time ago, I'd never take this man for granted.

His eyes crinkled at the corners. "If this is how you get when I cook, I'm going to live in the kitchen."

I ran my fingers through the thick, ebony hair that curled at his collar. "Promise?"

He tilted his head. "What happened to your hair?"

Right. I touched my dark brown 'do, suddenly feeling self-conscious. "My mom fixed it."

He touched a lock at my shoulder. "I like your wild child side."

"It's still there." I couldn't get away from it. "Only now I recognize myself."

Pleasure tickled down my spine when his eyes swept over me. "Well you look sexy as hell."

I felt it. I'd waited thirty years for a man to look at me like that.

He leaned down and brushed my lips with his once, twice. I sank into him, teasing the nape of his neck with my fingers, feeling his hands slide up my back and skim around my side until one of his hands cupped my breast. His thumb brushed over the nipple, teasing it, and I felt it down to my toes.

"You're going to burn your bacon," I said against his mouth.

"I like it crunchy," he said, drawing me closer, deepening the kiss until I couldn't think of anything else either.

His hard length pressed against my stomach and I ground against it, wishing we had a bed or a couch or hell—a kitchen table so that I could feel it where I needed it most.

I slid my hand down to cup him, and he jerked against me.

I could do it. I could take him right over to that table.

If the room had a lock. And soundproof walls. And was located in another house entirely. I trailed up his length, wriggled around the apron and began to slide a hand down the front of his jeans.

"Elizabeth Gertrude Brown!" My mother choked.

Dimitri and I broke apart, only I couldn't quite get my hand out of the front of his jeans, so he ended up dragging me with him.

Hillary stared at my hand, to us, back to my hand.

I wriggled it out as my entire body flushed pink. This was so not how I wanted her to meet Dimitri. Or Dimitri to meet her.

Holy Hades.

Meanwhile, he'd turned back to the stove, probably to hide his giant erection.

There was nothing I could say to make this better, so I cleared my throat and went for the obvious. "Hillary, I'd like you to meet Dimitri."

She brought a hand to her chest. "I…I did meet him earlier. He made me a delicious Greek coffee.. Thank you, Dimitri. We had a lovely conversation." She talked as if she were on autopilot.

I stifled a groan. Come on. What did she think I was? A virgin? I was thirty years old. Engaged, for goodness sake.

It's not like she caught us on the kitchen table—her favorite spot. Sure, maybe I'd thought about it, but she'd actually done it.

That should count for something, right?

"Your mom was telling me about your first date," Dimitri said, changing the subject as he finished flipping the bacon.

Oh, no. "Mom, you weren't telling him that." She did want this man to like me, right?

She winced. "Not so loud." She nudged around me and found the coffee pot.

Dimitri only smiled and began checking on some scrambled eggs he was keeping warm in the oven.

Yeah, okay, I could tell Hillary wasn't feeling so hot. Her hair was perfect. Her sleeveless eyelet shirt was pressed. But there was a slight rounding to her shoulders, and she was at least two shades paler than usual.

Maybe I could convince her she'd hallucinated the whole hand-in-the-pants incident.

Or maybe I was getting a tad bit desperate.

Still, I had to know, "What'd you tell him?"

"Little things," she mused, pouring herself a cup. She leaned back against the counter. "Like the first time you tried to say something romantic."

"Ugh," I said, as she calmly sipped at her coffee. I knew where this was going.

"Remember?" she asked, as if I hadn't tried to forget. "You called your little boyfriend, Matt Peterman. First you wrote a long letter to read to so you'd know what to say." My stomach tightened. I remembered. "And then you started reciting the letter when he answered the phone."

Yes. "I can't believe you told him that."

I glanced at Dimitri, who was calmly taking the bacon off the stove, as if I wasn't about to sink into the floor.

My mom didn't even notice. "Only it was the boy's dad who answered, and you confessed your love to Mr. Peterman instead."

Yes, yes. I knew. I was there.

"He handed the phone to Matt," I said, more to Dimitri than to her. It still stung to think about it.

"But you'd already hung up and ran." She turned to Dimitri, who thank heaven, wasn't enjoying the story either. "She's always been a little emotional," my mom said, by way of warning.

"I think it's sweet," he told her. "As long as you're not still dating him." He leveled his gaze at me.

"Ha. No," I said, amazed at his ability to deflect my mother. Maybe I could take lessons.

And for her information, I wasn't emotional. I was controlled. Ice. I'd relentlessly fixed that part of myself, to the point where I'd almost lost Dimitri, and the biker witches. Even now, I found it hard to open up.

As I was figuring out how to say that, Dimitri walked over and gave me a hug. He pressed a kiss against the top of my head, then against my ear. "I don't care if you have a sordid past. You're the best thing that ever happened to me."

I snickered against his chest, needing him like my next breath.

Hillary cleared her throat, but before she could say anything, Ant Eater's rusty voice called out. "Hey, eggs first. Then you can get all smoochy."

A bunch of the hung over witches filed into the kitchen. "You're alive," I said.

Barely.

They were wearing the same tea party clothes they'd had on yesterday. Only now, their ribbons were gone, their buns were flopping to the side and their lipstick—while never quite classy—had smeared. They looked like retired hookers.

Dimitri leaned close. "By the way, you're going to have to tell me what happened here."

As if I could explain it.

My mom straightened as best she could. Still, I noticed she'd propped one hand on the counter, like she needed it to hold her up. "We went a little overboard with the tea party yesterday. I know I stayed up too late." Her mouth twisted into a wry smile. "I can't do this like I could in the 70's."

"My eyelashes hurt," Grandma said. She rested her elbows on the table and her head in her hands.

Bob pulled up, with Pirate riding on his lap. As soon my dog saw there was no food on the table, he jumped down and dashed for the stove, as if we'd somehow run out of breakfast before he could beg for it.

Ant Eater collapsed into a chair, eyes bloodshot, her chin pointed down.

"Nice look," Grandma said.

The scribbled-on biker witch glanced at Frieda, who had rested her head on the rough wood table. "I got *her* beat."

Yes, well, I wasn't the one who'd told them to drink so much tea.

Luckily for them, breakfast was ready. It looked amazing. Dimitri had made his special scrambled eggs, with tomatoes and onions and cheese. There was thick sliced bacon and toast.

He served while mom and I handed out the plates. Every once in awhile, he tossed a bacon sliver down to Pirate, who ate it like he'd never see food again.

When everyone had been served, we each took a plate and joined the witches at the table. Dimitri sat next to me, and my mom, directly across.

I watched as Ant Eater dug a small pouch out of her sock. I mean, who wears socks and motorcycle boots with a dress? She tipped some grayish powder into her drink glass and passed it on to Grandma.

Hillary touched a perfectly manicured hand to her forehead. "I think I'm coming down with the flu."

Somebody was going to have to explain to her about the tea.

Or not.

I glanced around the table to the biker witches, who seemed busy looking at everything but me.

"Creely?" I prodded. She was the one who started it.

The engineering witch gave me an innocent look that wouldn't have even fooled Pirate. "Eat some bacon," she suggested to Hillary. "The grease will settle your stomach."

Hillary picked at her plate. "I don't normally eat bacon," she said, eyeing it wistfully. "At my age, everything goes straight to my hips." She tasted a small bite of eggs. "Oh, my." She tried another small bite. Then another.

"It's a Greek recipe," Dimitri told her. "Strapatsatha. My mother taught me. It's basically American scrambled eggs, only with feta, tomatoes and some onion grilled in olive oil."

My mom's eyes brightened and her cheeks flushed. "You spent time in the kitchen with your mother?"

Okay, maybe these two would get along.

Dimitri grinned. "She taught me everything I know."

"Did you hear that, Lizzie?" She asked, as if I wasn't sitting right there. "He cooks. He listens to his mother. And look at how he's dressed. He's wearing nice pants and a nice shirt." She directed a pointed look at my wrinkled outfit.

"Maybe he'll rub off on me," I suggested.

"Oh, he'll rub off on her all right," Creely snarfed.

My mom's mouth fell open.

Oh, goody. The biker witches were feeling better.

"Please. Do *not* say things like that in my kitchen," mom huffed.

"Because a kitchen isn't the place for it, right?" Ant Eater winked.

"Of course it's not...I don't know what you mean." Mom said quickly. Whether it was from the topic or because she really did remember what she'd said.

I ran my fingers down Dimitri's muscular arm—I loved his arms—and lightly caressed the olive skin at his wrist.

Dimitri grinned.

Mom frowned. "What I'm trying to say, honey, is that we know you like that dress but you didn't have to sleep in it."

I glanced down at my wrinkled sundress and

noticed the dirt streaking it. Pirate's paws must have been filthy last night.

She poured cream into her coffee. "A husband always appreciates it when his wife puts in the effort to look beautiful for him."

Good thing she didn't see the hot glare Dimitri shot at her. "Lizzie is naturally gorgeous, and I appreciate everything about her."

Hillary looked as shocked as if her toast had started attacking her.

Her eyes caught his and Dimitri stared her down until she found her coffee mug fascinating.

Great.

I touched him on the arm. "Can I talk to you for a sec, sweets?"

He didn't look so eager. Too bad. I led him past the stove, to the corner by the door. Then, as we noticed all eyes on us, he opened the back door and we ducked outside onto the porch.

"You don't have to defend me," I said, once the door had closed behind us.

It was a little chilly outside, but not biting. I wrapped my arms over my chest.

Sure, I knew he'd always love me, even when he saw me at my worst. Physically. We'd been to hell and back together and he still loved me. But he had to get along with my mom as well.

He opened his mouth then closed it. He clearly didn't get it. "That wasn't a defense. That was me telling the truth."

Through very rosy sunglasses. "You know what I mean."

"I can't help it," he said, "I want to protect you." He said it as if it were fact, like he didn't have a choice.

I glanced out over the early morning garden. "Okay." I'd give him that. His protective, loyal streak was one of the things I loved about him. I knew I could always count on him. "But this is my *mother*."

He frowned. "And you saw how she acted. You may be used to it, but I'm not. I won't ever be. If someone takes a swipe at you, I'll block it. If someone throws an axe at your head, I'll defend you. Even if it's against someone who's supposed to love you."

I got what he was saying. I really did. "Let's not start any fights, okay?"

"I didn't start it," he reminded me.

"Okay, well don't engage in any battles with my mom." That was my job. Even if I wasn't doing so hot.

He didn't make any promises. He ran a hand through his hair, frustrated. "Ten bucks says your dog's in there eating my breakfast."

I wouldn't take that bet.

"Come on," he said, opening the back door for me.

We walked in to a loud table of biker witches and a glaring Hillary. And Dimitri was right about Pirate eating his bacon.

"Are you done keeping secrets now?" My mom asked.

"I wish," I said, taking the chair across from her.

Dimitri loaded up a new plate, and I dug into my semi-cold one. It didn't matter. The eggs were amazing. I wished I could relax and enjoyed them.

I twined a pinkie with his, feeling solid. Dimitri had a way of making me feel safe. "I'm glad you finally made it."

He glanced at the witches, then back at me. "Me, too. A couple things happened last night," he said, lowering his voice. "I'll tell you later."

When we were alone. Okay.

My mom gave a tight smile as Grandma rose from the table and started taking her plate to the sink. "Thank you for the breakfast, Dimitri. Now I think we'll all agree when I say we have a lot of work to do today."

While she addressed the table, Creely slipped some gray powder into mom's coffee cup.

We all finished up at that point, and I managed to catch Creely by the prairie dress on her way out of the kitchen. "What did you just put in her drink?"

"Relax," she said, tucking a lock of green-streaked hair behind her ear. "It's a hangover remedy. We broke her. We fix her."

I glanced back at my mom, who was sipping her coffee with gusto. "What's in it?"

The witch gave me a pitying look. "Oh honey, you don't want to know."

Chapter Seven

This was one case where I'd have to trust the biker witches. Heaven help us.

Dimitri and I loaded up the dishwasher, and then I showed him up to his room, the one across the hallway from mine.

"Where'd you sleep last night?" I asked, as we climbed the stairs.

"The Red Skulls were nice enough to leave a couch open," he said. "I thought about trying to find you, but I didn't want to start opening doors."

I wished he had.

When we made it to his room, he ducked his head inside the masculine, blue and green space, then back out to look at me. "You've got to be kidding."

"House rules," I said. "I'm across the hall."

His lips quirked. "Did your mother say anything about me having guests?"

"Rule breaker," I said, as he drew me inside.

"Count on it," he said, his lips against my ear before he cupped my face in his hands and kissed me.

The sensation of it rushed over me and I melted into him and the sheer warm, sweet desire of it. The door slammed shut, and my back was suddenly against it. My body collided with his and I gave in to the sensation of completeness, belonging. Him.

At last I broke the kiss. He took the opportunity to nibble at my ear. "I can't wait to marry you," he murmured. I ground against him, making him groan.

Warmth flooded through me. "Me, too."

I touched his cheek, his strong jaw.

He kissed my palm.

I wanted this to be an easy, simple, fun wedding week, but, "I need to tell you about what I found yesterday." I took both of his hands in mine, drawing him over to the bed. He went quite willingly, happily in fact, until I began explaining to him about the old observatory.

The bed dipped as he sat next to me, and I handed him my cell phone with the pictures of what we'd found.

He studied it, stiffening as he enlarged the photo of the swirled design on the stone floor. "It's similar," he said, tilting the phone to see.

"I know," I said, trying not to worry. Failing. "That's Pluto. I think the planetary designs have something to do with the old observatory."

"Pluto's not a planet," he said.

"Thanks for reminding me."

He frowned. "It's clear that whoever built this had an occult fetish." He handed me the phone. "Let's hope it was a hobby and not the real thing. You didn't mention sensing any danger."

"This place feels okay." Slightly weird. Definitely creepy with that lady wandering around the garden. "I saw a ghost, but Pirate had no clue she was there. I'm trying to understand it, but..."

"This is the dog that likes to play board games with the recently deceased."

"Exactly." I knew he'd understand.

"Rachmort's getting in tonight. Let's show him the pictures, maybe even take him out to the site."

"Okay. Good." I liked that. My mentor was a leading necromancer and one of the foremost experts on demonic powers.

Dimitri drew me close, his cheek resting against the top of my head. His other hand moved up my side seductively. "Now let me greet you properly."

"Hmm," I said, kissing him lightly on the neck. "You mean I get more than crispy bacon?"

We shared a long, deep kiss.

"One more thing," I said, trying to stay focused. "And it's not even about the wedding."

"Too bad," he said, leaning in to continue what we'd started.

"My powers aren't working right lately."

He drew back.

"I couldn't levitate yesterday," I told him. "Not that I'm great at it in the first place, but I couldn't even get off the ground. Also, my protective emerald," the one he'd given me, "it's turning into jewelry instead of weapons."

He touched the jewel at my throat and it warmed slightly. "It's supposed to give you what you need."

Like a way to contact the ghost. I had a sinking feeling that the woman I'd seen in the garden was the same Elizabeth whose grave I'd visited.

She'd said she needed my help. If she appeared again, I'd try to make contact. *Less panic, more action.* Was I a badass or what?

Dimitri turned the stone and we watched the facets catch the light. "I wonder if our powers are merging, now that we're so close to being married."

I nudged him. "You mean I get to fly?"

He grinned. "You know what I mean. The longer we're together, I know I can sense your needs better. When you're on the mark, when you're hurting."

I nuzzled his neck. "When I'm horny."

His eyes darkened. "You know I won't let anything happen to you."

I dropped my head. "I'm not asking for protection." Sure, he was mister tall, dark, and dangerous, but I could take care of myself, too. I ran a hand along his arm. "Where were you yesterday?"

He flexed his shoulders as he glanced away, then back at me. "I'm trying to think of a way to give you the simple version," he said, irritation filtering into his voice. "The best way I can describe it is 'clan business.'"

"That's lame."

He sighed. "I know."

I swore some of these clans were worse than children fighting.

"Did you fix it?"

He didn't look happy. "I will. Eventually."

He wasn't the ruler of his clan. His sisters were. At least they'd be arriving in a few days.

"Okay." I knew he was dealing with a lot here. "Just call me next time."

"I tried," he said, frustrated. "Cell coverage is terrible around here. It's like living in the stone age."

I'd give him that. "Well, you had me worried sick."

"I didn't mean to do that," he said, embracing me.

"Be careful. I like you in one piece."

He grinned at that. "What else do you like about me?"

"This," I said, reaching up to brush a kiss over his lips. "This," I continued, touching my lips to his collarbone. "This," I murmured. He gave a small groan as I ran my hand over his waist, down to his thigh.

He leaned back on the bed and I climbed over him.

The door burst open behind us. "There you are." Hillary stood in the doorway, holding a clipboard.

Fricking biker witches and their feel-good powder.

She appeared completely recovered. Perky, even. Well, until she saw what I had in my hand. Again.

"I thought you two understood you have separate rooms," she said, her expression and her voice ice cold.

Dimitri sat up. "Listen, Hillary—"

"We do," I said tightly, cutting him off, holding his leg in a death grip.

She opened her mouth and then closed it. Finally, she said, "I'm calling a meeting so that we can go over our exciting week to come," she said. "Are you ready?"

No.

"Yes," I said, taking Dimitri's hand.

✝✝✝

I grabbed a shower on the way, a cold one, and changed into a lilac sundress and straw wedge heels. It was about the only thing that could halt this parade, and not for long.

Hillary waited while I got ready, then escorted Dimitri and me to the sitting room where—curse our luck—she'd recovered enough to set up a large message board on an easel. It was draped in white cloth, like some sort of fabulous surprise. We all knew better than that.

She stood at the front of the room, quite proud of her creation while the biker witches burrowed into various couches and chairs like students on a Monday morning.

No surprise that the couch at the very front of the class was unoccupied. I sat, trying to stay positive, and was rewarded when Grandma joined me. Dimitri took the spot on the other side and Ant Eater, who was paying the price for wandering in late, plopped down into the chair next to us.

"Your fault for making her feel better," I said under my breath to the gold-toothed witch.

She didn't even have the courtesy to look guilty.

At least she'd changed out of that god-awful tea party dress and back into her leather pants and black T-shirt. She had her sleeves rolled up and was half-heartedly playing with a vial that contained a glittering gold spell.

For reasons that escaped me, Hillary had changed clothes as well. She was a vision in white, with ivory skinny jeans and a lace shirt, set off with a thin gold chain around her neck and tiny gold ball earrings. Then again, this was the woman who gardened in sundresses.

What I'd give for a leather skirt and a matching bustier.

My mom clapped her hands together. "Okay, everyone. It's time to get started. Are you as excited as I am?"

Dimitri leaned close. "I would have been more excited if she'd have given us a few more minutes," he whispered in my ear.

Oh, Lord. Imagine what she could have walked in on.

Hillary would have had a heart attack.

With the flourish of a model from *The Price Is Right*, she unveiled a long dry-erase board. It was divided into subsections and meticulously filled-out in red, black and green ink, which frankly made it look more like an invasion plan than a wedding party schedule.

She tucked her blond hair behind her ears. "We have a packed week, and it's going to be so much fun as long as you follow the rules." She eyed the crowd, pleased as all get out to be running the show. "First off, in precisely seven minutes, we will begin the bonbon favor making party."

I swear I heard Ant Eater groan.

Dimitri shifted in his seat. "You don't need me for that," he reasoned.

"What? You only want to be here for the fun parts?" I asked him.

"Yes," he said, without hesitation.

Too bad. If I had to do it, it didn't seem fair for him to make an escape, simply because he had a penis. Even if it was a really nice one.

Hillary was on a roll. "Tonight at six o'clock sharp is the fork and knife barbeque. With a live band playing jazzy renditions of your favorite country hits."

"Elevator music," Grandma said under her breath.

I tried to ignore her because it was probably true.

Hillary pointed to the next board. "Tomorrow, at nine a.m. sharp, Ixia Papos will arrive from the Greek Institute to teach us some lovely ways to greet Lizzie's new in-laws. Then at eleven a.m. sharp…"

Dimitri sat like a statue, muscled arms crossed over his chest, staring into space. "I'd rather check out that observatory."

I eyed his strong, Grecian profile. "Not without me."

"Then let's get out of here," he prodded.

I sighed.

"Where are you going?" Grandma asked.

"Nowhere," I insisted.

"Okay, wedding favors!" My mother clapped her hands again. "You three. Pay attention."

He caught my hand and wrapped it in his. It was warm and solid. "Fine," he said. "I'm staying."

Okay, but I really could hack it. "In case you don't remember, I was the one who got you out of hell." He looked like he wanted to roll his eyes. "I was also the one who blasted that entire army of sex-on-wheels succubi."

"Then I kept you from incinerating yourself," he said under his breath.

Fair enough.

"Which time?" Grandma prodded.

"Shut it," we said together, a little louder than was absolutely necessary.

"Have you even been paying attention?" Hillary bleated, her cheeks reddening, "because I don't see how you're going to make tulle wrapped bonbon favors correctly if you're talking during the directions!"

"Sorry, Mom," I said quickly.

Did anybody really care about wedding favors?

I didn't. Then again, I was getting the feeling that this week leading up to the big day wasn't about me.

I wriggled a little, trying to get more comfortable on my seat. The couch was old, and hard.

At least Hillary hadn't heard what we were talking about. "We need to be more careful," I muttered.

"Or, hey, here's a thought—you could tell your mom you're a demon slayer," Grandma said under her breath, as if I could just blurt that out.

"I thought you were going to tell her," Dimitri said, as Ant Eater passed him a stack of white tulle. He looked at it like it might jump up and bite him.

"Take fifteen pieces and pass it," Hillary instructed.

He handed the entire wad to me. "I'll watch and make sure you're doing it right."

"No," Hillary strode over to our couch, heels clacking on the tile. "We need all the help we can get to make your wedding day perfect." She stood above him. Even sitting, he was almost at eye level with her. Too bad for Dimitri, Hillary had an advanced degree in dagger eyes.

He looked like a trapped bear.

"Love means making compromises," I told him, counting off fifteen squares of tulle and dropping them into his lap. Yes, he may be a hot-as-hell, badass shape-shifting griffin, but he still had to get along with his mother-in-law.

And if he was going to protect me from unseen dangers, he could at least make some wedding favors while he was at it.

"It can't be worse than switch stars," I told him. Handling them had taken years off his life. He'd grabbed an ice monster for me, he'd dealt with blood and guts and demon spittle. But a little tulle seemed to be his kryptonite.

If only our enemies knew his weakness.

He really did look miserable.

"Okay." Far be it from me to cause him undue pain. "Why don't you take off?" I asked. He wasn't doing any good here. And yes, my powers did feel strange, but I wasn't in any immediate danger. Besides, "I've got the Red Skulls." I gave him a small smile.

He looked from me, to the tulle in his lap, to the schedule boasting events like flower headdress weaving and a ribbon tying party.

"I'm out of here," he said, lightning fast as he stood. His griffin nature let him move a hair quicker than other men. I didn't know if I'd ever get used to it.

He kissed me on the head and was out the door before the tulle on the seat next to me stopped fluttering.

Typical man.

✝✝✝

After a half hour of wrapping bonbons into little tulle squares, I changed my opinion.

He was a smart man.

I struggled to twist the top of the little bag while trying to tie a thin silk ribbon around it. I slipped, and the side of my hand crushed the bonbon. Gah. I'd never been good at crafts.

"Just eat it," Grandma said.

"No." I'd already polished off the last three. Pretty soon, my mom was going to notice. No doubt she'd counted and catalogued every last bonbon.

It was like a sweatshop. As soon as I'd finish a stack, mom was ready with more tulle, more bonbons.

Wrap. Twist. Tie. Repeat.

"I don't know why we're out of bonbons already," Hillary fussed.

I pretended not to hear.

Wrap. Twist. Tie. Crush the bonbon slightly.

Good enough.

Hillary stiffened as Ant Eater held up her bonbon favor bag. She'd double wrapped it to look like testicles. Lovely.

"Candied nuts!" Luna hollered from the back, which had Creely grinning, and okay—me, too.

"Hold on. I'm coming!" my mother said, clacking over to Ant Eater.

She frowned when she saw Ant Eater's creation. "No, no." She took it gingerly between two fingers and held it up for the room, "Almost, but you see, we only want one ball in the sack."

"I prefer two," Ant Eater told her solemnly.

Hillary twisted her lips into a tight smile. "That's not how they're made."

Ant Eater raised both brows. "Have you seen any lately?"

That's it. "One ball," I said, standing and confiscating Ant Eater's treasure. "It's my wedding, and I want a one-balled affair."

The biker witches snickered, which was better than them rebelling.

"That's right," Hillary said, unsure of exactly what we were talking about.

I found a seat next to the gold-toothed biker witch. "I thought you were going to behave."

"I didn't think you'd be having a one-balled wedding," Ant Eater said, untying the bag and popping a bonbon into her mouth. "I know Dimitri's not going to go along with that."

"Ew. No comments about the groom, please. And stop tormenting my mom."

"Come on," Grandma said, "she's begging for it."

I glanced up. Hillary was in the back, inspecting a triple-balled creation of Frieda's.

Exactly who had *she* been dating?

"When are you going to set an example?" I asked Grandma's second in command.

Ant Eater ate her other bonbon and stuffed the tulle into the couch cushions behind her. "When were you going to tell us about the creepy observatory you found?" she asked, chewing.

I stiffened. "Who told you about the occult room?"

She smiled, showing chocolate teeth. "Pirate mutters a lot."

Unfortunately.

"I was going to tell you all when we had time." I glanced at Grandma. "And when you weren't drinking tea." It's not like I was holding it back.

Mom shrieked. All three of us craned our necks around. The bald witch was trying to walk the length of the room balancing an antique mantle clock on her head.

"Luna!" I gasped.

She startled and the clock fell. Frieda caught it at the last minute, but that wasn't the point.

"Control them," I ordered to whoever would listen.

My mom gasped again, and I saw that someone had added *Mike, the randy policeman* to the bachelorette party schedule.

Not that I was against Officer Naughty, but—

Ant Eater stood. "Listen to me, missy—"

"No," I said, drawing close. "You listen to me. Mom might not do things the same way we do—or anyone for that matter—but she's rented us an incredible old mansion, she's doing her very best, and you have to respect that. And her."

Grandma sighed. At least she looked guilty. "We tried, Lizzie. You saw us try."

"Try harder," I told her.

"Hey," Creely nudged me, "anybody up for some tea?"

I gave her a sour look. "You can't get my mom drunk every day."

The engineering witch had to think about that one. "Why not?"

Poor Hillary was busy fixing her schedule board, scrubbing like she was trying to dig through it with her eraser. I made my way over to her. "You doing okay?"

Her mascara was smudged and there were faint circles under her eyes.

"My society friends will be here in a few days. We don't even have half the wedding favors we need." Her voice went up a pitch. "And I can *not* have a stripper in this house."

"That's fine," I said, resisting the urge to rub her back a little. We didn't really have that kind of relationship. Which was sad when I thought about it.

"You need to help me. You need to support me." She started in on the board again. "And I'm beginning to suspect your new friends are seriously unbalanced."

"I'm not going to argue with you there," I said.

Ant Eater had Grandma in a discussion over in the corner while the rest of the witches had taken it upon themselves to start up an arm wrestling tournament.

"They'll stick to the schedule. I promise."

She let me take the eraser from her hand. "It's the only way I'll survive this," she said, making an attempt to smooth her hair.

Planning. Order.

I'd helped her keep it that way for most of my life.

And I could do it now.

"Give me a hug," I said, not allowing her much of a choice. I could feel her relax and was about to claim a small victory when the doorbell chimed. Three long bongs sounded throughout the downstairs.

Hillary drew back, sniffling a little. "I wonder if the band is here early. That would be nice," she said, dabbing at her eyes with the tips of her fingers.

"Nope," said a biker witch, who had leaned back dangerously far in her chair to peer past the curtained front window. "If I had to guess, I'd say it's the Greeks."

Bong.

Bong.

"That's impossible," Hillary said, frantically checking her schedule, "they don't arrive until tomorrow night's ouzo and olive bar reception!"

Frieda leaned over to take a look. "Well, there are twenty or so of them outside."

"And no one is opening the door," I said, hurrying for it.

Bong.

"Twenty?" Hillary would have shrieked if she weren't about to hyperventilate. "It should be five. Dimitri's sisters, their godmothers," she ticked them off on her fingers like that would change anything. "…some nice man who wrote to say he's lactose intolerant…"

I opened the door to an invading army. They'd taken over the porch. And the steps. And the driveway beyond.

"Lizzie!" Dimitri's younger sister, Dyonne, wrapped me in a hug. His other sister, Diana, had me from the side.

Some old Greek woman joined on in the other side. And a guy with a mustache behind her.

It was a big, fat Greek sandwich. And Frieda had it wrong. There weren't twenty random relatives outside the door. There had to be at least thirty-five.

Chapter Eight

Holy Hades. What were they doing here?

"Dyonne!" I clung to Dimitri's spritely, shorthaired sister while Diana let me go enough to kiss me on both cheeks.

"Traditional Greek greeting," Diana said, "grab whatever part you can get."

I grinned. "As long as you left Zeus at home." He was a monstrous horse. Diana liked to ride him in the house.

She laughed, tucking her long, dark hair behind her ears. "I've mellowed out a little."

"She's lying," Dyonne said proudly, finally letting me pull back.

Hey, who was I to judge? They'd lived their lives under a demon's curse, knowing they'd fall into a coma when they reached the age of twenty-eight and die twenty-eight days later. While some people—most—would have responded by withdrawing, these two had gone out of their way to eke every bit out of life.

Dimitri and I had saved them, but it was up to them to make a new life for themselves.

"Glad to see you haven't lost your edge," I said.

"Don't speak so soon," Diana's coin earrings dangled as she snuck a glance at the mass of relatives behind her. "We were trying to escape early."

"Before the new clan followed us," Diana added.

"You might want to work on that," I told her as assorted relatives started pushing past.

Diana leaned in close, her hair brushing my shoulder. "They caught us at the airport. While boarding."

"We tried to call," Dyonne added, "but nobody had an international cell phone. And then, by the time we got here, it was all we could do to rent a bus."

I glanced past the crowd to see a gray rental coach with its luggage doors open. The poor driver dragged suitcase after suitcase out of the bottom, aided by several muscular Greek men, jockeying for position.

Oy vey. "I see you still have your suitors."

The strongest females ruled Griffin clans, and since Diana and Dyonne were the only ones left of their particular line...

It didn't hurt that when I'd killed the demon who was cursing them, they'd absorbed the power of generations of griffin leaders. Pretty much every leader who had succumbed to the curse over the centuries.

So now, they had beauty, power and their whole lives ahead of them—not to mention a bunch of griffin warriors intent on wooing them.

Dyonne's short-cropped hair fell in layers around her eyes as she watched the men. "I told them whoever unloaded the most got to sit next to me tonight."

"We should have used them for the tulle bonbons," I said to myself.

Diana gave me a quizzical glance, but she didn't question.

This could be fun.

"Dimitri is off somewhere," I said. "I don't know where he is…or what he's doing."

Dyonne grinned. "I think I know."

Before I could grill her, I felt a pinch on my arm. "She is too skinny. You, too."

"Ow." I yanked back and turned to see a heavy-set woman wearing a white tunic outfit and plenty of gold jewelry. Her coal black hair was teased high on her head, and if I wasn't mistaken, she had a slight mustache.

Diana wrapped an arm around the woman, as if guiding her to give me a little more personal space.

It didn't work.

"Aunt Ophelia," she said, "meet Lizzie."

"Aunt?" I asked. The women in Dimitri's family had perished from a curse.

Diana caught my confusion. "Ophelia is from our new clan. When we joined, we gained about a dozen aunts and twice as many uncles. All unrelated, although you wouldn't know from the way they treat me."

The woman leaned in close. Way close. Her face was severely angled, softened by age, and her eyes were a striking shade of gray-blue. "Blessings on you, and may you have a dozen children."

I tried to laugh. But a dozen kids? "I have enough trouble with my dog," I told her.

"Ha!" She barked out a laugh, before it died on her lips. She brought a hand to her chest. "She understands me?" she said to Diana. Then turning back to me. "You there, you know Greek?"

Before she got too excited for me, I had to admit. "It's a demon slayer power." I could decipher languages.

It was most handy with ancient demonic texts, but hey, I'd use it where I could.

Wait. I turned to Diana. "Your new relatives know I'm a demon slayer, right?"

She looked at me like I was crazy. "Who doesn't?

Hmm…with a sinking feeling I realized I had more in common with a bunch of shape shifting griffins then I did with the woman who'd raised me.

I only hoped they wouldn't say anything to my mom until I had a chance.

In the mean time, Aunt Ophelia was studying me like a prized goat. "This is good," she said, fluffing my hair, examining the cloth of my dress between her fingers. In a minute, she would start checking my teeth. "You will have no trouble when you come to live with us."

"Er," I said, both glad and worried she'd overlooked the state of my dress, "I live here."

"My nephew Izzy is going to marry Diana," she said confidently, as if I hadn't spoken.

We'd see about that.

"Hello!" Mom said, drawing up next to me. She had that pasted-on smile that said she was about one second from a panic attack.

At least most of Dimitri's relatives had made it into the foyer, and into the hallway, and okay—it was getting a little claustrophobic in here. Plus, it didn't help that they were watching us.

"Mom, this is Dimitri's Aunt Ophelia. And his sisters, Diana and Dyonne."

Mom seemed to take comfort in the routine introduction, until Aunt Ophelia took over. "And this is Gelasia, Eugenia, Antonia," she said, pointing them out one-by-one. There were older aunts and uncles, some younger twenty-somethings, no kids. "Antony, Tony, Milo, Argo, Tony, Nick, Tony, Antonio…" She pushed through the crowd to cup a good-looking guy by both cheeks. My handsome son, Antonio."

He smiled widely and let her do it, even though he carried four suitcases stacked in his arms.

"He belonged to my old clan, but when I married his step father, he was a loyal son and came with me," she told my mom proudly.

"Oh. My," my mom said, no doubt thinking Ophelia was one slice short of a baklava. "If you'll please follow me this way," she said, breaking away to guide a few of the Antonio's up the stairs. She paused part way up. "I look forward to meeting each and every one of you. Some of you will find your names on the doors. If not, then, you can choose your own room on this floor or the third floor." She raised a warning finger. "Be sure to inform me so that I can make name plates for you."

A bunch of the Greeks stormed the steps after her, ready to claim their spots, while others began cozying up to biker witches. An older man—Tony?—broke out a bottle of ouzo.

He grinned proudly, his cheeks red. "Want to know how I smuggled it through?"

The biker witches whooped.

Talk about a universal greeting.

Diana hugged a startled Ant Eater while I caught up with Grandma. "I wish you spoke Greek," I told her.

"In a minute," she said, as Sidecar Bob wheeled into the room, his mouth split in a grin as he held a homemade marshmallow launcher.

How very biker witch.

He dug a jar of what looked like pink marbles out of the bag on the back of his chair. Of course, I knew better.

"Watch this," he said, dumping the contents into the launcher. "Fire in the hole!"

I winced as Bob pulled the trigger and fired a shot across the foyer.

Gasps erupted from the Greeks as it exploded in mid-air. Aunt Ophelia shrieked. Caustic smoke filtered over the room as flakes of glitter rained down. They felt cold to the touch, and—oh no—"She's shifting!"

This was not a threat. There was no danger. But try telling that to Aunt Ophelia.

Claws erupted out of her hands and feet. Her tunic tore in half as a thick lion's back emerged. Red, orange, and silver feathers cascaded down her shoulders and spine and formed wings as her bones snapped and re-formed.

And she grew. Huge. She was as big as a truck. Her blue eyes glowed as she turned to me and snarled.

Ant Eater stood next to me. Staring. "At least she's still in the foyer."

Yes. Well. "Is that good or bad?"

"I don't know," she said, refusing to take her eyes off the beast.

Aunt Ophelia snarled and rose to her full height, her head clinking against a wrought-iron chandelier.

"Somebody stop her," I gasped, envisioning an Aunt Ophelia-sized hole in the wall. A staircase reduced to tinder. Hillary in a dead faint.

The elder Tony scratched his chin. His other hand held a half-empty bottle of ouzo. "You want me to shift too?"

"No!" One griffin was enough. "Talk to her," I pleaded. "Reason with her. It was just a translation spell."

"That is unfortunate," he said as Aunt Ophelia let out a bellow.

Oh, my God. It hadn't really hit me until that moment. I had a house full of griffins.

Ophelia's son Antonio came walking down the stairs. He did a double take when he saw his mom.

"Can you help her?" I asked him.

He winced a little as she slid her claws over the tile floors, trying to get her feet under her. "Really, Uncle Tony," he said, "I know she's wanted to stretch her wings, but she could have waited."

Tony shrugged. "They scared her."

"Congratulations on your wedding," Antonio said, as if that were the most important thing right now.

"Thank you," I said automatically. Aunt Ophelia wasn't shifting back. And it's not like we could get her out the door.

"I know you and I don't know each other well," Antonio said, "but if you could talk to Dyonne on my behalf, I'd really appreciate it. I mean, I'm the strongest fighter on Rhodos. I've trained under Master Arcas. I know you don't know who that is, but trust me—he's the best. I'm fluent in a dozen languages."

And I was ready to scream.

It was rotten and it was wrong, but, I took Antonio by the arm. "If you can get your step mom to shift back in the next two minutes, I'll get you a date with Dyonne."

He broke into a grin.

"Mama!" he called. "Bee-sco!"

She swung her head from side-to-side.

"It didn't work," I told him.

"You will see," he said.

She bent her head and began to shift.

"What did you say to her?" I asked.

He shrugged. "She wanted my cookies from the flight. You have a towel?" he asked.

I realized with a sinking feeling that she was going to be naked. Nobody needed to see that.

Luckily, Antonio seemed delighted at the idea of removing his blue dress shirt. The guy had amazing muscles. Great abs. He tossed the garment over Aunt Ophelia.

Oh well. I had to give him props for showmanship. "If I didn't know better, I'd think you planned that."

"Me, too," he said, displaying his chest, as he caught Dyonne's eye. No doubt he was looking forward to his date.

✝✝✝

By late afternoon, we managed to get all of Dimitri's relatives assigned to rooms—not that they stayed there. The suitors were relatively under control (although I didn't relish telling Dyonne about her date), and my mom was still in one piece.

I considered that a victory.

"I don't know what I'm going to do," she said, as we stood near the long tables on the back porch, watching the caterers bring in food for the fork and knife barbeque.

In all fairness, the yard looked pretty good. She had small twinkling lights strung up. The witches had tapped a keg and everybody seemed to be having an okay time.

But I could feel the tension rolling off Hillary. "There's not enough to eat. The house smells like fireworks. If I didn't know better, I'd think they were having a frat party out here." She sighed. "I wish your father were here."

"He hates noise," I reminded her.

She gave a small grin. "Good point."

I had to give my mom credit. She was holding up well, all things considered.

Although I think the griffin in the foyer would have done her in.

"We've got cheese and bread in the house. We have olives," I said. Plus, Hillary always ordered too much food.

"Lonny Hard Rider trapped some rabbits," Frieda said, handing me a cup.

"There you go," I said, raising a glass to my mom.

So, Hillary's fork and knife barbeque turned into more of a roast rabbits on a spit kind of event, but everybody had fun.

Well, most everybody.

I kept waiting for Dimitri to show up, hopefully in human form, and join us. But he never did.

Diana caught me walking back from the front of the house, as if looking down the road would help flush him out.

"I don't like it," I told her. She of all people knew what kind of trouble he'd dealt with in the past.

She frowned. Didn't try to sugar coat it, which I appreciated. "I thought I knew what he was doing, but it shouldn't have taken him this long."

"Tell me," I said.

She winced. "I shouldn't. It's a griffin wedding tradition and I don't want to blow it." She took a sip from her cup. "But I am going to talk to him about it."

"Thanks," I said. I needed an ally.

†††

That night, a thick fog rolled in from the coast. And still, Dimitri was gone.

We'd moved the party into the kitchen, and the sitting room. And the dining room, if you counted the Koum-kan game. I was never any good at Greek rummy, but Frieda was having a great time. Then again, she seemed to be more interested in one of the cousins than she did her cards.

I sat in a chair in the foyer, with Pirate dead asleep on my lap. He'd been out in the garden all day. I could tell from the burrs and bits of leaves and bark I kept finding in his fur.

He stirred, growling under his breath as he dreamed. His legs churned, as if he were chasing something.

I jerked suddenly when I saw a shadowy form moving through the wall of cloud.

Pirate's eyes flew open. "I'm on it!" he said, flipping upright and nearly falling off my lap.

"It's fine," I said, as my own heart thundered in my chest. It was Dimitri. I could feel him reaching out to me. It confused me for a second, how he was reaching out to me. Then I realized he must have been using my energy—our combined strength—as a beacon through the fog. No doubt he could see lights in the fog below, but...

He didn't know how to land.

They didn't have fog like this where he was from. I dropped Pirate on the cushioned chair. "Stay here."

Of course, he didn't listen.

I felt Dimitri's harsh breath, the glide of air under his wings as he circled. "I'm coming," I said, grabbing my switch star belt off the hall table.

Luckily, Pirate met up with Bob and a piece of leftover rabbit at about the same time.

"Don't worry about me, Lizzie," I heard him say as I banged out the back door of the kitchen.

I needed to guide him in before he impaled himself on one of the jutting iron spikes on the roof, or went crashing into a cliff.

The fog was dense, the night cool. I unhooked the Maglite from my utility belt and headed for the most open place in the garden I could think of—the herb beds.

I could only see about ten feet in front of me as I made my way past the box hedges and the fountain. I gave a small shudder as the laughing centaur rose up out of the mist.

Once I hit the lavender beds, I turned my Maglite toward the sky and began blinking it. On. Off. On. Off.

This is not a house light. Or a boat light.

It is a landing light.

A trickle of sweat snaked down my back. "Come on, babe," I said to myself as much as to him.

There was nothing else I could do. I certainly couldn't see him. I hoped this would be enough. It had to be.

I felt rather than saw him land. He was a little farther out, toward the rose garden maybe. I ventured a step in that direction, then another. "Dimitri?"

It was the most isolating feeling in the world, like standing in the middle of a cloud. It was as if I could slip off the edge into oblivion, and no one would notice until it was too late.

I almost dropped my flashlight when he walked out of the fog like every fantasy I'd had rolled up into one. He was shirtless, his pants slung low over his hips. The tips of his dark hair curled under and a slick sheen of sweat coated his body. I wanted to devour him on the spot. Dang. "If I was only a half-minute earlier."

He shook his head and kept coming. "Would have been the best thing to happen to me all night."

"Still could be," I said, catching his arm as he bent down for a kiss.

The glow from my Maglite illuminated the space around us, but the rest of the world was a soft dove gray.

He drew his mouth over mine, almost making me forget my good sense.

Almost.

I nudged one well-defined pectoral. "You said you weren't going to scare me anymore." This was obviously a planned trip.

"Sorry," he said, caressing my chin.

I slid my hands down his chest. He was warm, delicious. "You're going to have to do better than that."

"You're going to have to trust me," he said softly.

Trust wasn't a problem. Worry was.

I tucked a lock of hair behind my ear and looked up at him. "Can I go with you?" I was good in a fight, or a negotiation. Besides, his last big secret almost destroyed his clan. He'd needed me then.

His expression softened, but he shook his head. "If I need help, I'll let you know. It'll be over before we leave for the honeymoon, though. I promise."

"I can't wait," I told him. We needed a break, some time alone. A loud bang sounded, and a cheer went up from inside the house.

We slipped farther back into the mist-drenched garden. Alone. Unseen.

He kissed me, long and slow. I could feel the heat of his fingers through my dress, the slide of his body against mine. The scent of sage and basil surrounded us as we explored each other.

He caressed the nape of my neck as he pulled his lips back. They hovered right over mine. "You want to take a walk in the woods with me?"

I couldn't help but grin. "Good luck finding any woods." We'd need all our luck to find the house again in this fog.

His lips bushed mine once. Twice. "Want to get lucky behind a garden bush?" I could feel the smile in his voice.

Hmm...I slid my arms around his neck. "I'm too neat and tidy."

He laughed at that.

And then he showed me exactly how dirty I could get.

Chapter Nine

God bless Dimitri and his ability to make me forget everything but him.

I caressed his shoulders. How I loved his shoulders. I ran my hands down his wide chest. He was already half-undressed, which was very convenient.

More than that, this was the man who was always there for me, loved me.

His kisses were gentle, teasing, and I soaked them in like warm rain.

At last, I had time to savor this man. So many times in the past, we were running from imps or a demon, trying to save someone or simply trying to survive ourselves. But here…now, I had him all to myself.

We were alone. Hidden. I could finally take the time to explore every delicious inch of him, and I intended to take full advantage.

Oh, yes.

His kisses grew deeper, more insistent as I drew my hands down over his hips and slid them over the notch of muscle that defined his waist. "This is one of my favorite parts," I said, dying to kiss it, completely unwilling to rush.

"It's yours," he murmured, sliding the straps of my sundress off my shoulders and drawing coursing wet kisses over my collarbone. I fisted the waist of his trousers, holding on tight as he slipped my dress down over my arms, trapping me against his chest.

"Perfect," he said, caressing my nipples.

"I—oh!" He laved one nipple, then the other. Between his mouth, and the blanket of fog, and the heady feeling of being trapped against him, I didn't think I'd ever felt more connected, more loved. It was us against the world and finally—finally we'd taken time for *us*.

It felt incredible to love him like this, to be with him. This is what we had been fighting for, for so long. This connection like no other. The pleasure of it washed over me until I was almost drunk with it.

I barely noticed when he slipped off my dress. I was drenched as he tore off my panties. And before I could wrap my head around it, he'd pressed me down onto the cool garden path. He kissed me long and hard as he pressed the warm, hard length of his body over me. I writhed against him, teasing us both.

"Wait." We needed to slow down. I wanted to stay here and feel him and be with him. But his kisses and his touch, and oh God, he found the core of me with his fingers, and with it, the searing heat that scorched through me, filling me with white hot pleasure and screaming need. "Dimitri!" I rolled him onto his back, covered him with my body and with devouring, eating kisses. I ground against him, tore at his pants until he kicked them off, so he was as naked as I was.

He was hot and hard against my core. I drew a long, desperate groan from him as I rubbed my slit over his cock, drenching him in my juices.

"Now," he said, pressing the tip of himself against me.

"Not yet," I said, sliding down again, torturing us both. But it was so good, so right, and even though we were on the knife's edge, I was greedy. I wanted more time, more kisses—as if kisses and touches and need alone could show this man what he meant to me.

His breath was ragged as he rolled me onto my back, found the tender spot at the nape of my neck. "Jesus, Lizzie, I need you so badly."

Hades, I needed him like I needed my next breath.

I dug my fingers into his hips as his cock shifted, sliding against the full wet center of me. We both groaned as he entered me hard.

God, he felt amazing. Even better when he drew my legs up and pumped his lean hips in a slow, steady rhythm that had me squirming against him.

"I. Love. You. So. Much." he said, with every hard thrust of his cock.

"I love you too," I whispered, trying to find my voice. I'd never loved anyone like I loved him.

He felt incredible inside me, over me, against me, as his body twined with mine. I felt every move, every touch tenfold. And I knew this was what it was like to be truly connected with someone. To be one.

His kisses were hot against my sweat slickened body. I opened myself to him fully—now and forever.

I gasped as his thrusts sped up, lost their careful rhythm. I ground against him, licked his salty shoulder, bit it as the pressure built, the pleasure mounted and bliss spiked through me.

His control broke. He drove hard and wild against me as I clung to him, coming harder, spiraling higher. Savoring every last tongue of fire that lashed through me, knowing that this is where I belonged.

A little while later, Dimitri let out a satisfied sigh as I snuggled against his chest. "I think we trounced our clothes," I told him.

He snorted. "Griffins like to be naked."

"I'll keep that in mind." I ran a finger along his arm, watched in satisfaction as the muscle flexed.

The man had a point. I didn't need clothes. I didn't need anything. Except for him.

He touched my cheek and looked down at me with such love it nearly tore me to pieces. "Thanks for guiding me in."

"Anytime, hot stuff," I said, reaching up for a kiss.

I was about ready for round two when…

"Lizzie?" A rusty voice echoed through the fog.

My lips tingled as they missed his mouth and grazed the stubble on his chin.

It was Grandma.

"We heard you screaming, baby," my mom said, out of breath. "We're coming!"

Oh my God. I bolted upright.

Chapter Ten

It sounded like an army tromping down the path. Lights cut through the fog. They were coming. Fast.

Dimitri and I rocketed to our feet. "Where are my clothes?" I hissed. Everything was dark and foggy and so not the way I'd planned this.

He tossed my dress at me, and it hit me square in the chest. It was like my arms weren't working anymore. I couldn't think. Except that this was becoming very mortifying very fast.

Pirate, barking like a fiend, headed straight for us.

"Lizzie!" He broke through the fog, misjudged the distance and slammed right into my shin. He bounced off, spun around and danced a circle. "Lizzie, you're alive!"

"Yes. Of course. *Pirate*," I pleaded. It wasn't like I'd set off to slay a demon.

My dog looked up at me, earnest. "You yelled, and then Dimitri started hollering. You sounded like you were being eaten alive."

In a manner of speaking.

"Don't worry. I called in the troops," my dog said, gleefully.

I glanced to Dimitri, who was barely in his pants. Hades, he had a nice ass. "What did you do with your shirt?" I asked him.

"Didn't bother putting it on," he said, as we both realized that I'd torn his top pants button right off.

He laughed, which made me snort. He knew I was a goner then. He reached for me, kissing me silly.

In fact, I was about to forget what was wrong in the first place—when my mom let out a huge gasp.

"Lizzie Brown! I thought you'd been murdered!"

At least Frieda, standing behind her, had the courtesy to cringe. "Noise travels in the fog."

Now they tell me.

"Hells bells." I touched my forehead against Dimitri's chest and wished that they would all go away.

He wrapped a protective hand around my waist. "She was guiding me in," he said, as if he wasn't standing there half naked with his top button torn and as if I hadn't—Lord help me—put my dress on inside out.

And were those my panties lying on the path at our feet? Yep. I was pretty sure they were.

I ventured a glance. The biker witches grinned.

My mom did not. "You were *screaming*," she said, slowly piecing it together.

Pirate circled around my feet. "You know what, come to think of it, she doesn't yell a lot when she fights. Let's see, there were the demons from Las Vegas, the demons from hell, the demons from—"

"Pirate," I snapped. "Stop trying to make this better."

At least Hillary couldn't understand him.

Still, let's face it, everybody knew what was up and I didn't like how they were all standing around staring at us. There was no way to exit this gracefully—not that I should have to—Dimitri was my fiancé for heaven's sake.

If anything, they should be apologizing to me.

Not that I was going to hold my breath.

"Let's go," Dimitri said, leading me away from the scene of the crime, effectively giving up on his shirt, my shoes, my underwear, his... You know what? I didn't want to go looking for it in the fog.

Hillary was going to think I was some kind of wild child when all I'd wanted was a half-hour alone with my fiancé.

Why did I even care what she thought?

Because she was my mother.

Frieda and Creely made a break in the line for us and we headed for the house.

Dimitri, smart man that he was, had rescued my light. He flipped it on to guide our way. He wrapped his other arm around my waist. "You okay?"

"For now." I couldn't guarantee anything once my mom got a hold of me.

The fog hadn't let up a bit. Still, we definitely knew the direction the search party had taken from the house. "I notice none of your relatives barged out after us," I said. The Greeks must be lovers, not fighters.

He glanced down at me. "They're here? Good." He let out a huff. "I asked my sisters for help with some clan business."

"Well, they certainly brought the clan."

His flashlight beam jerked. "What do you mean?" he asked.

He'd find out soon enough.

"When are we ever going to be alone?" I asked him under my breath, very aware of the parade behind us.

He gave me a slight squeeze. "Think of the honeymoon."

Yes, the surprise honeymoon. Dimitri had refused to tell me where we were going, only that it would blow my mind.

Frankly, that could mean anywhere, as long as Dimitri was with me. But right now, I needed some good news, or at least a goal to get me through to the wedding. "Tell me where."

He turned to me in surprise. "You really want to know?"

Yes. No. "Maybe." I could cling to the fact that going somewhere magical with this man. "Give me a hint," I said as he led me around the sage plants and up the back porch steps.

He drew a hand down my arm, leaving goose bumps in his wake. "Far, far away," he said, glancing back at the witches breaking through the fog.

He nuzzled my cheek. "Soft beds. Ocean views. Me naked."

"With a rose between your teeth?"

"That can be arranged."

I gave him a soft kiss on the shoulder.

Hillary cleared her throat. That's when I noticed she'd bypassed our little tête-à-tête and was holding the back door open for us. Dang. I could use her as a super spy demon scout—if she knew I was a slayer.

"Remember you are rooming separately until the wedding," she said to Dimitri. Probably to me as well.

He stiffened, and for a moment, I thought I was about to have another battle on my hands. I squeezed his shoulder and leaned up to whisper in his ear. "Let it go."

His gaze was hard, his jaw granite. Hell, he was probably grinding his teeth. But he held back. For me.

"Thank you," I wound my fingers with his as we entered the kitchen.

"You're welcome," Hillary replied behind us.

It was just as well.

He escorted me up to our rooms. I needed another shower. And to snuggle with him.

He ducked his head and gave me a long, slow kiss, then pulled back with a mock stern expression on his face. "Think honeymoon," he said, before he turned away, the muscles in his broad back flexing as he headed across the hall.

†††

I retreated to the bathroom for a long, hot shower. Afterward, I rubbed on some jasmine scented lotion and slipped into a sexy silk nightgown.

When I closed the bathroom door behind me, Pirate was curled up on the bed. He stood when he saw me. "Oh, no. You're going to kick me out, and I'm going to have to sleep on the sofa again. Or the floor. I hate the floor."

"Relax," I said, running my fingers through my freshly washed and combed hair. "It's only us tonight."

"For real?" He asked, leaping over the comforter he'd bunched up on the bed. "Because as your dog, I have to tell you I expect equal attention. Remember how we used to lay in bed all night, reading books and eating popcorn? We could do that." I sat next to him on the bed, and he immediately rolled onto his back. "Or how about we lay in bed and you rub my belly and tell me stories about your day?" I scratched the soft fur on his stomach, and he gave a happy wriggle. "Oh yeah. That's the ticket. Oh, Lizzie, I needed this."

He'd started to kick his back leg in tune with my scratches when there was a knock at the door.

Pirate flipped over onto his feet. "Aw hell."

"It might not be Dimitri," I told him, secretly hoping it was. My body screamed for round two. I was certainly ready.

"Um hum," my dog said. "See? No matter how loyal I am, this is what happens."

But I was hardly listening. My gorgeous, wonderful, adventurous man was going to get us caught. Again.

"Couldn't resist, could you?" I asked, opening the door.

But instead of my dream man, I found a very unhappy Hillary.

She'd changed into her version of loungewear—a matching velour outfit with some kind of a designer label on the sleeve.

"I'd like to see you downstairs, please," she said, her voice clipped, her fingers white on her clipboard.

"Can it wait?" I asked. I was all for planning emergencies, but not at eleven o'clock at night. Besides, I'd somehow managed to hold on to a nice, post-nookie mood. I didn't need to hear about placemats from a woman who was obviously annoyed with me.

"Now," she said, in a tone she hadn't used since I was a teenager.

I held back a sigh. She was lucky she was my mother.

Pirate turned in a circle and settled back in while I found my matching silk robe. "I'll keep the bed warm for you."

"You're a good dog," I said, closing the door behind me and following my mom down to the kitchen.

Lo and behold, the biker witches had turned in early. The Greeks, too. At least I'd be close behind. Hillary was not a night person. I went straight for the pantry by the refrigerator, thinking I might get some crackers. Or maybe Hillary had ice cream—when she turned on me.

"I can't believe you were outside—naked—sleeping with Dimitri!"

Oh, God. Just like that, I lost my appetite. I turned to face her.

Her cheeks were flushed, her expression hard.

"Okay." We might as well lay it out on the table. "I'm an adult. He's my fiancé, and we were *supposed* to be alone."

I was thirty years old, for goodness sake, old enough to be able to have a private moment, or three.

Hillary gripped her clipboard. "I have five days worth of parties and after parties," she said, pounding her finger against her finely tuned, color-coded notes. "I have ribbons that match napkins that match plates. I am killing myself. For you. To give *you* the perfect wedding. And what do you do? You sneak off and do vulgar things in my garden!"

Because I'd asked for artisan placemats, bonbon making parties and a three-ring circus. "This isn't about me." None of it was. "This is about you getting ready for your country club friends."

She wasn't even insulted. "How are you going to come back to Atlanta and live a good life if you *don't* impress these people?"

"Newsflash mom. I'm not going back!"

She looked like I'd slapped her. "You have no idea what you're talking about. Yes, you're in love, but Atlanta is your home." All the color drained from her face. "You'd better not do something insane, like move to Greece. Is he putting these notions into your head?

Like I didn't have a thought of my own. "Maybe if you got to know him, instead of picking fights with him, you'd realize he's not like that."

She snorted. "It's hard to talk to him when you always have a hand down the front of his pants."

"That's not fair," I snapped.

"You want to know what's not fair?" I'd never seen Hillary snarl. But she quickly hid it. She took one deep breath, then another. She set her clipboard down on the kitchen island behind her, held up her hands like I was the one attacking her. "I tried so hard to have a baby," she said evenly, controlled. "When I adopted you, all my dreams came true. I simply wanted to give you a good life, to have a perfect daughter. And you fight me at every turn."

I wasn't fighting. In fact, my problem was that I hadn't pushed back for the majority of my life. I stewed in silence, which didn't help anybody. It was only when I came into my powers that I began to realize I didn't have to be the person my mom wanted me to be. I could be me.

The biker witches had given me that gift. They may have dragged me to it, kicking and screaming, but they taught me to let go, to make my own choices, to believe in myself. I didn't live my life afraid anymore. I knew who I was.

In fact, if I had any sort of guts, I'd tell Hillary I was a demon slayer. She needed to know. And now was the perfect time.

My heart sped up and my voice caught in my throat. "Mom—"

There was no going back.

"Wait." She set down her clipboard with a sigh. "I know we're both under a lot of pressure with this wedding, but you're my daughter, and I've been dreaming about this for so long." She took a deep breath. "Now, let's both try to smile. I have a surprise for you." She walked to the large closet by the back door. "I was going to save it. I should." She drew a clear garment bag out of the closet. "But I don't know what you're going to do anymore." Inside, was a wedding dress.

Mom, I'm a demon slayer.

"This was my dress. I'd like you to wear it," she said, as more of a fact than a request.

Disappointment welled up in me. I wasn't sure if it was from the lost chance at a confession, or that I was going to have to let her down again. "I have a dress," I said. I loved it. It was so me.

She closed her eyes, as if she'd expected this particular failure, too. "This dress is couture," she said, unzipping the bag and holding up an off-white gown with one long, elegant sleeve and one arm left bare.

"You're missing a sleeve," I told her.

"That's the style," she said, proudly.

She turned it around and showed me a waffle-like design on the back. It was like nothing I'd ever seen before and like nothing I wanted to wear.

"Thank you, mom. I'm honored." I was. I really was. "But I want to wear my own dress." Maybe a few years ago, before I'd broken free, before I'd learned to stand up for myself, I would have bowed under the pressure to give up my gown. But not anymore.

The sadness in her expression nearly broke my heart.

But it didn't break *me*.

"We'll think about it," she said, as if we hadn't settled it already.

I couldn't do this anymore. "I need to get to bed."

"Well, that's true," she conceded. "You don't want bags under your eyes."

As if that were my biggest problem.

I gave her an awkward wave goodnight and headed out of the kitchen.

I'd lost my chance to give her the truth. But in a way, I think I'd given her all the truth she could handle for one evening. There was nothing for me to consider. This was who I was. She needed to accept me.

Or maybe I was taking the easy way out—only giving her the truths that I had to—leaving out the ones that were soul-deep.

It would come to a head sooner or later, if only I could find a way to make it easier.

Chapter Eleven

The next morning, I woke up with bags under my eyes. The tragedy.

Of course I hadn't slept well. I just wanted this week to be over. My dog was nowhere in sight when I made it out of the bathroom.

"Pirate?" I asked, noticing the hall door was slightly open.

Sure, he never liked to sleep in, but he usually let me know when he was going to wander.

I slipped on a pair of yellow wedge heels that went with my daisy print sundress.

"Little dog?" I asked.

I opened the door to peek out into the hall and almost ran smack into Creely, who wore leather pants, a zebra print top and was carrying her own version of Hillary's clipboard. "Oh, good. You're awake."

"What are you doing?" I asked, almost one hundred percent sure I didn't want to know the answer.

She raised her brows, a Kool-Aid green lock of hair falling in between them. "You said you wanted us to play nice. We are. Now, I want to go over some options for the post-wedding kegger."

"Absolutely not," I said, stepping out into the hall. "You said you were going to listen to my mom."

Hopefully better than I listened to her.

"We tried." She shrugged. "Now we're going to do it our own way."

"What about me?" I'd asked them to get along.

She shot me a quizzical look. "You're just the bride."

And here I thought this wedding was about what I wanted. I don't know why I kept clinging to that notion.

The doorbell rang downstairs, and Pirate let off a frenzy of barking. So that's where my dog was.

Creely kept talking. "Don't worry. We're going to do the reception up fancy, with clear plastic glasses and whatnot, but I tell you, it's going to be a bitch to get a beer truck up the hill out front."

"Hillary will have a heart attack," I said to her, and myself. I said it slowly, so she would understand.

I started to walk around her, to check out who was at the door. Because, let's face it, Creely wasn't budging.

"Neal is getting his old hair band back together," she said, in true biker witch style.

"Neal?" I gaped. Grandma's off-again, on-again, hippie lover Neal? "She can't behave around him."

"Says the woman who banged a griffin in the fog."

Lovely. "I'm going to pretend I didn't hear that."

She shrugged. "Neal's band is good. At least, they used to be."

Creely angled her clipboard away from me but not before I saw the note to stop by the dollar store for balloons and slip-n-slides.

"I'm not going on a slip-in-slide."

She gave me the "duh" expression. "It's for after you and Dimitri leave. We've got to do something to the Electric Slide."

I couldn't believe this. "How about you do the

dance," I said, heading for the stairs, "like normal people?"

She laughed like I was making a joke.

The door opened, but I couldn't see who was arriving. I glanced back at Creely. "Don't think you're off the hook."

She merely grinned.

When I reached the foyer, mom was closing the door.

"Who was that? I asked. My mentor, Rachmort, was due to arrive today, although he'd probably be in the foyer if it were him.

"It was no one," my mom said airily.

She looked a little too innocent for my taste, like Pirate after he broke into my last box of Girl Scout cookies. "Mom..." I prodded.

She waved a hand. "It was a mistake. I fixed it."

Dimitri walked in from the hall. "I saw the UPS guy leaving. Did you get your dress?" He stopped, checking his watch. "The tracking said it was supposed to be here by ten."

No. She wouldn't. My insides hollowed, and I felt myself begin to shake. "Mother, what did you do?"

"I'm taking care of the details for you." She drew up her defenses. "We agreed you'd wear my dress," she said in a rush, as if were the most obvious thing in the world.

Only I did not agree to anything of the sort, and oh my God—she sent back my dress. I rushed past her and threw open the door. The truck wasn't even a blip on the winding drive and my dress was gone. Vanished. Kaput.

I spun to face her. "What were you thinking?" I yelled, the words burning my throat. "This is *my* wedding," I advanced on her. "That was *my* dress!"

She brought her hands up to her chest as if I'd struck her. "You didn't see it. It was plain."

"It was mine!" I screamed.

She backed up. "It was short," she said, stammering, her gaze searching for anything but me. "This wedding is going to be a production and your dress has to live up to that. The one you picked out was a dress for cocktail party."

"Get it back." I ordered.

She brought a hand to her chest. "Lizzie, I—"

"Get. It. Back." I repeated.

My head was going to explode. Dimitri stepped up, but I held out my hand before he got any closer. I didn't want him to make this right, unless it meant getting my dress back.

"This ends now," I told her. "I'm not a prop in a show to impress your friends. I've gone along with the teas and the planning and all of this production that I didn't ask for and I didn't want. All I wanted was to wear *my* dress, and you fucked that up. I'd rather walk down the aisle naked than wear your dress."

I spun and ran straight into Dimitri. Dammit. I was shaking. I tried to pull away, but he caught me. "Hey," he smoothed my hair out of my face, "listen to me. I'll get it back for you if I have to fly out and land on top of that truck."

My throat felt tight. "Thanks." We should have just gone to Vegas, done it biker witch style.

Dimitri pulled out his cell phone and started the tracking process.

And if that didn't work, I wondered if Dimitri was serious about shifting and hijacking the truck. That had to be illegal on about seven different levels. I still wanted him to do it.

Ophelia came from the sitting room, not doubt

drawn by the noise. "Oh, my." She wrapped both hands around my arm. At least she cared. "We can fix it for you, kopelia mou."

Maybe. I hoped. "Do you know someone at UPS?" I asked.

She patted my arm. "No. I'm sorry, dear. But we have a gift for you that will make you feel so much better."

She'd obviously never had her wedding dress replaced.

"This way," Ophelia said, guiding me into the sitting room, where the Greeks had erased Hillary's white board and instead used it as a place to keep score for their Biriba tournament.

Good.

"Come, come," Ophelia said to the biker witches gathering at the fringes of the room. "This is for everyone."

Dimitri stood in the foyer, with his back to us, on the phone, tracking my dress. I was glad he could handle it, because right now I was afraid what would come out if I opened my mouth.

I stood, trying to calm the shaking that radiated from my core as Ophelia directed her fellow matriarchs with trays of drinks that looked like mimosas. She pressed one into my hand and I sipped. Definitely some kind of Greek liquor in it, but it was sweet and frankly, I could use a stiff one at this point.

The couches were full of various aunts and uncles, although I did notice the younger cousins gave up their seats for some of the biker witches.

Diana and Dyonne were two of the last to arrive. They gave me questioning looks—probably wondering why I looked ready to strangle someone—as Ophelia drew me in front of the big, bay window.

Ophelia was flustered, excited as two of the aunts made their way through the crowd with a bundle tied in black silk.

She brought her hands together as if in prayer, then touched them to her lips. "My little bride," she said bringing her hands down, clasping them against her breast. "We are so happy, so honored to welcome you into our family and our clan. We are Artamae, the hunters."

Yes, from Rhodes. Dimitri had shown me pictures of the ancient gates to one of the cities the clan founded. The carvings of the sacred deer were still visible on the walls. In old times, the people could see griffins and would make offerings of the best kills from their hunt. When I'd squicked out a bit, Dimitri reminded me that I liked deer sausage. He'd had a point, I supposed.

"You are our family now," Ophelia said.

I took a deep, calming breath. "I'm glad," I said. I really was, even as Dimitri lowered the phone and turned to give me a glance that said all was definitely not well.

"And so," Ophelia said, her eyes growing misty again, "we have made your wedding gown!"

I gripped my drink glass. Not another one.

"It is our tradition," she said. "Each woman in the clan gives something to the dress. Some choose the silk. Only the best. Some work tirelessly on the stitching. Hand done. Every bit. Some work hard to inspect each and every bead for the bodice…"

Hillary stood, stone-faced, at the back.

She deserved it.

"We keep adding and adding and working until," she unveiled the dress. "You have this!"

Creely spit her drink.

I would have, too, except I was frozen in place.

It was made of silk, all right—yards and yards of silk, like a Southern Belle intent on drowning herself. And there were beads...everywhere. On the bodice, down the front, streaking over the sleeves, wound around the high, choking neckline like snakes. And these weren't pretty, dainty glass beads or pearls. They were shaped like sunbursts and seashells and I even spotted a few sand dollars among the complete and utter chaos.

"Damn." Creely said.

"Wow," I said, trying to recover, but the light was catching the sequins on the poof-ball sleeves, and frankly, the whole thing was such a train wreck, I couldn't stop looking.

But it was made with love, given with no strings attached.

The Greeks weren't trying to change me, or hurt me. Ophelia and her clan only wanted to make me happy.

In fact, it was perfect. If I couldn't have my dress, this was the next best thing simply because it was the exact opposite of everything my mom was trying to force on me. If Dimitri pulled off a miracle and got my dress back, I'd find a way to bow out of this graciously. But if not, revenge was best served with a million seed pearls.

"As you may have heard from all the yelling," I said, "I have a dress picked out. Still, there's been an accident." I started to warm to the idea, and to my mom's shock in the back. "If my dress doesn't arrive," which it would, it had to, "I would be touched and honored to wear this dress."

The Greeks cheered.

My mom dropped her cocktail.

Ophelia held up the dress while I took another look at what I'd agreed to wear. Danged if it didn't make me smile. I couldn't help it. I had to admire it. "The bow on the butt is huge."

"That is mine!" An elderly aunt called out from the back. Her relatives on either side patted her on the arms, congratulating her. "I hand sewed each sparkle."

"That must have taken forever." There were sequins all over it. And there were matching bows on the sleeves. "And butterflies on top of the bows."

My mother looked like she was going to hurl.

I, on the other hand, couldn't get over it. I could wear it twelve times and still see something new every time.

"The butterflies are mine," said a somewhat shy, younger women, seated on a couch near the front. She wrung her hands together, tucked her already-tucked hair behind her ears. "I wanted even more, but they said it could get busy."

"If you want to add more, feel free," I told her, fingering the large silk insects on each shoulder of the dress. "The more the better."

She blushed.

Bring 'em on.

At this point, Hillary had recovered enough to start making her way to the front. "As gorgeous as this is," she said, sidestepping Greeks, "I really must insist Lizzie wear my old gown, for sentimental reasons."

"You're over-ruled," I told her. "Now," I addressed the room, "who wants to see me try on my dress?"

The Greeks were ecstatic. Mom looked ready to faint. And I was trying to figure out where to go to change.

"Try it on over your clothes," Ophelia insisted. "As much as you can."

"I'd love to," I said, as she began unhooking the dozens and dozens of extremely large buttons that ran down the back.

"Each of these is handmade," she said. "Some are more fine than others, depending on the skill of the button maker."

Ophelia and Grandma held the dress open to me. I stepped in as the young woman from the front rushed up to help me into my sleeves. They had a loop that went over my middle finger, effectively covering half my hand and making it look like I was wearing part of a glove that attached to my sleeve. It was a design at least twenty years past its prime. Perfect.

"You will love this," Ophelia said, starting with the strangling buttons at the neck. "Dimitri will love this."

I think Dimitri would love it if we could skip to the actual wedding. Come to think of it, that would be my choice, too.

They turned me toward the window in order to work the large buttons in the back.

The dress wrapped around me too tightly. I tried to move and adjust a bit.

"Vivi, Antonia!" Ophelia called.

Two more sets of hands joined in the prodding and tugging. Oof. There was so much fabric.

It was hard to stand still. The inside lining was prickly. The seams stabbed under my arms. The lace dug into the base of my throat. It tightened as they slipped the buttons closed. This was worse than wrestling an imp. I should know. And at least with minions of the underworld, I could stab them and put us both out of our misery.

I swallowed, tried to speak but nothing came out. They'd probably crushed my windpipe.

Dots formed in my line of vision as Grandma gave me a vicious tug from behind. "Suck it in," she ordered.

I whooshed out a breath, brought both hands to my stomach and tried to cast a smile over my shoulder at the array of in-laws on the couches.

This is so much fun.

For other people.

I turned back and came face-to-face with the ghost. I jolted, which caused the hands at the back of my gown to pull back harder.

It was *her*. The woman from the garden.

She stood on the other side of the window, wearing an old-fashioned, high-necked white gown. She brought her hands to her throat.

"What?" I croaked. I was drowning, suffocating.

She watched me silently.

I looked down at my own hands, ready to draw them to my own throat, when a trickle of blood leaked from my right sleeve.

I stared at it, horrified, unable to speak or even scream as the trail of blood thickened. It dripped from my fingers.

Holy Hades.

Look at me! See me!

Searing pain raced up my arms and down my back, breaking through the paralyzing cloud that had formed around me. Still, I couldn't move. I couldn't beg, plead, tear this dress away and run.

I craned my neck around. The people on the couches talked and smiled, nodded to each other and to me. They didn't see. They didn't *know*.

The woman at the window pressed her hands against the glass.

I gasped against the heat burning through my veins. It was getting hotter, turning molten.

More blood spotted my sleeves as the front of the dress caved in on itself, soaking itself in red as my life seeped into the beaded fabric.

Chapter Twelve

At last someone screamed

Then another.

And another.

I couldn't think past the blood and the pain. I was seized by the primal need to move, run. Escape.

But I was paralyzed. Trapped in my swiftly weakening body. I could do nothing except stand like a statue, bleeding out on the floor.

The terror stole my breath and my mind. My veins were ready to burst with fire.

Get the dress off. Get the dress off.

Ophelia cried out, twisting her fingers around the collar around my neck, strangling me, making it worse. She shrieked and retreated.

Diana whimpered as she yanked at my buttons. "They won't come off!" She turned me around, sheer panic seizing every movement. Her own hands were bloody as she yanked at my sleeves.

"Incoming!" Ant Eater hollered, as she hurled a spell jar at my feet. It broke open with a hiss, sending plumes of green smoke and ash up into the air. I breathed better for a startling moment, before the horror crashed down again.

Dimitri tore past them all. His shirt was off and his pants were half done, as if he'd been preparing to shift.

Instead, he reached for me with hands that had turned to claws. His eyes were orange, savage as he ripped the sleeves from my arms with his bare hands. He bit the lace at my neck with his teeth, ravaged it away and yanked the rest of the dress free.

I stumbled back against the window. My sundress was drenched in blood.

He chased me, grabbed me and pulled me against him. He kept me from falling as he hissed in agony from the mere act of touching me. "Hit her again!" he ordered.

Hillary screamed. The griffins roared.

Biker witches pelted the floor around us with jars. Several smashed through the window. They came from everywhere at once, a blinding, gut-wrenching jolt of magic.

My stomach heaved. My skin burned. I wanted to curl up and die on the spot. If it weren't for Dimitri holding me up, I think I would have.

I slid down a few inches.

He propped me up.

"I've got you," he repeated against my ear like a mantra. Like he needed to believe it. I did, too.

My breath came in hard bursts. The sulfur in the air stung my throat and my eyes. Dimitri's skin was scorched where he'd touched me.

Grandma stared at us, her hair wild, her eyes wide, muttering, "shit, shit, shit."

The burn had turned into a blistering, throbbing ache. It pounded with my heartbeat. I was afraid to look down. I didn't want to see the damage. Not yet.

This attack was so much worse than anything before because I hadn't even seen it coming. Most of the time, I could prepare myself for injuries, expect them. But now I'd been ravaged by my own wedding dress.

Creely gulped, fought to keep her eyes level with mine. "Frieda went to get Battina's supplies."

The healing witch. We'd lost her in battle. What I wouldn't give to see her now.

Ophelia let out a screech. I followed her gaze to the floor and saw the wreck of a dress twitch. Dimitri had tossed it onto the floor near a couch. Now, a lump, like a trapped animal, formed under the yards of tulle and ribbons. It started to move.

My first instinct was to reach for a switch star, but my arm wouldn't budge.

Creely hit it with a spell jar and it stopped. For now.

Of course, the lump was still there.

"Don't anybody go near it," Dimitri ordered, in the understatement of the year.

Frieda rushed through the throng of startled onlookers. She carried a colorful carpetbag. Battina's supplies.

The blond biker witch made a wide arc around the dress and opened the bag on the floor in front of us. She rifled through the contents for a moment before drawing out an old Dawn dishwashing detergent bottle, now filled with a goopy green and brownish colored liquid.

"Hold your breath," she said, standing. She leaned away as she squeezed it over my arms, my chest, my neck, and Dimitri's chest.

It cooled my skin instantly. I still throbbed, but I could think. And yes, it was gross—with bits of sticks and bark—and it smelled like a month-old latrine, but I didn't care. Frieda snapped on a pair of Battina's gloves and began gently smoothing the goop over our skin. I watched as it soothed the redness from Dimitri's chest. And at last, I was brave enough to look down at my own arms.

The skin was ragged, torn and blistered. My fingernails were gone.

I looked away, tears burning the corners of my eyes. I was alive. That's what counted.

"You'll be fine," Frieda said, going back and drawing out another bottle.

What else was she going to say? *Sorry, but there's no way you can fully recover from this.*

"How many do you have?" Dimitri asked, his voice tight.

Frieda glanced at him, and I could tell she was tempted to cage her answer. "This is the last one," she finally admitted.

"Use it all on Lizzie," he said.

I swallowed hard, tried to speak. I understood that I'd freaked out a little. Truly, this wasn't going to be pretty for any of us. "Don't," I croaked, my throat raw. "I'm not an invalid," I managed to complete the sentence on a whisper, but I'd made my point. I didn't need them treating me with kid gloves. I was stronger than that.

I had to be.

Dimitri pushed out a breath. "I hate to ruin your noble moment," he said, with that old, familiar warmth I'd come to count on, "but I can heal better than you."

Nodding, I managed a throaty, "Good point."

I let Frieda bathe me with the entire contents of the last bottle. Lord, it felt good. I closed my eyes as the cool gel-like liquid soothed my skin. Amazingly enough, I was actually happy when the harsh throbbing gave way to an angry itch.

Maybe that meant I was healing.

"Bad news. You need a manicure," Frieda said.

I opened my eyes to a super close-up view of the witch. She gave a small smile as she touched her hands under my palms and brought them up for me to see.

My nails were back. Ragged, but whole. My skin was actually in one piece.

Thank God.

Battina, too. Bless her dear departed soul.

I flexed my fingers. They were stiff but whole. And, dang, I was going to need a shower. "Frieda," I said, as she finished packing up Battina's supplies, "do you think you can grab my switch star belt? It's in my room." I'd nail the dress as soon as Creely and Grandma were finished with it.

The two witches knelt next to the dress with what looked like a test tube kit. Biker witches stood over them, spell jars as the ready, as Creely and Grandma drew fibers with tweezers and dropped them into various tubes full of blue, red and purple liquid.

Frieda stood behind them, her hands on her hips. "You think you might want to keep your switch star belt with you next time? Oh, demon slayer?"

"Strangely, I think I've figured that out." Although, truth be told, I'd been too compromised to throw a star. Still, I needed to keep my weapons with me at all times. I wasn't safe anywhere—even behind the wards.

Diana lingered nearby, her hands covered in the same healing goo Frieda had used on me. Dyonne was busy keeping my mother upright. Hillary looked as if she'd been to hell and back.

Suddenly, one of Grandma's test tubes spit fire and sparks.

"What is it?" Dimitri asked.

Grandma leaned back on her haunches. "Spittle of Cerberus," she said, not happy at all.

"What is that?" Hillary protested, pushing against Dyonne.

"Three headed dog of the underworld," Creely answered automatically. "Let's test again to make sure."

"Poison." It settled in my stomach like a rock.

Somebody had tried to kill me.

But truly, hadn't I known from the moment I saw blood?

Hillary freed herself and stumbled toward me. "This doesn't make sense," she said, her tone pleading, wobbling on her heels as she tried to find her footing. "Lizzie?" she asked, as if I could somehow put her back in her normal world where organization triumphed, society was king, wedding dresses didn't try to kill the bride.

"Mom—" I began. Oh geez. "I don't know where to start?"

"How about with the truth?" Grandma muttered.

"Yeah, right." Oh, hell.

"What have you done?" Hillary asked Ophelia. Her words were sharp, her tone angry. I knew that voice. That was mom regaining control, damn the consequences.

"It is not us," Ophelia protested as mom advanced on her. "The dress was fine! We tried it on Antonia right before we left our villa!"

"You tried to poison my baby." Hillary said, her voice low and controlled. She looked ready to hit Ophelia.

Ophelia snarled. Two more griffins joined her.

That's when Dimitri honest-to-God roared.

"Stop fighting," he ordered. "We have an emergency. Someone is trying to kill Lizzie." His eyes were orange again, or maybe they'd never changed back. He clutched me to his side, every inch of his body hard, feral. His voice was clipped, measured. "I don't imagine the guilty party will admit to this heinous attack, but I do promise I will find you."

He spoke to the Greeks, the witches, and my mother.

A stone cold silence fell over the room. Naturally, it was Hillary who broke it. She tugged at her pearls, her voice hard, her cheeks flushed. "Will someone please explain to me what the hell is going on?"

It was the moment I'd dreaded since I came into my powers. "Mom," I began, my voice scratchy. She already knew, right? She had to know. She'd seen spells and partial griffin shifting and me asking Frieda for weapons.

This had to turn out okay. Maybe.

Hopefully.

"Okay," I looked to my confused, desperate, on-the-edge mother. And pointed at Grandma. "They're witches."

Hillary gripped her pearls. Hard. "I don't believe in that."

"Those jars, the ones that spit smoke and energy—those were spell jars. Powerful ones."

"There—" She stammered. "There has to be another explanation."

While I was on a roll, I took my fiancé by the arm. It wasn't hard because he was still helping to hold me up. "Dimitri is a shape shifting griffin."

She shook her head. "I don't even know what that means."

Come on. "He just roared." Then again, it wasn't like she'd ever picked up a paranormal romance. Or even watched *Buffy* on TV. "Think werewolf, mom. But bigger, with wings."

Now she had both hands gripping her necklace. "Lizzie Brown, you stop playing with me this instant. We have things to do. I'm sure we're off schedule..."

"Hillary," Dimitri said. For added proof, or maybe because he had an ornery streak, he locked gazes with her and changed his eyes from mocha brown to startling green, and then orange.

She let out a small squeak.

Frieda picked that moment to clomp up with my switch star belt. "It sure got quiet around here," she said, handing it to me.

Dimitri helped hold me steady while I buckled on my weapons. "Mom," I said. This wasn't the way I'd wanted to tell her, what with the poisoned dress and me all shaky and her standing there with her mouth moving up and down with no words coming out. But in for a penny, in for a pound, "I'm a demon slayer."

She watched me, speechless, as I took several shaky steps toward the poison dress.

"Stay back," I said to Hillary. "I have weapons. You just can't see them."

"Oh," she half-barked, half-squeaked.

Grandma and Creely had finished by then, and the dress was alone. It wasn't dumb, though. Whatever had hold of it skittered the dress sideways a few inches as I approached.

"Could be possessed," Creely offered.

I didn't know and I didn't care. With fingers that were still a bit shaky, I drew a switch star out of my belt. I aimed. And I hurled it.

The star ripped through the fabric. *Skeeetch!* It cried out as if it were alive. A wave of sulfuric fumes hit us as the dress caved in on itself and a bright blue flame shot out and up.

We retreated a few steps and watched the flame consume the dress. When the magical fire died down, all that was left was my switch star, gleaming in a pile of ashes.

That's when I realized I had a massive headache. My arms and legs felt weak. "I think I'm going to pass out," I told Dimitri.

Grandma drew a spell jar. "You think you're in trouble again?"

No. "I'm beat."

Mom stood behind her, watching me as if she were seeing me for the first time. "You're a demon slayer," she said, as if she were trying out the words.

"Yes," I told her. I hoped with everything I had that she could accept me.

"Lizzie can also talk to her dog," Dimitri supplied, helpfully.

Hillary's eyes rolled to the back of her head and she fainted dead away.

Dyonne, bless her heart, was there to catch her. I sure couldn't have moved that quickly.

"Come on," Dimitri said, "let's get you some rest, too."

I took one last look at my mom as they moved her to the couch. "Maybe you shouldn't have told her about Pirate," I said, as he helped me out toward the foyer.

"Yeah," he said, bracing my arm, wrapping his hand around my back. "The dog was the problem."

CHAPTER THIRTEEN

I fell asleep within seconds of reaching my room. When I woke, Dimitri was gone. He'd helped me shower before putting me to bed, and I hadn't even gotten to enjoy it. My head pounded and the skin on my chest and arms felt tight. Diana sat by my bedside with a glass of water and a Tylenol.

She gave a slight smile. "Try this."

I leaned up, taking them from her. "A little conventional, don't you think?"

"Never underestimate a good pain killer."

I looked down at my chest and arms. They were slightly pink, like I'd gotten too much sun, but they were whole. "Where's Dimitri?"

Diana flattened me with one hand. "He's out patrolling the grounds."

"In his condition?" I hadn't seen the extent of his injuries, but if he felt even a fraction of what I had, he should be in bed next to me.

He was in no shape to shift or fight.

We didn't even know who'd wanted to kill me, or why.

Yes, I was a demon slayer, but that meant I had hundreds of enemies. How was I going to even begin to know where this attack had started? And worse, how to stop it.

"You try keeping a two-hundred-pound griffin inside," Diana said, clearly worried as well. "Dyonne is downstairs, routing the griffins a new one. Someone has to know who poisoned the dress."

"It may not have come from one of the griffins," I said. Yes, we hadn't had great luck with the clans in the past, but it didn't mean the Artemae were guilty by the sake of their blood. Besides, I smelled sulfur. This was demonic.

There was a knock at the door. Grandma pushed her way inside, followed closely by Creely.

"The wards were never breached," Grandma said, by way of greeting.

"How is that possible?" I asked. "Nobody can sneak poison from hell past your barriers."

Creely exchanged a glance with Grandma. "You shouldn't," the engineering witch grunted.

"What the hell does that mean?" Diana barked.

Creely crossed her arms over her chest. "Shit. Beats me. I'd say whoever booby-trapped the dress came from inside the wedding party."

Grandma glared at her. "Makes sense," she said grudgingly.

There was another knock at the door. What was this? A fricking party?

My mentor, Rachmort, poked his head around the door, and if I didn't feel like death warmed over, I would have rushed over to hug him. The wrinkles around his eyes and the angle of his cheekbones gave him an air of jocular authority.

He removed his black top hat and ran a hand thorough his mop of white hair. If anything, it made his wild white locks stand up even more.

Zebediah Rachmort was a necromancer, a legendary demon slayer instructor and a cursed-creatures consultant for the Department of Intramagical Matters'

Lost Souls Outreach program. Today he wore a brown dress jacket, an olive green waistcoat and brown pants with pinstripes.

His white hair reminded me of Einstein's, while his Victorian-era clothes, neatly clipped sideburns, and large gold watch fob looked like something out of a Dickens novel.

It was impossible to tell how old he was. The man seemed almost timeless.

He was my sounding board. My rock.

"Ant Eater told me what happened," he said, reaching into his pocket for a blue nugget of what looked to be a chalky type of gem. He handed it to Grandma "A little something extra for the wards."

She and Creely left to go use it as Rachmort ambled toward my bedside. He sat heavy on the chair that Diana had vacated and watched me, elbows resting on his knees.

He fiddled with the humongous gold and copper ring on his middle finger. It looked more like a compass than a piece of jewelry. "It's good to see you. Alive."

"If you look at this as a fun learning opportunity, I'm going to slap you," I told him.

He merely grinned. "I'd hoped to talk to you about so many other things." He dropped the humor, gave a slight shake to his head. "I don't think any of your wedding guests are trying to hurt you."

"But you heard what Grandma and Creely said." No one came in from the outside.

He shook his head, watching me carefully. "Regretfully, I believe one of your guests is possessed."

It took me a second to process that. But damn. It made sense.

Diana frowned. "How could they get a demonic

poison past the wards?"

In typical Rachmort fashion, he embraced the discussion like a professor with a pupil. "The biker witches protect against threats from the outside. Strangers. They don't protect against good people, or invited guests who happen to carry dangerous weapons." He held up a hand while he used the other to root around in an inside jacket pocket. "If that were the case, I'd have been zapped for carrying my hell fire." He gave a slight grin as he produced a round globe with a searing yellow and orange flame inside. "Pretty, isn't it?" He held it up for us to see. "It could send you straight to hell." He set it on the bed.

Diana and I both shrank back.

Rachmort didn't notice.

"Oh, and I forgot I had this." He drew a cackling insect from his jacket. "Not to worry. Theodore is trained. You should see Petite Ice Nymphs in the wild. Nasty buggers."

"Can you put that away?" I asked.

He seemed surprised at that. "Oh, sure."

Diana took another step back. "Why do you even have that stuff?"

"I counsel the black souls of purgatory," he told Diana. "This makes me easier to relate to. You have to know your audience. Anyhow, back to our problem, I can tell you unequivocally that dangerous items can make it past the wards."

"Yes," I said, "like Cerberus slobber."

"So what got in here?" Diana asked. "When did it start?"

I tried to think back. "I don't know. I took some grave dirt on the way here, but I'm not possessed. And it wasn't evil."

"You have to invite it in," Diana said.

"Unfortunately you don't," Rachmort said, regret

coloring his voice. "There must be a pathway however. That's what makes it tricky."

How was I supposed to find a pathway when I couldn't even count on my demon detector senses working? *Think.* "If we don't know 'how' then we need to figure out 'who'." I sat up on my pillows, glad no one tried to stop me. My head was feeling better and my voice was, too, now that I was using it. "The only demon who is after me—at the moment—is the Earl of Hell." At least that was the only one I knew about. "We locked him up, though."

"Don't rule out your Earl," Rachmort said. "Zatar isn't one to stew for centuries."

I reached out with my demon slayer senses, tested the space around us for as far as I could reach in my weakened state. "I can't feel him," I said, "even before the dress incident. I didn't sense any demons. I'd know if someone is possessed. I'm a slayer."

"Except that you didn't see it coming," Rachmort said. "Did you?"

"No," I whispered.

He was right. My powers had been compromised.

Hadn't I known in, in some way, from the minute I stepped on this property?

"Can you help?" I asked Rachmort.

"I don't sense demons," he said, "but I will work to see if I can determine which of your guests could be stricken."

"What do I do?" How could I fight this evil if I couldn't even sense it?

A boom went up outside, and I heard biker witches cussing.

Boots tromped up the stairs and the door flew open. "Rachmort, can you get down here?" Grandma asked.

He nodded, and stood to go. "Be careful," he told me by way of parting.

"You, too," I said.

At least I was sitting now. I swung my legs over to get out of bed.

Diana caught them. "I promised I'd take care of you."

"You did," I told her. "Now I've got to figure out what's going on. Hand me my leather pants." My legs were smooth, maybe a little red. And weak. Otherwise, you'd never know I'd been poisoned.

"You're worse than Dimitri," she said, as I stood slowly.

"Thanks," I said, managing to stay upright.

"I didn't mean it as a compliment."

"So how the hell are you going to find a demon you can't even sense?" she asked me, as if I wasn't having enough trouble putting my pants on.

"Simple," I said, zipping them up and fastening the button. "I'm doing it the old fashioned way."

†††

I was extremely quiet, and kept to the right side of the bannister as I headed down the main staircase. There were still small groups of Dimitri's relatives gathered in the sitting room. They leaned their heads together, talking quietly, fearfully.

My legs still felt a little weak, and I took it slow. Still, I didn't want to bring any attention to myself or have to hear about how I should be in bed. Recovering was one thing. It was something else to sit around doing nothing while someone or some*thing* tried to destroy us.

When I made it outside, I saw a pair of biker witches at the far end of the drive, right before it sloped down. They were working with a group of objects on the ground. Spells, most likely. To my far right, I saw a plume of smoke erupt from the dense gardens on the side of the house.

"Lizzie!" A wet nose found the back of my knee, and I nearly stumbled off the porch. "I told you one of these days I'd be able to sneak up on you."

Yes, well I wasn't quite myself this evening. "Where have you been, Pirate?"

He stood as tall as his stubby legs would allow. "Your mom threw me outside for barking. Can you believe it? I was only trying to tell you your dress was here."

The dress was the least of my problems now.

"You think you can help me with something, bub?" I asked, bending to scratch his knobby head. As soon as he saw me reach down, he got so excited he couldn't stop moving. I hit his ear, snout, his nose. "I need to search the estate, see if we can find more of those markers, like the one you saw in the observatory."

"Oh, I will be good at that," Pirate said, falling in next to me as I started walking. "I have been all over this place. Running. Chasing rabbits. Running. Did you know there's not a fence? I could run until I fall over. In fact, I did that. Flappy had to bring me home."

"Which way?" I asked. It was more a question for myself than for him. The sides of the house looked clear. It would be hard to hide something on open ground. The gardens in the back, however, left all kinds of possibilities.

"Dimitri is making sure everything out front here is safe," Pirate said, starting to head that way.

"Let's go out back," I said, making it several feet before Pirate realized I'd done the opposite.

He rushed to join me. "What is this? Some kind of super secret mission?" he asked, his stubby legs going a mile a minute as he kept up with me.

"I'm afraid they're going to try and make me stay in

the house," I said to him, as I double-checked my switch stars. No telling what we'd find out there.

"I get it," Pirate said as we neared an arched trellis that marked the entrance to the side garden. "When I want to be in, people throw me out. When I want to go out, no one ever opens the door."

I opened my demon slayer senses as we neared the garden. I detected nothing. I focused on something new—the slight hum of my switch stars. In the past, I'd always been able to detect their subtle power. Now, I couldn't even feel that.

What had we gotten into?

"Be careful, Pirate."

He snorted. "Careful? Shit. Any creeps out here better watch out for me."

Yes. Fear the mighty Jack Russell Terrier and the injured demon slayer.

I still had my powers. That was evident enough by the way I'd nuked my wedding gown in the sitting room. But I didn't have my instincts, and that was dangerous.

It felt like I was going in blind.

We made it through the herb garden, and instead of heading through the roses, like last time, we veered into a covered garden. It swallowed us up. The archway didn't end with the trellis, rather the wiry top extended over us, forming a tunnel as climbing vines grew up and over us on both sides.

"This is like a cave!" Pirate said.

"Have you been this way before?" I asked, noticing the spider designs on the tunnel supports.

What was it with this place and spiders?

"Of course I've been this way before," Pirate said, every step light as he streaked out ahead of me. "I've been everywhere."

I reached out to touch one of the iron spiders. It was slick and cold. "How long does this go?"

"I don't know," my dog said, turning a corner, "I usually run!"

"Pirate, wait!" I dashed after him, afraid he was about to spring a booby trap or barrel headlong into something treacherous or heck—unleash a curse.

Instead, he stood at the end of another tunnel that led to a large, dry pool that held the battered husks of plants. Water lilies, I assumed.

"Are there any markers in there?" I asked, approaching slowly, saving my strength.

"Lemme see," Pirate said, scrambling up the side and basically tipping head first into the mess. I could hear him crunching around in the dead leaves before I got close enough to see him.

"Well?"

He leapt from pile to pile like a tiny stag. "It tickles my tummy!"

"Pirate, focus."

"No crazy markers, but that lady don't have a face."

For a second, I thought the ghost was back, and then I saw the statue overlooking the pond. It was some kind of a water nymph, with flowing robes and hair. She held her hands out, palms cupped toward the sky. And Pirate was right—she had no face.

"Looks like the people in the observatory," Pirate said, looking up at her.

"Those weren't people." They were very creepy statues.

I scanned the bottom of the pond, glad for once that Pirate had stirred things up. The bottom was slick, red tile, with no markers in sight. I walked the perimeter of the pool and checked the base and robes of the statue to make sure.

They were clean.

Hades. I wasn't sure where to go next. Several paths branched off from our little clearing, like spokes on a wheel. I counted six, including the one we'd just used.

"What way is the best, bub?" I asked. He'd been down some of these.

Pirate lay down in a sunny spot. "Oh, I don't know. I don't like to pay attention to *where* I'm going. Spoils the surprise, you know?"

No, I didn't. I'd had my fill of surprises lately.

"Hold on," I said, as if my dog was going anywhere.

I opened up my demon slayer senses and reached out, hoping, praying I'd get at least some sign of where we should go.

Nothing.

Lovely. I sighed, not sure what to do. Yes, I could pick a path, any path, but we only had about two hours of daylight left. I could get some biker witches to help us look. At this point, we were all on equal footing— searching without the benefit my demonic warning system.

"Help me," I said, to no one in particular.

A filmy mass hovered on the path up ahead and left. I froze, felt my heart speed up as she began to take shape—long, fluttering hair, a rounded face. It was the ghost I'd seen from the window as I was being sucked dry by poison.

She stood, watching me, wearing that same old-fashioned wedding gown.

She beckoned me with a long, bony finger.

"Oh, hell."

"Ha! You cussed. This must be serious. What did you find? I'll eat it."

"Can it, Pirate." Things had changed.

I didn't know if she was evil or good. A helper, or a creature that wanted to lure me to my doom.

Now or never.

"Come on, Pirate," I said, leading him toward the darkened path.

Chapter Fourteen

The dead woman had to pick the darkest, twistiest path. We followed her anyway. She wanted to show us something, and as far as I was concerned, the more I could learn about this place, the closer I was to determining what in Hades was happening to me and to my possessed wedding guest.

Of course, I have to admit it was a bit nerve wracking when the path took a sudden twist and we lost sight of the clearing behind us.

"Stick close, Pirate," I ordered.

For once in his life, my dog listened. He kept his nose to the ground and ears up as we trailed the ghost deeper into the garden.

The tangling vines above us grew thicker. The air was heavier with every breath, every step. The ghost widened the distance between us. I could still see her, barely, on the shadowed path ahead. She hovered higher as the path twisted once more.

"See that?" I muttered to my dog, "she's changing." She was even beginning to fade.

"I still don't see anything." Pirate sniffed the air. "Can't smell her, either."

I stepped past part of the trellis that had fallen in. It had broken in several places back here. Tree branches shot through, garden debris spilled onto the path. It was as if the entire structure was under siege.

"Do ghosts even have smells?" I was afraid to take my eyes off her as she passed through a waterfall of wild ivy.

"Everything has a smell," he said, as if it were obvious. "Like this place? It smells like rotten flowers and mucky dirt."

I didn't need his nose to tell me that.

"It's actually kind of nice," Pirate mused. The leaves to the left of me crackled as he paused to bury his nose in a pile of dead foliage. "Um hum. I'm detecting floral tones with a touch of dark oak. Dry, with a surprising boldness."

"Focus." I knew he was a connoisseur, but we didn't have the time.

It worried me that the dog with such a natural affinity for specters couldn't contact or see this one. Of course, all the ghosts Pirate had met had been benevolent.

I rested a hand on my switch stars, wondering if they even worked on the dead.

"Well, I think this is a very nice path," Pirate said, as I stepped over a fallen log and he ducked under it. "This is fun, right?"

Not when the garden grew darker. My stomach grew heavy with dread. I didn't need demon slayer mojo to tell me something was very wrong here. I could feel it in the way prey senses a predator. It was as if we were being watched, hunted. Lured closer for the kill.

There would be no one to help us out here. We were on our own.

The poisoned wedding dress was only the beginning. I had no doubt the next strike would be more violent.

I stumbled a little as I stepped into a hole. It seemed that everything I'd counted on was crumbling underneath my feet.

Snap out of it. I blew out a breath. I was a demon slayer. I had to be out here. I couldn't hide the second I was in danger. And yes, something wanted to kill me. It's not like that was unusual.

"I'm glad they're trying to axe me," I muttered to myself. Better me than someone I loved.

Pirate spun, scattering leaves. "Who's got an axe?"

"No one," I said. No sense worrying the dog.

I had enough on my mind for both of us. We were nearing a third twist in the path and so far, Pirate hadn't once tried to race out in front. Sure, I'd told him to stick close, but that never stopped him before. Pirate always had to be first.

My dog might not be able to sense the specter in a more traditional sense, but I had no doubt that he knew, somewhere in his doggie subconscious, that she was there.

The ghost disappeared around the bend. I rubbed my sweaty palms on my dress and followed. When I made it around the corner, I was shocked to see that she'd stopped. She was waiting for me.

Slowly, she turned to face us. Her expression was unreadable, her hair, a tangle of curls. It floated in the ether like a halo. Her body had mostly vanished. I could see straight through her to the wall of ivy on the other side.

We were at a dead end.

I suddenly felt claustrophobic, trapped. I desperately wanted to look behind me. It felt as if I had my entire back exposed, like something could sneak up at any moment. But I didn't dare take my eyes off her.

"Help me." Her words floated between us.

She faded into the shadows. Gone.

Pirate hit me with a wet nose to the shin. "What's she doing now?"

The shock of it brought me back. I glanced over my shoulder at the shadowed path behind us. "She left." As far as I knew.

I turned to see if she was above us, lingering on either side. I tried to sense her in the air. There was nothing. It was as if we'd been dropped down the rabbit hole.

"You mean she brought us to a wall?" Pirate asked, venturing out ahead to sniff.

"Yes." She'd taken us straight into a dead end. "Maybe there's something unusual about this spot." There had to be a reason why we'd come here. I reached out to touch the barrier. "We might be able to slide it or push it out of the way."

"Oooh," Pirate warmed to the idea instantly. "Like MacGyver!"

"You know that's not real," I said, anxious to get out of there, knowing I couldn't until we found whatever the ghost had been trying to show us.

"It's not just a TV show. It could happen," Pirate insisted as he tried to jam his nose underneath the wall.

"Remind me to dog-block Nick at Night," I said, running my hands over the corners of the wall, trying to find a gate or break in the structure.

"Now that's cruel."

I didn't find an opening in the traditional sense, but I managed to pull some ivy back. We weren't looking at a solid wall, but another iron trellis. This one was welded onto the path, obstructing us.

"What do you have in your demon slayer belt?" Pirate prodded. "What we could really use is a paper clip, a rubber band, and about twenty pounds of explosives."

"Try switch stars and magic crystals." Actually, Pirate's idea wasn't half bad. "Stand back," I told him.

I drew a switch star from my belt. The blades churned. My body tensed. "Now." I hurled it at the uppermost joint holding the trellis.

The switch star spun on its axis, sawing straight down.

I shielded my eyes as it spit wood dust and leafy bits.

"Nice!" Pirate said, ducking behind me. "Here I thought those were strictly for killing bad guys."

"So is that as good as MacGyver?" I asked, reaching to catch my weapon as it boomeranged back to me.

"Well, it's no hang glider made of duct tape," he said, while I sheathed my star.

At least he was honest.

I shoved at the trellis, forcing it back through the undergrowth on the other side, grunting as the aged metal creaked and protested. My hands grew sweaty and my entire body itched.

"You're doing great, Lizzie!" Pirate said from behind me.

"I always wanted my own personal cheerleading squad," I said, managing to shove it back a few feet.

My knees still felt a little wobbly from the wedding dress fiasco. Or maybe I was simply strung out. I gathered my strength, braced one hand on my switch stars, and ducked around the corner to see what was on the other side.

More dense garden. A couple of bees.

Frick.

"Maybe it's buried," Pirate said, inspecting the garden-turned jungle, kicking at the dirt.

In that case, we'd need Indiana Jones as well as

MacGyver. For lack of a better idea, I kicked at the dirt with him. We found nothing.

I glanced up, hands on my hips. The sun was beginning to set. We didn't have a ton of time left.

My dog brushed through the undergrowth. "Oooh...I definitely smell something dead over here."

"No dead things," I said, automatically, ignoring his overly dramatic sigh.

I didn't get it. "Why would the ghost take us out here if there wasn't anything to find?"

She'd shown up when I was being poisoned. She'd helped lead me to the abandoned observatory. I wouldn't be shocked if that was her in the graveyard at the market.

"What do you want to do?" Pirate asked. "Because in a minute, I'm going to need to start rolling in the leaves over by that dead thing. I can't help it. And you're going to get all mad. And you're going to give me a bath. I hate baths. But I can't help it. Haven't you ever heard of instinct?"

Hells bells.

"Okay, come on," I said, heading for the path.

He popped his head up, scattering leaves. "We're going back?"

"There's nothing out here." Cripes. "At least it's nothing I can detect." I'd never missed my demon slayer intuition more.

"Cheer up," Pirate said, taking the lead, "at least we know nothing's gonna eat us this time."

Small comfort.

We wound back up the path, past all three twists. I kept an eye out, although I didn't know what I expected to find different this time. Whatever it was, I didn't see it.

"We missed something," I said, once we'd reached the dry fountain.

It was the only explanation.

It killed me. We were blowing a big chance here. This could be the break we needed. If only I were in tune enough to see it.

Pirate turned in a circle and sat. "So what are you going to do if we bump into something creepy? Or find one of these markers?"

Hopefully not run for my life.

Something was here. I knew it, even if I couldn't sense it anymore. It was evil. It had already infected at least one person I cared about, and it wanted me.

I needed to learn more about the threat before I had any hope of discovering exactly what was happening here.

He stood and shook off. "Okay. Well, let's try another path."

"That's not the solution," I said, a little harsher than I'd intended.

"You got a better plan?" My dog asked, rounding the fountain and taking off down a different trail.

"No," I said, following. He disappeared around a corner. "Hey," I said, picking up my pace, "Don't get too far ahead."

But Pirate had begun to run. Curse it. His ears flopped, his tongue lolled to the side as he took one corner, dashed hard and took another one.

"Wait!" I stopped cold. *One corner. Two corners.*

I took off after him. If I had to guess right, we'd round a third corner—which we did. Before the dead end.

Pirate sat in front of a wall of ivy, exactly like the one we'd broken through. He was panting, happy. "Nothing to see here!" He said, a little too gleefully for my taste.

"Wrong, buddy," I said, catching my breath, a wave of dread crashing over me.

There was a reason the air felt heavy here, why plants died and no insects screamed. I hadn't noticed the utter, deeply disturbing silence before, probably because I'd been so consumed by the ghost. Now, it was all I could do not to escape, run and keep going.

"Pirate, we found the third marker. Remember the way it looked back at the observatory? The centerpiece, the six wavy lines coming off it. Three turns each."

We weren't looking for it. We were standing on it.

†††

I have never gotten out of somewhere so fast in my life. I didn't even care that a startled Dyonne saw me racing back into the house.

She almost dropped the platter she was rinsing in the sink. "You're supposed to be in bed."

I blew past her and barged down the hallway to the sitting room.

"Where's Rachmort?" Groupings of Dimitri's relatives looked up from their tea and coffee. I must have missed dinner entirely.

"I'm here," he said, emerging from the dining room, pipe in hand. "You ran right past me."

I really was losing my edge. "We need to talk. Somewhere private," I added glancing at the crowded sitting room, the group playing cards over in the dining room.

He nodded, as if this were not at all unusual. It made me wonder exactly what he did in his normal job.

Meanwhile, Pirate had found Ophelia and her leftovers. I left him to it.

"This way." Rachmort led me up to the second floor, then down the hallway to a small doorway that led to another, more stark landing.

"You know this house better than I do," I mumbled as we began to ascend the steep, narrow servant's stairs.

"My room is up here," he said, with his trademark good humor.

"We can get you switched." I was embarrassed my mom did that.

He shook his head. "I asked for it. I like my privacy," he said, producing a small vial of liquid from his coat pocket.

The hallway was undecorated, the doors stark and old. We stopped at the third door down and Rachmort dabbed a fingertip's worth of the liquid on the lock. It clicked open and he led us inside.

His room was Spartan, containing only a small bed and a dresser. I didn't feel comfortable sitting on either one, so I remained standing. "I found the second marker."

He nodded solemnly. "I thought you would." He looked at me closely, caging his words. "Dimitri showed me the photo you took of the first marker. I've seen it before."

"It's bad, isn't it?" I could tell by the way he was acting. "Don't sugar-coat it. I need to know what I'm dealing with here."

He nodded, still watching me. "The markers are very specific calling signs. They're meant to gather power, to direct it." He stepped closer, towering over me. "Lizzie, I'm afraid these markers are pathways, designed to enable a demon to cross over."

Oh my God. "What if we destroy them?" I could take a hatchet to the stone one. Maybe. I didn't know how I'd level half the garden.

"You'd need to find them all first."

"Maybe I did," I said, wildly hoping. Praying.

"There are always three," Rachmort said. "And if they are drawing planetary power, they will be arranged in a straight line. It would be my guess that the observatory is the first marker."

"Okay, so the garden is the second. Come to think of it, if we cut a straight line from there, we'd hit the observatory." Dang. Rachmort really was good.

He placed his glasses on the dresser. "So you have the observatory," he said, positioning them toward the back. "Then the garden maze," he said, digging in his pocket and producing a pink-and-green flecked gem the size of a golf ball.

"What is that?"

"Limbo bargaining chip," he said, dismissing it. "Now where is the third marker?"

"Let me think. We have the herb garden, some crazy statues, the back porch... The house." A chill prickled through my veins.

Holy Hades.

"It might not be a straight line," I said, grasping for straws at that point.

"Come," Rachmort said, leading back out to the stairs, up to another landing, and another. There was a locked door at the top. He took care of it in an instant with his little vial.

"I need to get some of that stuff," I said, as he applied it to the lock.

"I'll take you to see RaeRae next time we're in limbo."

"Oh, great," I said, my enthusiasm waning. RaeRae, an otherworldly oddities collector, drove a hard bargain.

We walked out to the center of the parapet. "Dang. You can see everything from here."

Rachmort pointed. "There's the observatory."

It was a small tower among the trees at the back. "There's the fountain Pirate and I saw." The rest of the marker was hidden under the trellises, but the center of it lined up perfectly with the observatory.

They were spaced evenly, about fifty yards apart. And fifty yards in, in a straight line from the fountain, was the house.

"We're standing on top of it," I said, fighting the urge to flee, to run, to leave and never come back.

Rachmort took me by the shoulders, forced me to look up at him. "You can fix this, Lizzie."

"Maybe so, but we need to get my family out of here." Yes, Hillary had picked this evil house. I had no doubt now she'd been compelled into it. She'd told me she had to have it. She didn't even understand why. Now I knew. Something wanted me here.

"You can't leave," Rachmort said, the wind catching his wild gray hair as the sun set behind him. "The demon has a hold on someone. That person can't leave now or the demon will remain with them. They'll deteriorate, Lizzie. They'll lose their soul."

"So then forty other people have to stay?" They'd all be in equal danger. This was a nightmare.

"You have to make the choice, Lizzie."

It was crazy. "How can I possibly choose?" I couldn't.

That's when it hit me: would I leave if Dimitri were compromised? Never. Grandma? No. One of his new clan members? I was ashamed at the direction my thoughts had taken.

"Okay," I said, "nobody comes, nobody leaves. I'll destroy all the markers."

"At once," Rachmort said. "You must destroy them all at the same time."

He had to be kidding. "How am I going to do that?"

"I don't know. You're the demon slayer. Once you do that, the demon can no longer use the markers to draw power, and then all you have to do is exorcise the hell spawn."

Oh, sure. Piece of cake.

I'd figure it out later. "We need to warn everyone," I said, heading for the stairs.

"No." Rachmort caught my arm. "You absolutely cannot tell anyone. Not even your fiancé. Whoever is compromised will tip off our target."

"I'm marrying him in two days and I can't even tell him this?"

"You can't even tell your dog."

I couldn't believe it. "What if you're compromised?" I asked.

He shot me an apologetic glance. "Then you're screwed."

We tromped down the stairs, my mind swimming with possibilities. I couldn't imagine whom the demon had targeted, or when they would attack.

"Act as normal as possible," Rachmort instructed. "Be on your guard. We must not tip off the possessed. Hopefully, we'll catch him or her during his next attempt on your life."

"Now doesn't that make me feel good?"

"This isn't about you, Lizzie. It's about finding that marker."

"I will," I told him. I didn't have a choice.

Chapter Fifteen

I searched for Dimitri and found him in his room as he was coming out of the shower. Just my luck, I didn't even get to appreciate it.

"We need to search the house," I told him.

He paused before he finished wrapping a towel around his waist. "What are you doing out of bed?"

"I feel great," I said, knowing neither of us remotely believed that. "Besides, we have bigger problems. What if there are more weapons hidden in the house?"

Like a third marker.

It was a plausible explanation, without telling him anything. Hades, I felt like a jerk.

He watched me, running a hand towel over his hair, spiky wet from the shower. Water droplets clung to the strands at the nape of his neck. God, he was sexy. He also knew I was holding back on him. I could see it in his eyes.

"Let me get dressed," he said simply, before grabbing a pair of jeans off the end of the bed. Dang. I loved that curve of muscle at his hip, the long sinewy lines of his body. He tugged on a black T-shirt. "Enjoying yourself?"

"Next best thing to undressing you."

He gave me a saucy grin as he sat on the bed and tugged on a pair of motorcycle boots. "You're going to pay for that when you're feeling better."

I watched as the muscles in his chest and arms worked. "I hope so." I couldn't even tell he'd been hurt.

"So you think there's something dangerous here." He stood, tucking in his shirt. "Is there a particular place you want to start?"

That was the trick. "I have no real leads. Only a feeling." The knowledge that we would find the third marker somewhere in the house.

He nodded. "Then let's start at the top and work our way down."

We headed for the stairs Rachmort and I had used. He seemed so sure of himself and the direction we were headed. "Wait. Have you been up here before?"

"I was curious," Dimitri said, opening the door for me. "I saw the towers from the outside, and wanted to see where they led."

We started climbing. Dimitri and I both liked to explore new places. At the same time, I had my suspicions about his time in the towers. "You were avoiding my mother, weren't you?"

He grunted. "Name one guy who goes to a bonbon party."

"You."

"Not for long."

Touché. I struggled to keep my breath even. The steep stairs were doing a number on me since the attack. My legs ached, my chest heaved. The adrenaline I'd had while running up with Rachmort was shot. I didn't need Dimitri to see I was struggling, lest he send me back to bed.

At last, we made it to the top.

Dimitri tried the door to the parapet. "Locked," he said, giving the handle one final twist.

"It wasn't before?"

"Not a few days ago, no." He gave a final glance at the door. "I can fly up and take a look on the parapet if we don't find anything inside the house."

"It can wait," I said. I'd get Rachmort to take me back up, in case Dimitri was compromised.

God, I hated to think of him housing a demon, all because of me. I hated lying to him. Damn, this whole thing was so frustrating.

"Hey," he said, taking my hand. "What's that look for?" His lips brushed mine. "If there's something in this house that can hurt you, we'll find it."

"Thanks," I said, hugging him tight. Hades, I wished I could be sure it wasn't him hurting me. That would kill him.

His arms wrapped around me lightly, and he patted me on the back. I could tell he was a little confused. Oh, well. He was going to marry me. He'd better get used to it.

I drew back. "Okay, let's see what we find." And hope we got lucky.

The start of our search was less productive than I'd hoped, mainly because most of the rooms on this floor had been taken over by Dimitri's relatives, and the doors were locked.

I was willing to bet there was nothing in the demon slayer handbook about that.

"Are you sure you can't use your evil sensing powers?" Dimitri asked, trying yet another barred door. "We wouldn't have time to go through every room even if they were unlocked. Besides, Aunt Zizi will beat my ass if she catches me going through her nighties."

Frick. He was right. "Okay. New plan. How about we search the public areas?"

He gave me a sideways glance as he tried yet another locked door. "You do realize that the odds of anyone hiding a weapon in the dining room are zero to none."

He still thought we were looking for poisons and such. This was ridiculous. "Let's also keep an eye out for evil markers and omens," I said, as casually as I could. There. I didn't tell him. I hinted. He deserved a hint.

He knew something was up. Of course he did. He wasn't an idiot. "Lizzie," he drew it out, expecting me to say more. He waited, not giving me an inch.

"Trust me, okay?" I said, falling back on a loophole he'd used, oh, about a thousand times.

He knew it, too. He pressed his mouth closed, unhappy. But he didn't say anything.

We searched both the third and the second floor hallways before moving down to the foyer. The wood walls in the entryway were beautiful. I hadn't taken the time to really study them before. They were hand-carved in intricate flower and wildlife motifs. I did catch the occasional wooden spider, but that was all. No markers.

It was getting late and the sitting room was clearing out.

"I'll take the front by the windows, and you take the area by the dining room," Dimitri said.

So he thought. I'd have to figure out a way to search the whole thing.

Frieda and a bunch of biker witches walked over. She held a cup and saucer, and I was tempted to sniff her tea. "What's the problem?" she asked.

"Lizzie lost her earring," Dimitri said. The lie came from him so smoothly I almost believed it myself.

"We'll help you look," Frieda offered, much to the annoyance of a few of her companions. They followed Dimitri to the front of the room while I headed the opposite way. There was a card game going on in the dining room, boys versus girls. That should be fun.

"Lizzie," my mom entered from the hallway. Her hair was flawless. She'd re-done her nails and changed her outfit. Only her eyes betrayed the impact of this afternoon. She was wary, scared. "Are you okay, honey?"

I was ready with a formulaic answer when she rushed to close the distance between us and gave me a real, genuine hug. It felt so good that I almost forgot about our mission down here.

"I'm fine," I said, swallowing some unexpected emotion. At least I had to think I would be. I drew back to look at her. "Are you? How are you doing with the demon slaying and the biker witches and," I searched for a way to say it, "Dimitri's claws."

She brought her chin up, steeling herself. "I'm going to be fine," she said, in a way that at least told me that she was determined to make it true.

Mom took my hands, running her fingers over them and inspecting them, like she couldn't believe I was really okay.

I let out a breath I hadn't even realized I was holding. "I'd meant to tell you sooner." I really had.

She nodded a few too many times. "I can see where it would be...difficult." Tears filled her eyes. "I'm worried about you, honey. Your grandmother says these kinds of attacks happen to you more often than not. I realize she'd hoped to make me feel better, but I don't want to see you go through this. When you hurt, I hurt."

I knew she meant well. And I hated to put her

through this, but, "Mom, I can't stop being a demon slayer."

"I know." She quickly wiped away a tear. "I'd never ask that."

That stunned me. "You wouldn't?"

Creely stood behind mom, giving me the thumbs up. I wondered exactly what the biker witches had told Hillary.

"It wouldn't stop you anyway," Hillary said.

"True," I said slowly, waiting for the other shoe to drop. This wouldn't be the end of it. Not by a long shot.

She folded her hands in front of her. "Tell me what I can do to help."

That part was deceptively simple. "You have to keep going," I told her. We needed everyone to stay, to have fun. My mom was great at organizing groups. "Only," I didn't quite know how to tell her this, but, "no more guests."

She looked at me like I'd sprouted horns. "Your wedding is in two days. Of course there'll be more guests. We have the VanWillens, and the Frosts. Pipsi Carmichael and her fiancé. Oh, and of course Matt Shott and his lovely girlfriend, Kimmy. Matt owns a hockey team."

She didn't get it.

"Look, mom—"

"Your father arrives tomorrow."

"No, mom. Listen to me. There's still a danger." Heads in the dining room swiveled our way. "A slight one," I amended. "We don't know who or what is after me. So let's keep this wedding small, and then we can have a nice reception somewhere later."

A furrow formed between her brows. "We'll talk about it," she said, reluctantly. She knew I had a point.

"You said you wanted to help." I was relieved to see

her nod. "I don't want to be responsible for anyone else getting hurt. Right now, the witches and the griffins can defend themselves, the VanWillens cannot. No more guests, okay?"

She began to argue, then simply said, "okay."

Mom helped me search the back of the sitting room until we ran into Dimitri's family. Then she hit up Dimitri with a load of questions on what it was like to be a griffin. I was glad for her curiosity. It meant I could covertly re-check his section and hit the dining room as well. I have to admit I did feel bad for the guy, having to answer things like:

Do you eat...food?

Yes. I wanted to ask her if she remembered the time he fixed breakfast for us.

Exactly why do you want *to fly?*

Because he's fricking griffin, mom.

And, *What happens to your clothes when you shift?*

Mom went red after that one. Some things, you don't want to know about your daughter's fiancé.

Dimitri, bless his heart, was unfailingly polite. I could tell mom felt better talking about it. Maybe the truth wasn't so bad after all.

We searched the kitchen together, my mom trying to make us snacks the entire time. I settled for an artesian cheese sandwich but forgot it on the counter as Dimitri and I readied ourselves to descend into the basement.

I kept a hand on my switch stars and he took the stairs before me. They were incredibly steep. Narrow as well. A chill seeped up from the cavern, along with a pungent, musty odor. A single bulb above lit the stairs, its light dying as it reached too far underground.

"Let me go first. I'm a demon slayer."

"You're injured," he said, starting down. "Don't

think I don't see how you keep leaning up against the wall."

He had me there. My entire body ached. "I have the weapons."

Dimitri reached up and pulled the chain for a second, dangling bulb. This one lit parts of a gray floor that stretched out into the darkness.

"You know," I continued, worrying a bit when I began getting light headed, "demon slayer. Demon attack."

He cursed and stepped aside to let me pass as we neared the bottom. My palms were clammy and my knees were weak.

"Ready?" He asked, pausing to search for a light switch.

I drew a switch star. "Ready."

Light bathed the space at the bottom of the stairs. The walls were made of stacked stone, painted white. The floor was concrete. And that was it. No storage. No ping-pong table. No demons. As far as I could tell, whoever was in charge of renting out the place didn't seem to use the basement.

"I don't get it." There had to be another room, a secret space with those faceless statues and maybe a few minions of the devil.

Dimitri and I followed the basement around a U-shaped bend and came to a door to the right. I nodded at him, switch star in hand, and he threw it open.

"Ha!" I drew my star back, ready to throw, until I realized it was a utility room, lit by the same ceiling lights as the rest of the basement. "This is way too normal."

Dimitri glanced at me, then back inside the room. "We might as well check it out."

We thoroughly searched the small utility room because, well, where else were we going to look? But as I expected, I didn't find any demonic markers behind the water heater.

I didn't understand it. The house had been a bust.

My entire body ached.

Logically, there had to be something down here, or maybe upstairs or *somewhere*. I severely doubted we'd find a demonic marker hidden in a random bedroom. But those were the only places we hadn't searched. That and the parapet.

"Maybe it's in the garden," Dimitri said, taking one final look behind the furnace.

"No," I said, heading for the stairs.

All I wanted to do was crawl into bed.

His footsteps were heavy behind me. "You asked me to trust you. I get that. But this will go a lot easier if you told me what the hell we're looking for."

"I'm too tired to argue." My legs ached. My chest and arms still felt tight from the poison's effects, and I'd swear I hadn't slept in a year.

I didn't even protest when Dimitri led me into his room instead of mine.

"It'll be the least of your mom's shocks for today," he said, closing the door behind us. We eased our shoes off and he drew me into bed.

It was so soft. Perfect. I curled into the warmth of his arms. "I love you," I said, and before he could answer, I was asleep.

†††

The next morning, Dimitri and I made up from our tiredness the night before. He was acting perfectly normal, although he certainly made love like a man possessed. Very refreshing.

Afterward, I curled next to him, naked, wishing I could tell him what was happening with the marks. Of course, it was impossible, for his sake and for mine.

I purposely kept my head tucked against his chest. I

couldn't look at him as I said, "my mom wants me to make wedding doves today."

He drew back, trying to look at me. I kept my head down.

"Lizzie, we're in the middle of an attack."

"I know, but I promised. She wants us to glue sequins onto the backs of these fake birds she got at Michaels."

He forced me to look at him then. "Are you okay?" He searched my face, looking for evidence of an addled brain. I didn't blame him a bit.

I pasted on my best smile. "Sure. In the mean time, can you and the griffins make sure the grounds are secure?" I did worry about what was out there in the garden, and what could be approaching from any direction. We weren't safe in this house, not until I could find and destroy the markers. Dimitri may not be able to help with that, but if I had the griffins protecting the house, I'd feel a lot better while I looked.

He ground his jaw tight. "Fine. But I know you're not gluing doves."

Okay. Caught. "What if I said I was making rose petal sachets?"

His eyes were steel, his expression hard. "Be careful."

Easier said than done.

We showered together and dressed with our backs to each other. I felt for him. I really did. I knew what it was like to have your partner, the person who is supposed to love and trust you above all others, go rogue with no explanation or apology. But I didn't have a choice here.

He left to gather the griffins while I set out to investigate what we could have possibly missed inside the house

This place was old, with plenty of nooks and crannies. Well, everywhere except for the basement. I stopped at the second floor landing and closed my eyes. I reached out, trying to feel the energy of the house, to sense any disruptions that may lead me to the third marker.

Nothing.

I shoved my hands into my pockets. "Cripes." It was worth a try.

Maybe there was a hidden part of the house, or a secret passage. I could really use the ghost right about now. "Help me," I said, as I ran my fingers over the paneling on the second floor landing. I moved down each stair, feeling the wall as I went. "Help me."

That's when Creely nearly ran me over.

"Watch it," I told her.

"Hey, sorry. I thought you might actually be walking down the stairs."

"I'm looking for hidden passages."

She stopped a few stairs below me. "That's an outside wall, sweetheart."

"I know that. But wouldn't this be a great place for a passage? You could make it a foot or two wide in this spot. Nobody would suspect."

She looked at me like I was nuts. "It's a load bearing wall. In an old house like this, of course, it would be a foot thick."

Yes, well some of us weren't engineers.

She gave me a cock-eyed look, clearly deciding if she should stay and harass me, or if she should continue barreling through the house.

"Come here," she said, heading down the stairs. "The trick to discovering any kind of hidden room or structural oddity is to look at what you can see."

"Have you been brewing more tea?" I asked, following her down.

"No, look," she said, as we stood in the foyer, with our backs to the front door. "If we went outside, you could see that the walls are built in proportion on the outside, so no secret passages there. Then you simply move forward," she said, leading me through the house. "The sitting room is out. No missing spaces, so to speak. I've already checked the dining room." She shrugged. "I suck at cards."

We moved farther back into the hallway.

It was old and had these neat woodcarvings.

"Now I wonder what's behind that wall," she mused.

Was this a quiz? "It's the stairs."

"No. The stairs are toward the front." She tilted her head, studying it. "That back part doesn't line up."

I leaned forward to look.

"See?" She continued, starting to get a little excited. "The kitchen doesn't go that far back into that space."

No kidding. I knew Creely was smart, but this was something else. "You think it's something?"

I checked the kitchen. It didn't extend back this far. It was true—there was some missing space. "I'll bet something *is* behind here," I said, running my fingers over the carved mahogany paneling.

"Yeah, but how do we access it?" she asked, taking a look into the kitchen.

"That wall is really plain." It would be hard to hide anything.

"Doesn't mean they didn't."

I heard her checking things out in there while I worked finding anything unusual about the hall paneling.

There were lions with claws bared, fighting what looked to be centaurs. It was like they were in a jungle with these wild looking flowers and plants that sprouting up everywhere. They were as big as the animals. Then you had the cosmos above, with swirling planets and stars.

After a while, Creely joined me. We did a systematic check. It was slow going, and I almost started to doubt, when Creely touched a lever. It had been perfectly hidden in the scrollwork of a toothsome creature holding a battle shield.

"Amazing," I said as the door swung open on a dark room.

"Logic. These things are never in plants or bunnies," she said, moving past me, feeling for a light.

There wasn't one.

Oh great. I was about to go into a hidden, dark room with someone who may be possessed. I blew out a breath. Problem was, I needed to see this through. I'd have to be on my guard.

We heard the back door to the kitchen open, and then my mom's voice as well as Grandma's.

"Quickly," Creely said.

I unhooked the Maglite from my switch star belt and followed her into the secret room.

Chapter Sixteen

The air was stuffy and stale.

"I'm shutting the door," Creely warned, before it clicked closed behind her.

Darkness enveloped us, save for the beam from my flashlight. "Do we know how to get out?" I asked, shining my light over the wood paneling she'd closed.

Creely's rusty laugh cut through the gloom. "That wasn't your goal, now was it?"

Yeek. I hoped she was joking. It was hard to tell sometimes with biker witches. The truly awful thing is that I wouldn't know whether or not she was out to kill me, until she tried.

It was eerily quiet.

Creely moved slowly through the murky darkness. I had to keep my head about me or I'd put a switch star through her by accident.

A thick burgundy carpet covered the floors. I didn't see how we were going to get under it in order to check for a marker. Dark wood bookshelves lined the walls. I shone my light up.

The room had two stories worth of shelves, with a walkway on the top level. There must have been a rolling ladder at one point. I didn't see it now. The room didn't have any windows. It wouldn't. We were in the very center of the house.

Unease prickled at the back of my neck. I didn't like the lack of exits. It made the place feel closed in, tomb-like.

An ornate wooden desk dominated the center of the room. Creely eased into the leather chair behind it. She struck a match and lit one of the thick white candles on the desk.

"You think you ought to be setting fires in here? I asked, coughing a little against the sharp smell of the match.

"At least I'm keeping my cigars in my pocket," she said, lighting two more candles off the original one.

Fine. As long as we didn't burn the house down.

Creely took a look at the desk. I kept an eye on her while I searched for any more passages, or any interesting books.

Grimoire of Pope Leo, 1740

Spiritual Lessons from the Brownings

Fléau des Démons et Sorciers I pulled the cracking black leather book off the shelf. It was a black bible. Our library owner may have started off as a hobbyist, but he'd ended up with some pretty twisted reading material.

And back it went. I'd seen enough dark texts to last me a lifetime.

I turned in a slow circle, my light hovering over the dusty volumes on the shelves.

"Take a look at this," Creely said, hunched over an old journal with a cracked green leather cover.

"What'd you find?" I asked, moving to look over her shoulder.

"I don't know. It was behind a false panel in the desk." The first page revealed it was the personal journal of Stuart T. Russell.

"Hey," she said, swiping my light and turning the

book around so she could get a better angle. "That's the guy who built this place." She paged through the journal while I tried to see. "He was a fancy pants railroad baron."

"You know about him?"

"I like his taste in architecture." She shrugged. "This isn't a well-known building, but it's been on my list of places to see. It says here that Russell broke ground in 1889. Finished in 1891. Ha."

"What?"

"You want to know what's funny about that?"

"I will if you tell me."

"He was a freak about the occult. They like to do things in threes. Three years to build. Three spires along the top of the house. Three main paths in the garden." She glanced back at me. "Don't tell me it was a mistake that the herb garden is laid out in a pentacle."

I'd been too busy looking at the markers.

She pressed the book open to a page filled with pen and ink drawings of spiders. They were creepy looking, certainly ugly with their long legs and fangs. Occult symbols for death and rebirth were etched into their bulbous bodies.

"What is it with spiders in this place?" I asked, running my finger over the yellowed page.

"Spiders are an occult symbol in themselves," Creely said. "They're linked to treachery and death in a lot of cultures. Think of the Greeks and how Athena turned Arachne into a spider. Or how the Christians have linked spiders to an evil force that sucks blood from believers."

I liked this place less and less all the time.

"What's the point in all of this? A smart guy like Russell had to have a game plan. What did he want?"

"Maybe he wanted to be the best crazy Victorian occultist he could be." Creely kept paging through the book.

"Give me a second." I closed my eyes and focused on the book. I pictured it in my mind, I tried to feel the essence of the man who created it. I opened myself to its energies, its power.

Nothing.

I don't know why I kept trying. Except that I refused to stop doing everything I could, merely because I was compromised.

Creely kept my light trained over the yellowing book as she paged through an array of sun and moon symbols, as well as nonsensical messages written in capital letters.

"*See me now.*" I read. "*I am here.*" "*Build my garden.*" There were pages of them.

"You can read that?" She shook her head. "Of course you can." Her light hovered over the words. "What language are they using?"

"I have no idea."

"It looks to me like a code," she said. "Different occult groups used to make up their own languages."

It made sense.

Creely paused, thinking. "They'd get messages from an Ouija board and record them."

"Why was he using a Ouija board?" He had markers. It was the difference between two cups and a string versus a cell phone.

"Maybe he didn't have anybody to talk to," she said, missing the point. "I think he was some kind of recluse."

"That's sad."

"Yeah, there was this huge scandal. I forget the story. Then boom, he's stuck here."

"Oh yeah?" I said, warming to it. "What happened?" It may help me figure out this house.

Creely thought for a moment. "He may have been the one of the guys funneling money off the top in the Credit Mobilier scandal. No. Wait. Wrong railroad." She rubbed a hand over her chin. "Lizzie Borden was the one with the axe."

"These Victorians were a feisty bunch"

She slapped her hands together. "I got it. Russell was the one who killed his virgin bride on their wedding night."

"What?" I demanded. For the first time in my life, I made a biker witch jump. "We have a dead bride in this house?" Of course we did. Hadn't I seen her? She was certainly wearing white.

"Nobody ever figured out for sure if he killed her," she said, backtracking. As if that made a difference. She was dead and I'd seen her.

I walked straight into the darkness, spun back around, and fought the urge to throttle Creely. "When was somebody going to tell me about this?"

"I just thought of it," she said, defensively. "Now I'm sorry I did," she added under her breath.

"This is lovely. An occult house with a dead bride."

"Chill, Lizzie. We're here for your wedding, not hers."

Yes, well I didn't know if the ghost realized that or not.

For all I knew, I had vengeful poltergeist bridezilla on my hands. She was there at the attack, watching me as I choked. "This is a dangerous place."

Creely set the book aside. "Come on. You could get attacked in Chuck-E-Cheese, so don't go blaming everything in this house."

"Tell me about his wife."

She sighed. "I don't know. She was way younger

than him. I think she lived on a farm north of here. I doubt she came from a hugely rich family because they didn't do a ton of investigating after she was strangled on her wedding night."

"Sure. Why would they?" I started to pace. I'd be willing to bet I'd stood on her grave when Grandma and I had visited that farmers market.

Hadn't we seen the remains of an old farmhouse? Her headstone had been large, and expensive no doubt. Given by a guilty husband? Or perhaps bought by a family who could do nothing else but mourn.

I recalled the inscription on the stone. "Her name was Elizabeth, wasn't it?"

Creely shook her head. "I have no idea."

"Yes, well, I'm pretty sure I've seen her ghost," and cripes—I had her grave dirt in my locket. I had to get rid of it, but not here in the house. Somewhere away from the markers. "She wants me to help her."

"Don't." Creely said, closing the book and stuffing it into the back of her jeans. "You don't know what you're dealing with in this house."

Understatement of the year.

The kicker was, I couldn't control that. I just had to be on my game, and hope for the best. How sad to reach a point where a gothic bridal ghost was the least of my problems.

I stood for a moment, hands on my hips, thinking. I couldn't worry. Or wait. The only thing I could do to change any of this was to find that third marker.

"There's something we're not seeing," I told the biker witch.

Creely grinned, like it was a challenge. "Then let's hit this sucker."

We attacked Russell's office. We picked the locks on the main desk drawer and Creely cracked the combination on a safe hidden behind some books. We found a metal case with another magical diary of sorts. This one had an art nouveau type pentacle, which made Creely roll her eyes.

There were handmade talismans, a round altar cloth with the light and life cross and the six-pointed star on it. We came across a few wands that Creely declared 'no better than twigs' and a crystal ball with a crack down the middle.

"Amateurs," the biker witch muttered.

"When did this guy ever have time to run a railroad?" I asked, as we laid out all the stuff on the desk.

"I don't think he had many guests in here," she said, eyeing the bookshelves.

I followed her gaze and saw that the ceiling was painted with a scene from revelation. Or at least I hoped it was biblical. I cringed inwardly. It sure wasn't white magic.

Finally, I crawled under the desk and was rewarded with a handful of dust bunnies. And a few spiders. Ick. At least these were alive and of the normal variety. I rubbed my hands on my dress.

"Come, oh bride to be," Creely said, as she started blowing out the candles. A chill ran though my veins and I stood as fast as I could. Then again, if Creely had wanted to kill me, why hadn't she tried already?

The biker witch stood by the wall that opened to the hallway. "As much as I like insane nightmares, I think we've seen all there is in here."

No. This couldn't be the end of it. I tried to think, to imagine where else we could go.

I stood thinking for a moment. "Creely, do you need a couple of big stone walls to support a house like this?"

She shone the light at me, catching me in the face. "Care to be a bit more specific?"

"Stop," I said, as she lowered the Maglite. I blinked back the dots in my line of vision while I tried to picture the U-shaped bend in the basement. "Would you need two parallel load bearing walls about fifteen feet apart?"

"No." She began heading for the exit. "What's going on?"

She had no idea how tired I was of that question.

"I think there's a room directly below us." There had to be. "It's at the center of the house, walled in on all sides. I have to get down there."

She sighed, checked her watch. "You know your mom's throwing you a wedding shower in about a half hour."

I'd totally forgotten. "What day is it?"

She gave me an exaggerated bug-eyed stare. "Call in the necromancers, hell's heated up."

Ha, ha. "The wedding shower can wait."

The biker witch snarfed. "Have you met your mom?" She ran a thumb along the scrollwork on the wall, searching for the hidden lever.

"Creely. This is important to me. I'm the bride. If I want to find a secret room instead of sit there and get presents, it's my choice. My wedding."

She turned to me, looked me up and down. "Well, why the hell not?" She dug through her front pocket and produced a book of matches. "Gotta keep the bride happy." She handed me my flashlight on the way over to the desk. Then she relit the largest white taper candle and held it aloft. "As my gift to you, I will get you into the secret room under the creepy occult mansion."

"Thank you," I said, meaning every word. "It's so much better than hand towels."

She gave me a long look, the candlelight accenting

the lines on her face. "Let's hope you still feel that way once you're down there."

We searched the bookcases again. We searched the floor. And then I saw a book on Pluto.

"Don't read," Creely said, inspecting the bookcases, trying to find a hidden lever.

"Don't worry," I said, opening the first page.

She stopped searching. "Is this a demon slayer instinct?""More of a gut feeling. This is a book on a planet—"

"Pluto's not a planet," Creely said automatically.

"—shelved with a bunch of books on demonology. I paged through and almost dropped it when I saw the center of the book had been cut out, and a key neatly inserted. It was made of iron and nearly as long as my hand.

"It would be hard to lose that one," Creely said.

"Hard to hide it, too." If someone went through all this trouble, it was probably important. I tucked my Maglite under my arm started digging it out.

"Give me your light." Creely snatched the light, nearly making me drop the book. Which made the key pop out. Okay, two birds…

She shone my light into the space where the book had been shelved. "Bingo."

There was an antique keyhole built into the wall.

"That wasn't so difficult, was it?" Creely asked.

"Speak for yourself."

I handed her the key and she inserted it into the lock. Then I stood back, my right hand on my switch stars as she pushed the door to the bookcase back. It resisted for a moment. The hinges groaned as the door reluctantly swung back into a darkened stairwell.

It was lined with old brick and ornamented with crude, hand-painted images of spider webs. A concrete, spiral staircase wound down into the abyss.

"Happy wedding shower," Creely said.

I took the flashlight from her and shone it down the stairs. They were steep and winding. It was impossible to know what lay at the bottom.

"My present is down there."

I started down the steps. Meanwhile, Creely went back and grabbed her candle. "Damn. I wish I'd brought a few spell jars."

"Let's hope we don't need them." The air was musty and chilly in the passage. I fought off a shiver as we descended, our footsteps echoing off the stairs.

Whatever awaited us down there reeked of stale incense and rot. This had to be Russell's crowning achievement. It was hidden at the very center of his home, well concealed under his precious books and occult artifacts.

As we reached the bottom, I gasped. Holy hell. He wasn't an occultist. He was a Satanist.

My flashlight shone directly on a skull. Then another, then another. They were stacked along the walls, a macabre collection dedicated to death and the dark arts. Some of them were even decorated with gold gilt paint and lacquer. As if the gilded age tycoon couldn't even leave death unadorned.

"They don't look human." Creely said behind me.

"That one is." I pointed my light at a gold-painted skull that sat on top of a pillar, like a macabre bust. It was adorned with a dull red jewel between the eyes.

At the center of the room stood a black stone altar, with black tapers on either side. "Fuck it. I'm not lighting those," Creely said.

I didn't blame her. I also noticed neither one of us had moved from the very bottom of the stairs.

I'd heard of places like this, dedicated to the dark arts. "This is a black chapel."

The biker witch let out a low whistle. "It ain't Disneyland."

"I wonder if this is what's blocking my power." I didn't feel the heavy press of evil, like I should. Only the very real, very human instinct to run.

"Let's get the hell out of here." Creely said, obviously feeling the same.

"Give me a minute." I forced myself to take one step forward, then another. The floor itself seemed tainted, the air I breathed, impure.

My flashlight snaked across the chapel. I walked behind the altar, like a dark priest would. I stood at the very center of the house, the vortex of evil.

There, carved into the black altar, was the third mark.

CHAPTER SEVENTEEN

That was it. I hated to turn my back on the dark chapel, but I wasn't about to have Creely behind me, either. I let her take the lead as we made tracks up the stairs and through the hidden office. She battled with the secret door we'd used to get us into this mess while I guarded her back.

She'd needed my light to find the latch, so I was left with a candle and my switch stars. I kept an eye on the bookcase we'd closed behind us. Nothing seemed to follow from below. Yet. For that I was eternally grateful.

"Got it." Creely let the door swing open.

"Thank God." I doused the last candle and followed her out. She slammed the door behind us, and I didn't blame her a bit.

We were met by a startled Frieda, who stood a few feet away, stopped cold by our sudden appearance. "Err…" She fiddled with her hair. "People are looking for you."

"In a minute." I didn't care who they were or what they wanted. I had a creepy grave dirt issue to address.

I wasn't about to empty it inside the house. Who knew what that might do?

It would have to be done outside, completely off the property. I didn't want this dirt anywhere near the house, or the land.

After that, I'd have to wash the necklace and purify it. I wanted nothing to do with the demented railroad baron or his dead bride.

I jogged down the winding drive, all the way down to the main road. Gargoyles stared down at me as I put one foot in front of the other, trying not to think about what I could have around my neck.

What I'd worn this entire time.

My body warmed from the run. Despite it, I felt cold inside. I half-expected Elizabeth to appear and try to stop me.

I hadn't even heard the ghost's voice until I stepped on that grave. Her grave. Well, no more. She could haunt someone else.

I reached the road, crossed it, and picked my way through tall spindly weeds to the cliff face on the other side. There would be no way for Elizabeth to contact me again. Or at least I'd do my level best to make it so.

Salt tinged the air, along with a cool breeze off the water. I stopped a yard back from the edge of oblivion. Call me crazy, but I didn't trust the sturdiness of the land so close to a sheer drop off. I glanced behind me, making sure I was alone. This would be the perfect opportunity for murder.

The area behind me was deserted. So far.

Dry grass crunched under my feet as I forced myself to take one tentative step forward, then another. A car whizzed past. The ocean churned below.

With shaking fingers, I grasped the clasp of the locket, ready to release the dirt into the waters below.

It wouldn't open.

I pulled harder, the cool metal biting against my fingers.

"Come on." It wouldn't budge.

Sweet switch stars. I had to get rid of this tainted dirt. I felt sick with it. Claustrophobic. I needed the grave dirt off of me. Now.

Come on. Come on. I struggled against the enchanted metal.

It was as if the fricking thing were welded shut.

I wanted to collapse and cry. Maybe I would have if I hadn't been so petrified of the cliff, and the ocean, and what could happen if I let my guard down for a second.

There was only one thing left to do and, Hades, I wasn't even sure I could pull it off.

Dimitri had gifted me this enchanted necklace soon after we met. It was meant to be with me always, to protect me. Back when I was first learning my powers, it had been impossible to take off. Now, I had to change that.

"I'm sorry, Dimitri," I said, focusing every bit of my power and concentration on the task ahead. "I renounce our agreement," I said, feeling the sting of my own betrayal. It had to be done. "Though the emerald was freely given" —I paused before I could force myself to say the words out loud— "It is no longer freely accepted."

I could almost feel his heart break a little from here. Dimitri would understand why I broke our protection bond. He had to. He may not, however, be so generous about what I planned to do after I removed his family heirloom.

I grasped the necklace on either side, felt it hum in protest as I lifted it slowly. It grew heavier every second, but I kept going until I was free. I felt strange without it. Naked.

The necklace dangled from my hand, its bronze

cord in sharp relief against my clutched hand. I tried one last time to open the locket, with its gleaming teardrop emerald.

This necklace had given me so much joy, and anguish.

I focused on the good times. The time it had morphed into a crazy medieval helmet. The time I'd had to wear it as a Las Vegas stripper bra. I felt it pulse with energy as I held it over the edge of the cliff.

This was better than taking a chance that it was acting against me. I had friends to worry about, family as well. Dimitri would have to understand.

The metal chain hummed and went liquid. It attempted to cling to my hand, to wind itself up and around my wrist. I brushed it away. "Goodbye," I said, as I tossed it over the cliff.

It stuck to my hand.

"Frick." I tried to peel it away. It stuck to my other hand. "Oh, come on."

It was weak, most likely from the grave dirt. Still, it would *not* let go. The chain grasped at my hand. The locket stayed completely intact.

I could hit it with a switch star, not at this range. Can't say I wasn't tempted.

Of course it had attached itself to my throwing hand.

"This is the way it has to be," I said, giving it one final, violent toss over the edge.

It clung to my middle finger.

God bless America. It was official: I hated this necklace. I hated the ghost, and I needed to punch something except there was nothing to hit. I swung my arm around anyway. The necklace went with it, swinging by the chain, and smacked me hard on the cheek. My head rang and my skin stung.

"Fine!" I yelled to nobody in particular. This was such a mess.

I trudged back to the mansion, with a throbbing left cheek and a necklace attached to my throwing hand.

Frieda stood on the front porch, sneaking a smoke. She knew better than to say anything as I stormed past her.

The second I walked into the house, the necklace let go and collapsed in a heap onto the floor in the foyer. I was tempted to leave it there. Instead, I scooped it up in the wide skirt of my sundress and hurried it up to my room. Once I got there, I opened the top dresser drawer, cleared out my underwear, and let go of the necklace. It willingly dropped inside.

That settled it. I'd be sleeping with Dimitri tonight. I didn't want to be anywhere near that thing.

I clutched the dresser as a heaviness descended on me. It wound in my stomach, cold and evil. I didn't understand what was happening for a second until a sickening realization clicked into place. My demon slayer senses were waking, prickling like a blood-starved limb as they came back. Along with them, came the horrifying realization that we stood on cursed ground.

It screamed at me. I tried to breathe through it. Sweat slicked my body. Searing hate slashed at me, and I had to force myself to shut down a little.

Damn. If I'd felt a tenth of this on the first day, I never would have set foot inside this house. I could even feel the markers, pulsing.

Nausea hit me in waves as I tried to shut down more, to block the potent energy of this place. I had to get my friends and family out of here as soon as I could.

That meant destroying the markers. I shoved myself

away from the dresser and stumbled toward the door. Every step I took, I tried to shut down a small portion of the cavalcade of emotions that threatened to overpower me.

Fear.

Longing.

Hate.

One-by-one, I closed myself off. Until I felt the vicious energy as a muted throbbing at the back of my skull.

I paused for a few minutes at the top of the stairs, until I felt balanced enough to make it down all the way. Frieda stood talking with Ant Eater at then entrance to the sitting room.

The blond biker witch's eyes widened when she saw me. "Are you okay, sweetie?" She scrunched her face, as if afraid to say the next part. "You look like…"

"Hell," Ant Eater finished for her.

In this case, the curly haired witch wasn't too far off.

"Where's Rachmort?" I asked.

Ant Eater cocked her head. "In the dining room."

I found him at a large mahogany table, with a half-eaten sandwich at his elbow, playing cards with Pirate. He'd propped up a book so Pirate could display his hand with nobody peeking. My dog was standing on one of the nice chairs like he belonged there.

Rachmort peered over his cards. "How about…three of hearts."

"Ha!" Pirate pawed the edge of the table. "Go fish!"

The necromancer drew a card from the stack while my dog's tail wagged itself into a blur. "I am so good at this game. There should be a championship. I would be the Go Fish Ace!"

"I hate to interrupt your game," I began.

"Then you stay over there," Pirate said, "I'm winning."

Too bad. "Rachmort, I need to talk to you."

The necromancer glanced at me. "I forfeit," he said, laying his cards down. "You win."

"Yyyes! Zam!" Pirate hopped off his chair. "You see that, Lizzie?" He followed us as I motioned Rachmort into the kitchen. "Let's go best seven out of ten."

"Pirate, I need him alone," I said.

My dog kept coming. "Twelve out of fifteen?"

"Why don't you finish my sandwich?" Rachmort asked.

"Let's take a break." Pirate trotted off.

Luckily the kitchen was deserted. Rachmort and I crouched over the island. Even still, I leaned in closer. "I found the third marker. In a secret underground room, in the dead center of the house."

Rachmort whistled under his breath.

He didn't know the half of it. "This guy who owned the house, Russell, was seriously into the occult. He had hundreds of books on it in the library, a bunch of messages from a Ouija board, and a black chapel underneath it all."

That surprised him. Hades, it had shocked me, too. Rachmort scrubbed a hand over his mouth, thinking.

"So what do we do?" I asked. Now was the time for action.

The necromancer walked a few paces toward the kitchen table, then back. Then away, then back.

Oh, come on.

"Patience," he reminded me, rubbing at his chin. "We have to think."

"I'd rather destroy the markers."

He sighed, as if he'd given up on something. "If he

was reading how-to books, it doesn't seem like he was magical at all. I'd peg him as a novice. A poser."

Of all the... "I am *not* dreaming up any of the weird things happening in this house. This is real. Besides, you saw the dress."

My mentor held up a finger. "What I'd meant," he began, then paused to think again. I opted to grind my teeth as he kept his finger aloft for an extra few seconds, no doubt to drive me nuts. "Is that an individual who is connected to the magical world would not need the Ouija board."

"That's exactly what I thought. Why didn't he use the dark marks?"

Rachmort tapped his finger against his lips. "If our home owner was not a magically gifted individual, he would need to rely on outside learning as well as an outside power source. Hence the library and the dark marks. Apparently he was a *learn as you go* sort of man."

"Right," I said, chastened. That made a lot of sense, actually. I joined him on the other side of the kitchen island, planted my back against it. "Russell didn't have power of his own, so he had to create the dark marks. Still, he couldn't use them by himself."

"To power those dark marks, he'd need to have help from a demon. Then our occultist could do magic." He folded his hands over his chest, pacing again. "If wasn't careful— which I doubt he was, a demon could very easily escape. It's not like one of his little books would warn him of that possibility. Research is fine, but in this case, it would fall woefully short."

Dang. "You think he let a demon escape?"

"I'm almost sure of it," Rachmort said solemnly. "Well, that is, as long as he powered his markers."

Wait. I walked over to my mentor. "You said the demon would add the power."

"Yes, but our occultist would need a soul connection in order to create an opening."

"You mean sacrifice," I said, dread creeping over me when I remembered the skulls we'd seen in the chapel. "I saw a human skull down there."

Rachmort nodded, solemn. "Then it seems he found his victim. You must break the soul connection in order to break the markers."

I had a pretty good idea who the victim had been.

She had been young, less affluent, a sacrificial lamb from the start.

Then again, I didn't want to assume too much. That kind of thinking got people killed—or worse. This time, it wasn't only me on the line, but also the life and soul of my possessed wedding guest. I needed facts. For all I knew, the dead woman could have been in league with the demon to get revenge on her murdering husband.

Help me could have been short for, "Help unleash this demon."

I needed answers. Now. Before things got worse.

"I think I need the Cave of Visions," I said to myself.

Rachmort barked out a laugh.

Yeah, I knew my track record wasn't great.

The Cave of Visions was basically an express line to the other world. It opened up all kinds of possibilities—from finding the answers you sought, to losing your soul, and pretty much everything else in between.

The last time I'd tried to go in, I'd been sucked through by a bunch of sex demons in Las Vegas. But I'd learned so much since then. I was a better demon slayer, stronger. I wouldn't let my guard down again.

Of course, convincing the witches was another thing.

The Cave of Visions was a last resort, which seemed to fit our situation perfectly. I didn't know what else to do.

Rachmort wasn't exactly cheering my decision, but he didn't argue with me either. He placed a large hand on my shoulder. "While you're in there, do try to see who wants to kill you."

"Good point." I'd do that.

How bad was it when discovering the identity of my potential killer was the least of my problems?

††††

"Absolutely not," Grandma said.

I'd found her on the back porch, brewing up a large pot of leaves, sticks, dead bugs and from the smell of it—mint.

I gave it a brave whiff and regretted it. It smelled like road kill and chewing gum. "Don't tell my mom you have spiders in her soup pot."

Grandma sighed, tossing her gray hair over her shoulder. "First of all, she's renting. Second, she knows."

"Who do you think helped us carry it out here?" Creely asked. She opened a cooler and pulled out a couple of beers.

"You've got to be kidding."

I watched Grandma crack the beer open, thinking it would go in the pot. I should have known better. "Your mom's okay," she said, taking a long drag, wiping her mouth on her sleeve. "She said she wanted to help and she is. Now if we could get her into some better clothes."

"Don't even try it." Hillary wore heels to the grocery store.

"How does that look?" Grandma asked, glancing into the pot.

Creely took a look. "Needs more spiders."

The engineering witch ambled off the porch, presumably to go catch some.

I turned to Grandma. "I find it interesting that you'll brew up spells to protect us, but you won't build a Cave of Visions so that I can see who is trying to kill me."

"She does have a point," Creely called. "We'd be attacking the source of the problem."

"She'd want to go," Grandma said, her eyes boring into me.

I met her harsh glare. "I need to go in." I didn't have a choice.

Grandma gave a long look, stirred the pot, then caught my eye again. "I'll make you a deal. We'll build it. I go in."

"I'm the demon slayer," I told her.

She drew her chin up. "My coven."

I'd have to figure out a way to get in around her.

"Frieda!" Grandma called. The blonde witch's head popped up in the rose garden. "I need some turtle knees on the double. Send Ant Eater after the lizards and the Girl Scout Cookies. See if you can get Thin Mints. Meanwhile, I'll recon some shelter."

Fantastic. It was really happening. For the first time, I felt like we were on the right track. "Thanks, Grandma. I feel better."

She gave me a stern look. "You won't in a second."

"What's that supposed to mean?"

The door banged open behind me. "Lizzie Brown." My mother stood, hands on her hips, a disapproving glare directed at me. "Your wedding shower was supposed to start two hours ago."

As if I had time for presents and party talk. "I was dealing with demon slayer things, mom."

It didn't appease her in the slightest. "Are you finished?" she prompted.

I glanced at Grandma. "Pretty much." At least until they built the Cave of Visions. "How long is it going to take to get the cave going?"

Grandma sipped her beer. "Two, three hours."

"Well then come in the house," mom ordered, "I'll get everyone back together and get a new batch of coffee going."

Grandma snarfed as I followed my mom into the house. "Have fun with your tea towels."

Ha. I'd just be happy if nobody tried to poison me.

I should have known to be careful what I wished for.

Chapter Eighteen

My mom had decorated the sitting room in true Hillary Brown style. She'd dressed the coffee tables in lace and scattered several generations of silver-framed family wedding photos over them. She'd topped end tables with vases of white roses, tied with aqua bows. Several decorative dress mannequins, upholstered in silk, wore mom's collection of vintage lingerie.

Because, you know, that's exactly what I needed right now.

Most of Dimitri's relatives were already seated, and about half of the biker witches gathered on the low-slung couches and chairs. I guess you didn't need an entire coven to build a Cave of Visions.

"This is your place," mom said, leading me through the various seating groupings to a chair across from the bay window.

Our guests were talking among themselves, excited even. Everything felt so *normal*, at least for me. I was used to living in Hillary's world. Still, I couldn't help but glance at the spot where I'd nearly been killed the last time we'd all gotten together like this.

"There's too much sun over by the window," my mom said, mistaking my interest. "We don't want you back-lit in the photos."

The horror of it.

Dimitri entered from the foyer as I was getting ready to sit. He wore a rich blue button down with black pants and looked, in a word, delicious.

I dodged my chair and went to give him a quick kiss, which turned into a longer kiss. He felt great.

A few of his in-laws giggled and I could feel my mom's disapproval boring into my back.

The saucy grin he gave me made it all worth it.

He tucked a stray lock of hair behind my ear, growing serious. "How are you doing? I heard the witches are working on the Cave of Visions."

I rested my hands on his chest, feeling the warmth of him under his crisp shirt. "Only once I'd like to try and get something past you."

"I'm going in with you," he said, as if it were a done deal.

Never in a million years. But I wasn't about to get into it with him in front of a room full of people. "We're doing my bridal shower first," I said, hoping to put him off. Maybe I'd be finished with the witches before he even realized it.

But he didn't leave, like he usually did at the start of most any estrogen-inspired pre-wedding event.

"Sounds good to me," he said, exchanging a wave with Aunt Ophelia as he led me to a chair festooned with bows.

I didn't get it. "What's your angle?" I asked, sitting. He stood behind me, showing no signs of an imminent escape.

Dimitri leaned close, his lips against my ear. "I have a rule," he said, his warm breath caressing my skin. "I stick close when my fiancé is about to open a present from someone who wants to kill her."

Good point.

My mom stood watching us, chewing at her

immaculately glossed bottom lip. "This is really a girls' event...The rest of your male relatives are," she struggled to sound casual, "well, they're drag racing. In the sky. Or so I'm told." When Dimitri showed no signs of budging, mom—bless her heart—decided to roll with it.

"All right," she said, addressing the guests, "we are so glad to have you ladies here at our last big event before Lizzie and Dimitri walk down the aisle. While this isn't exactly how we'd planned it, what with it being four hours late, and the mini smiling bride ice sculptures having melted and the hors d'oeuvres eaten hours ago...when we thought we were going to start..." She looked a bit lost before regrouping. "It doesn't matter. None of it matters. We are all together now, and we have so many wonderful gifts for Lizzie and Dimitri."

I tried to smile at the smattering of polite applause. In truth, it made me a little uncomfortable to be the center of attention. A bit guilty, too, because my guests didn't need to get me anything. A lot of them had already spent a fortune coming here. They'd stayed, even after my mom had unveiled her party schedule. And they wanted the best for me. There was nothing else I could ask. Besides, it's not like Dimitri and I were setting up house. We were still holed up at a safe house/hippie commune owned by Grandma's friend, Neal.

Mom had stacked our gifts onto a small table. The dress mannequin behind it wore her wedding dress, with the one bared arm and the silk skirt. It was a subtle, yet direct barb. I chose to ignore it. I'd sooner wear the antique lingerie down the aisle.

The eyes of the room were on me as mom handed me the first gift, a large and heavy box wrapped in silver paper.

It had to weigh at least fifty pounds, and it took up my entire lap. "Thank you," I said, determined to enjoy it. I noticed the wedding bell pattern on the wrapping paper. How sweet.

Aunt Ophelia stood, "It is from the entire Rhodos clan!" She announced to stomping feet and cheers.

Dimitri moved in next to me, his hands curled into fists, his body tense.

This was his own clan. Still, if he was worried, I needed to proceed with caution as well.

My breath came a little quicker as I opened the box. I dug through the tissue paper to reveal a bronze, triangular-shaped shield, as long as my arm and as wide as my entire chest.

The Greeks let out a collective, "Ooooo."

I tried to hold it up, but frankly it was difficult with the box on my lap and the sheer size and weight of it. The metal was decorated with fancy scrollwork and pictures of deer, and it didn't have any handle inside that would make it a shield. Instead, buckles dangled from the edges.

"I love it!" I said.

"You do?" Ophelia pressed.

"I do!" I said, wondering how rude it would be to follow up with a *What is it?*

Diana rescued me. "This is a piece of griffin armor," she said, turning it around in my hands, so that the point end was toward the top. Lovely. I'd been holding it upside down. "It's meant to protect the right wing in battle," she added, taking it from me with an apologetic glance.

"I have never owned anything like it," I said, truthfully.

"What is she going to do with that?" I heard a few of the biker witches muttering.

"It's tradition," Ophelia shot back. "A bride gets her armor before the wedding. How else is she supposed to have it for her wedding night?"

"She needs armor on her wedding night?" Hillary asked.

"Why not?" I asked. It might not go with the sexy little outfit I'd bought, but we'd improvise.

When it was all said and done, I'd unwrapped two wing pieces, a breastplate, a collar (for wedding night fun, according to Ophelia), and a set of bronze tipped spikes for my front and back claws.

Hillary may have leaned on Diana once or twice for support, but she remained remarkably composed. Go Mom.

Dimitri, on the other hand, stalked behind me like a caged beast.

On the way to handing me another gift, his sister Dyonne knocked him with her elbow. "Do you mind? You're making everyone nervous."

"You could have fooled me," he said, alert as he surveyed the room. It was true. While we definitely had two camps: the bikers and the Greeks, they seemed remarkably at ease, given what had gone down with the wedding dress.

Then again, they didn't know everything else that was happening in the house, or even among themselves.

Melody, the Red Skull's new head of weapons stood. "Now this is more like it," she said, as Diana handed me a canvas, bedazzled Wal-Mart bag. Glass clinked inside.

Dimitri glared at the witch with the spiky black velvet choker. He seemed ready to strike as I drew out a recycled Smuckers jar filled with a brackish green liquid.

"Protection," she said, "for your wedding night."

The biker witches laughed, and I wasn't sure if she was joking or not.

"Toss it at anything that attacks you," she said, quite serious. "It's set to stun."

"Thanks," I said, well aware that this was the first gift I'd gotten that I could actually use.

The next jar was full of a pinkish sludge with bits of leaves and flower petals stuck in it.

"Ahhh," the witches murmured.

"What is this?" I asked, detecting a faint smell of turpentine.

Flava, a skinny witch in a black miniskirt, crossed her legs and grinned at me. "Dab a little behind each ear whenever you want to get him in the mood," she said, winking. "Works like a charm."

The biker witches guffawed. I glanced up at Dimitri, who didn't appear too enthused.

But you know what? This was nice. I opened a Tie Him Up spell, a Tie Him Down spell, some lavender bubble bath.

Everyone who could be here was together. I was receiving some interesting, well-intentioned gifts, and so far, nobody had tried to kill me.

It was a good party.

The gift table was almost empty when my mom handed me an envelope. "I'm glad you're here for this, too," she said, patting Dimitri on the shoulder.

He might be man-of-stone, but I couldn't help getting choked up a bit when I opened the simple, cut-out-card of a bride and groom and found the deed to a condominium by the shore.

"Mom, this is too much." It was off the California coast, near where we were staying with the witches. Only it was our own place. Tears flooded my eyes as I reached for her, wrapping her in a tight hug. She exhaled, holding me close.

"I only want what's best for you, honey."

"But you said…" She'd wanted me to move back and be somebody else and live in Atlanta, and I couldn't do that.

"I changed my mind," she said, simply. "You changed it." She glanced up at Dimitri. "I hope this is okay."

"It's perfect," he said, smiling down at her. "Thank you."

"We'll have to ward it," Melody said.

Yes, well she was the weapons expert. But that was a technicality. Yes, we'd make sure it was safe, and yes, we'd make it our own once we were back from the honeymoon. That's not what made it so special. It was the fact that my mom bought it for *us*.

"Your father still has to sign the papers, but he gets in tomorrow," mom said.

"So you did this last minute," I said. Of course she did. She never would have considered something like this even a week ago.

She gave a small shrug and seemed to grow embarrassed. "Now," she said, moving over to the gift table, "let's see what else we have for you."

"I've already gotten so much," I said. It was the truth.

Mom smiled and I could see she was genuinely having a good time. "This one is so pretty," she said, handing me a pink wrapped box with tiny doves on top.

Dimitri tensed as I opened the white silk ribbon and tore through the paper. I hadn't even touched the lid of the box before it flew open. Mom shrieked. Dimitri roared as countless shards of God-knows-what hurled straight for my face.

He leapt in front of me, taking the brunt of the blast as we both rocketed backward.

"Curses!" Melody screamed, as spell jars broke and griffins bellowed.

I shoved Dimitri off me as the curses shot to the ceiling like demented wasps. I cut through them with a switch star as a swarm dive-bombed me.

Chaos erupted. Dimitri was down, bloodied. I stood in front of him, taking out as many as I could before he grabbed my legs and took me down, rolling me under his body as another wave struck.

"God damn it," I pounded against his chest. I needed to fight. I rolled him, forcing him onto his back, which scared the hell out of me because the only way I could pull that off is if he were really hurt.

But I needed to move, to think. Curses came from the underworld. They'd either kill you or take you straight to hell. I didn't know what kind we had on our hands, but I didn't want to find out.

The fact that Dimitri was still, here, among the living mean that these things were meant for me.

A demon wanted me.

Well, screw that. I hit the curses again. And again. Taking some out, leaving far, far too many.

My eyes stung from spell dust, and griffin magic, and the sheer power glut in the room. But nothing we'd done so far had destroyed enough of these things to make a difference.

One of them could end me.

They gathered at the ceiling, ready to strike again. There was no way I could get out, nowhere to go. Not without leaving my friends and family behind. Besides, these things would catch me, and I wasn't about to be nailed in the back.

The third wave descended.

Dimitri tried to stand. I deliberately stepped away from him, toward *them*, and readied myself for the attack.

CHAPTER NINETEEN

I ran for my wedding gifts. The griffin armor lay in a pile under gift bags and spell jars. Curses whistled through the air behind me as I heaved a piece of bronze wing armor from under the mess and forced it in front of me like a shield. I held tight to the inside buckles, the metal digging into my skin when the blunt force of multiple curses slammed against it.

They threw me back, knocked me onto my side. I curled my legs underneath and clutched the armor in front of me like my life depended on it. Because it did.

Curses sprayed like a hail of machine gun fire. Then, abruptly, the attack ended.

A suffocating stench clouded the air and the silence that accompanied it was almost as scary as the flying curses. My mouth felt dry, and my arms were weak and shaking.

"Lizzie?" My mom was the first to reach me, crawling on her hands and knees, her white pants suit stained with soot, the pink rose dangling lifelessly. "Are you all right, baby?"

"Hold up." Slowly, I lowered my shield. I drew a switch star for good measure, but there was nothing left to attack. The curses lay imbedded in the griffin armor, dead.

The room reeked of magic, and I saw spots for a second as the witches and the griffins collected themselves off the floor. I crawled over to Dimitri, who looked like hell.

The curses had sliced his face and arms. His shirt was a total loss, and he had one hand over his left shoulder.

"Give me a second," he said, laying on his back, recovering.

I hovered over him, tried to remove his hand from his shoulder. "Can I see it?"

"No," he said, resisting.

Men.

I ran my fingers through his hair, which was probably the only part of his body that didn't hurt. "I'm so glad you're okay," I said, hoping I was right, infinitely grateful he'd stayed for the shower. He'd saved my life. Again.

My mom joined me. "Oh, my," she said, looking down at him. "I think I have some Band-Aids upstairs."

He shot her a you've-got-to-be-kidding glance, but didn't answer.

I stood and helped mom to her feet, Diana as well. The griffins and witches were all starting to recover— more or less. At least no one appeared seriously injured. I wasn't feeling too steady myself, when Mom pounced on me with a surprise embrace.

She managed to catch me on the side. "You have an awful, awful job," she sniffed against my shoulder.

"It's not usually this bad," I lied. I hated that she had to see this.

She pulled back. "Someone wants to kill you!"

I couldn't argue with her there. It happened more often than I cared to admit.

Melody was over opening windows. I was glad to see Dimitri had decided to sit up. That's when Frieda burst in the room.

"Sweet Jesus!" The blond biker witch spun on her heel. "I knew it." She turned to holler at someone behind her. "Get in here! I told you I smelled magic."

Ant Eater swore under her breath when she saw the mess.

She side-stepped Frieda as the other witch began helping people into chairs. "You can't hear a thing inside this latest Cave of Visions," Frieda muttered to herself.

Ant Eater was more interested in me. "What happened?"

"Demonic attack," I said, lifting the shield from the ground. There had to be at least five dozen tiny curses embedded in the bronze shield, any one of which could have pierced my flesh.

The gold-toothed witch inspected the mess. "Those are the poison kind."

"How can you tell?" Dimitri asked, staggering over to join us.

"They have tails that curl back, like a scorpion," Ant Eater said, tracing the spine of one with a lime green polished nail. "That's how they sting you."

"Damn." He shook his head. "I didn't get a good look at them. I was trying to—"

"Dive in front of them," I said, finishing his thought.

He at least had the courtesy to look properly chastened. "I was betting they didn't want me."

"That's a big bet." One that could have left me without a fiancé. "I'm glad it worked out."

He shook his head. "You and me both."

Someone wanted me bad.

Ant Eater shook her head. "I'll let your Grandma Gertie   know."

"They were in the pink box with the doves." I glanced at my mom. "Did you see who put that one in the pile?"

Her eyes were wide as she shook her head, 'no.' I wasn't surprised. The person who wanted me dead wasn't stupid, just determined.

Dimitri hefted the armor from me as the griffins gathered around it. Griffins were known for their loyalty, as well as their strong and ancient protective magic. I was incredibly grateful for both.

Ophelia led the pack, clucking over the damaged armor. "I hope you don't take this the wrong way, but I am so very glad you could use your wedding gift."

I supposed that was the ultimate goal.

She ran a hand over the damaged bronze, careful not to touch the curses. "Do not worry, momo. We will fix this up so you can wear it on your wedding night."

"Thanks," I said, not about to argue.

Dimitri stumbled backward, and it took both Diana and Dyonne to keep him upright. Darn it. He was hurt worse than we'd thought. His shoulder was bloody and he looked pale. Ophelia rushed to him and placed the back of her hand on his forehead. "Those vile creatures did not waste their stingers on you, but it seems they robbed some of your energy. It's best you rest."

Dimitri locked eyes with me.

"I'm not going to do anything risky without you," I said quickly.

"Famous last words," he answered, without a trace of humor. Okay, so he had too much experience dealing with me.

"I know I need you," I added. "At full strength."

I smoothed back his hair and went to give him a sweet kiss on the forehead. He dipped his head and countered with a blazing kiss that rocketed through me.

It was exactly what I needed after the horror of the evening. All too soon, he broke away with a saucy grin. "Don't do anything stupid."

"Too late," I muttered to myself, he walked up to his room, on his own power.

This entire week had been a mistake. I never should have placed everyone I loved in one location. It was easy pickings for a demon. I didn't know what I was thinking.

That was the problem. I wasn't thinking. Instead, I was trying to have a normal life, to pretend I wasn't charged with killing the spawn of Satan. Now it had come back to bite me. I was the Demon Slayer of Dalea, whether I liked it or not. There were some luxuries I simply couldn't afford anymore.

My mom let out a gasp behind us, and we all turned. But it wasn't another attack. She drew a silk dress mannequin upright and about cried when she saw what remained of the wedding dress she'd displayed— her dress. The skirt was ripped down the middle. It had burn marks from the battle. Glass from several spell jars had ripped holes through the delicate fabric.

"It's ruined," she sobbed.

"I'm sorry, mom," I said. Even though I never would have worn that dress, I hadn't wanted it to end like this.

Mom nodded, wiping at her tears. "If this is the worst that happened..." she trailed off, unable to say anymore.

I knew. We all did.

Frieda stood with her hands on her hips, surveying the mess. "Now we really need to go into the Cave of Visions."

It appeared as if she'd been working hard on it. Her lemon yellow jeans were dirty at the knees and she wore her hair tied back in a scarf.

"When will it be ready?" I asked.

Frieda gave a desperate sigh. "Come on. I'll show you," she said.

We headed out into the hall and back toward the kitchen. "Now mind you," she said, "there's no pet store within fifty miles, so I suggested we catch lizards." She rolled her eyes. "Do you know how hard it is to catch a lizard?"

I didn't even want to know.

"How long of a walk do we have?" I asked, hoping it was a good distance.

I should have specified that we be far, far from the evil center of the property. I hadn't. I'd overlooked that part. Still, even if the witches didn't know about the dark mark inside the house, I had to believe they'd feel the disturbance on some level and choose to avoid it.

We stepped out onto the back porch, and Frieda led me around the side, toward several trellises of purple rose bushes.

"Here we are!" She said, stopping at the entrance to an old root cellar that led directly into the basement.

"Oh, frick." I didn't need to crack open my powers to know this felt wrong.

Frieda's face fell. "It feels dark, doesn't it?" She glanced down at the hole. The weathered wooden doors had been thrown open, and we could see several witches down in the pit, weaving wards. Frieda shook her head. "I told Grandma. Ant Eater said it. Hell, I think we all said it at one point." She trailed her hand over the quartz crystal choker at her neck. "Still, you know your Grandma has the final word."

As if she'd heard her name, Grandma began climbing the old wooden ladder out of the cellar.

"Limit those wards," she said to the witches still inside. "I don't want you to interfere too much with what needs to come through."

"I'm all for some limits," I said, especially after what had happened at the shower.

The Red Skulls were usually more cautious.

Grandma shook out her shoulders like a cage fighter before a match. "I can handle it."

Maybe she could, maybe she couldn't. It didn't matter. "I'm going down first," I told her, daring her to argue.

Grandma looked me up and down. "What the hell happened to you?"

"She got caught in a curse attack," Frieda answered.

Grandma's eyes narrowed, and I shot a glare at Frieda. "Thanks for ratting me out."

"Yeah, because you were going to hide that," the blonde witch shot back. She must be stressed. It was rare for Frieda to lose her cool. "You know as well as I do that the Cave is dangerous," she spoke to the group, while her gaze remained fixed on me. "You can't go in rattled or injured."

"I'm fine." I snapped. Because I wasn't, not really. But I didn't have a choice.

The remaining witches climbed out of the hole while Grandma gave me the stink eye. "You think this is fucking easy?"

"I know it's not." I'd been once before. It sucked. But it was what I had to do to get answers, and I was prepared to brave it.

Grandma began running her hands through her long gray hair before, dropping them. "We don't even have any animals."

It took me a moment to realize what she was saying, until Ant Eater walked up next to her and solemnly handed her a Ziploc bag containing three live crickets.

"That's it?" I asked. The biker witches usually used guppies. They were enchanted so that the demon would take the life of the fish as it reached for the soul of the person in the Cave of Visions. You had three guppies, and when they were dead, you'd better run like hell.

Ant Eater didn't look happy. "We should put this off."

"No," Grandma said quickly. "It's ready now." She said the next part under her breath, but we all heard. "We might not have the magic to fire it up again."

Great. We had one shot, and it was already screwed up.

Still, I'd moved ahead under worse circumstances. I wasn't crazy about heading down there with bugs for protection, but if Grandma was going for it, I didn't want her doing anything without me.

The sun had begun to set over the ocean cliffs, leaving the rest of the world in a twilight haze. The witches began lighting candles while I rested my hand on the Maglite at my waist. I had more going for me than I gave myself credit for. I had my weapons, my wits. A fair amount of desperation.

The ladder leading up from the cellar sizzled with an unearthly blue current. A blaze of blue smoke trailed up into the night sky and—jumping Jesus on a pogo stick—pearly white snakes as long as my arm slithered from underneath the cellar doors. Large, flat heads thrust from both ends of the creatures as they hissed, spewing bursts of flame at each other and anyone else that wandered too close.

Damn it. "You're using cold magic again, aren't you?" It was stronger, harder to control.

Great at isolating demonic magic.

"Let me guess. You're the expert because you saw me do it once." Grandma leaned in close, her face flushed. "I'm using everything I've got right now. This entire place gives me the creeps."

That was saying something.

The urge to explore the cellar clawed at me, which was an awful sign. My powers were insanely attracted to things that wanted to eat me, possess me or chop me in half.

"Get everybody assembled," Grandma said, once the sun had dipped under the horizon.

We still hadn't decided who was heading up this little party. "I'm going in," I said.

She cursed under her breath.

The witches formed a semi-circle around us. They moved with military precision, dozens of Red Skulls carrying blue and silver candles.

Grandma handed me the bag of crickets as the circle closed behind us. I felt the energy build. Along with it, evil pricked over my skin.

Dimitri was going to kill me for going down there, but it's not like he could help me anyway. I had to do it alone.

"Link hands," Grandma ordered the witches. The power intensified. She stood between me and the entrance, as if she could shield me from what I'd find. "You know what to do, right?"

"Yes." Mostly. We both knew this wasn't an exact science. The last time Grandma tried it, she ended up in the first layer of hell.

"Trust the snakes," she said, as we stepped over one. It hissed and singed my boot. "Watch the crickets." A glow formed along the circle of witches surrounding us. I saw Creely, Ant Eater, Sidecar Bob. "Use the goat skull."

"Aunt Evie's?" She was the previous slayer, and we sometimes used things of hers, objects that held another generation of strong magic.

Grandma nodded. "It'll help you focus your strength."

An eerie blue layer of smoke collected at the edge of the pit. I looked down into the darkness.

Grandma stood next to me. "Light a candle. Focus on the demon and watch the crickets."

"Okay." Piece of cake. I tucked the edge of the cricket bag under my belt and tried not to notice as the creatures struggled to escape. It was too late—for them and for me.

Grandma watched me, stone faced. "If it grabs you, run. Try to get it off first. We don't want it following you." Practical until the end. She drew a necklace out of her shirt. Attached was a Ziploc with a twirling silver spell. "I've got the queen of anti-demonic spells here, but without any wards set up, it's worse than tossing a pop tart at a pissed off lion."

"You won't need it," I said. I could handle it.

I placed a foot on the top rung of the ladder and wished Dimitri was here. Times like this, I needed his strength, his protection and support more than anything. It would have been nice if I'd had my necklace to protect me as well. I clutched the ladder tighter and began my descent into the freezing cellar.

Hell was cold. It was the absence of love and light. And I felt every bit of it as the pit swallowed me up. The air grew heavier. The cold, colder.

My breath puffed out in front of me. The place smelled like raw dirt.

Halfway down, I drew my Maglite out of my belt and shone it down onto the floor below. The skull had been placed a short distance, away, near a stone wall that formed the foundation of the house. The other three walls were made of packed Earth.

I placed the candle in the center of the narrow space,

with the crickets next to it. They leapt and struggled against the bag.

Focus. If I panicked, I was done.

I lowered myself onto the floor and sat cross-legged in front of the gnarly-looking goat skull and the red candle.

Now or never. I struck a match and lit the wick. A bright blue flame shot up, dancing off the walls of the cellar. It felt like I was in a tomb. A trickle of sweat snaked down my back. The rest of me shivered.

I'd said I could do this and I would.

The Red Skulls murmured chants over me, their words mingling with the dancing flame of the candle.

I purposely removed my hand from my switch stars, where it always rested when I was nervous. Instead, I focused on the three markers I'd found. I pictured the one deep in the old observatory, surrounded by faceless statues. I pictured the marker that had been carved out of the garden, the one that had swallowed me whole. And I thought about the marker carved into the black altar itself, the one that stood on the other side of this wall, hidden in the basement of the house.

The back of my neck pricked and my breath came in starts. I pushed the air in and out of my lungs like it had gone liquid. My nerves thrummed and my body stiffened as an image formed in front of me.

It was the ghost. She lay chained to the black altar, arching away from it as the dark mark churned under her like a saw blade. It caught her back, sucking her down. She screamed as her body changed from solid to ghostly. I watched as the dark mark devoured her whole.

I shot to my feet, every instinct screaming for me to turn away, to run, to try and save her.

I am the virgin sacrifice. Free me.

"How?" I pleaded.

Holy hell. The ghost's soul was powering the markers. I had to free her. I had to end this.

You are the final sacrifice.

What? I turned away, the shock of it ripping me from the vision. No! "Wait. Hold up." I didn't understand.

I turned back toward the flame, stumbled when I almost stepped on the bag of crickets. I shouldn't have bothered. They were all dead.

My time was up.

Forget it. I needed to break through. I could not fail. But it didn't make any sense. The ghost powered the portal, not me.

Unless...

She thrashed again against the power of the dark alter, her agony and death on a constant loop.

My throat was dry, my voice hoarse, as I asked the most important question of all. "If I die, what happens?"

The dark marks churned, black magic sizzled, a violent storm ready to unleash itself on everyone I loved.

Then I saw Zatar, Earl of Hell.

He had the scaled body of a lizard and the face of an angel. His features were striking, beautiful. He must have been a heart-stopper before his fall. His hair was long and golden and he wore the silver and white wings of an angel.

"You—" I began, shocked. I'd locked Zatar away. There was no way he could touch me.

Unless he did it through someone I loved.

"Who did you take?" I demanded, ready to bargain, to force, to do anything I could to get answers.

"It doesn't matter," he said. His voice was like music and the wind, haunting and beautiful. It was like nothing I'd heard before. I had to force myself to stand my ground. "I have you."

A blast of power knocked me off my feet.

I hit him with a switch star, then another, then another. They barely slowed him down as he reached for me.

Holy mother. He wasn't supposed to be here. He was in hell. For as long as I lived and breathed.

Which at this rate...*don't think about it.*

There was nowhere to run, nowhere to hide.

I dropped my switch stars and drew deep down inside myself. I needed more. I was half angel, a detail most people, including myself, overlooked. Angel power didn't come with nifty weapons or a gang of biker witches, but it did come with something else.

I let it build inside me, trusted it even as the Earl bore down on me, I focused every bit of light and goodness I had and blasted him backward, straight through the stone wall and back to hell where he'd come from.

Shocked and shaking, I remained rooted in place as the air warmed around me. The candle crackled, and for the first time, I dared to look upward. The storm doors had been blasted completely off. Stars shone in the night sky.

"Okay," I said, knees still a little too wobbly to attempt a climb. Still, I knew what to do. It may be crazy, and it may get me killed, but at least I had a plan.

Chapter Twenty

I climbed out of the cellar and stalked past the startled witches.

"What did you see?" Grandma demanded, grabbing my arm. I shook her off.

"Zatar." My worst nightmare. I hadn't been able to beat him before. I'd thought it would be enough to lock him away in hell.

Fat load of good that had done.

Creely grabbed a spell jar, ready to attack. Only we didn't have an enemy. Not in the flesh.

"Lizzie—" she began.

I didn't hear the rest. I needed to focus. "I think I'm onto something," I said. If what I had planned would even work…

Frieda moved to block my path. I dodged her.

I opened the door to the kitchen and let it slam behind me, knowing they'd follow. I didn't have time to spell it out. I had to get the necklace with the grave dirt. Somehow, I had to free the ghost and disable the marks before the demon got his claws in me or anyone else.

Now that I was on to him, he'd move fast. I didn't know how much time we had.

I stalked down the hall and up the stairs, my mind tumbling over itself. Looking back, there had been a reason why I'd felt compelled to grab the grave dirt. Sometimes, I just *knew*. Hadn't the necklace clung to it? It had actively fought me when I'd tried to take my only connection to the ghost and dump it out over the ocean. It was still protecting me.

If I'd been thinking that way, I would have realized something was up when Pirate hadn't been able to see the dead bride. Pirate loved ghosts. He played with them. But we weren't dealing with a soul who was free to strike up a game of Parcheesi. The woman was trapped, and Pirate had lacked the connection to the locket, and the grave dirt inside.

I touched my fingers to my bare throat. It was no mistake the specter hadn't appeared since I'd given up the pendant. At the time, I'd been worried about hurting Dimitri by breaking our bond. Now, I could see it was a lot worse than that.

Twisting the doorknob to my room, I said a quick prayer, made my way over to the dresser. I opened the drawer and gasped.

There was an empty place where the necklace should have been.

Yes, I'd feared it, maybe I should have expected it, but it stunned me to the core. The emerald was pledged to me. Mine. I couldn't even throw it off a fricking cliff. It was wholly and totally bound to me.

Unless Dimitri was compromised.

He was the only one I knew who could touch it like I could.

By all that was holy, if he had taken it, I didn't know what I'd do.

It was clear someone had been in my dresser. My underthings had been neatly folded. As always. Now they were scattered as if they'd been caught in a storm. Bottoms mixed with bras and slips and, oh hell.

I dug through the mess, hoping, praying it was still there. I tossed panties, socks, everything out onto the floor.

There was no good way for the search to end. I'd felt it deep down in my gut.

The necklace was gone.

"Fuck!" I slammed my hand down on the dresser, staring down at the empty drawer.

Dimitri's door opened. "What's the matter?" he asked, no doubt startled by my outburst. Oh, no. I wasn't ready to face him yet.

He wore a blue t-shirt and jeans. His hair was mussed from sleep, and it was clear he still felt the effects of the earlier battle downstairs. A half-dozen witches crowded the hall as well.

There was no hiding my discovery. I tossed a stray bra off the dresser. "Someone stole my emerald," I said, still trying to wrap my head around it.

Dimitri flinched. "That's impossible."

He knew better than to say things like that.

He advanced on me as soon as he'd recovered from his surprise. "I can't believe you took it off."

Yeah, he was hurt. I would have been, too. But dammit. "Stay back." I moved to the other side of the open drawer. "I mean it." He didn't look possessed. His eyes were deep green, his voice clear. But it was the easiest explanation for my missing emerald. I needed time to think.

He kept coming. A purple bruise had formed at his collarbone. His face was raw from where the curses had streaked across his skin. His mouth was tight. "What the hell is wrong?"

Hades.

If he knew what I'd seen in the Cave of Visions,

would he attack?

Oh my God. I loved him. I needed him. I couldn't put a switch star through his heart simply because he was possessed.

Grandma moved in right behind him. "Tell us what happened," she said, grim, as if she were afraid of the answer. She tried to move in on the side of me, but Dimitri blocked her. "We have a right to know what's going on," she added.

"I can't." I bit back.

Even if I wanted to show my cards to my potentially possessed fiancé, it would still be hard to accurately describe what kind of shit we were in.

And I'd burned through my one big idea: Grab the necklace. Use the grave dirt and the ghost to power down the marks.

Now, I had nothing.

I was on my own.

And Zatar was coming.

Grandma's mouth set in a hard line. "I told you we shouldn't have let you go into the Cave of Visions."

"You *what*?" Dimitri roared.

"It was a last minute thing," I said quickly, retreating to the window. Hell. "You should be more upset about the necklace anyway."

If he was in his right mind.

His eyes narrowed. "We'll make a list," he said, still blocking Grandma. "What kind of trouble are we in?"

"It's complicated," I said. And getting worse all the time.

Ant Eater and Creely joined the crowd behind Grandma.

My hand drifted to my switch stars. *No.* There had to be a better way.

If I could only see him clearly, if I knew he was on my side, then I'd have something to go on. A partner I could trust. But I couldn't let down my guard for anyone, not even Dimitri. Rachmort had warned me of this very thing.

Another unpleasant thought intruded. There *was* a way to see inside him. If I was willing to bet my life he wasn't compromised.

Truth be told, it wasn't even up for debate at that point. For Dimitri, I'd do it.

"New plan," I said to the assembled biker witches. "I need everybody to leave Dimitri and me by ourselves in here."

Grandma balked. "Because leaving you alone has worked out so well for us."

Dimitri glared at the witches. "I can remove every last one of you if I want."

They grumbled, but they retreated. Score one for Dimitri. He'd tamed the biker witches. For the time being.

Now I was alone with my potentially possessed fiancé.

He didn't look too happy about it, either. "How the hell did the emerald even leave your body?"

It hurt to say it. "I had to renounce our bond in order to get the emerald off."

He brought a hand up, running it through his hair until it stood up in spiky clumps. A lesser man would have questioned my devotion, but not Dimitri.

"I didn't have a choice," I said quickly. "I was afraid of it." I'd leave the part out about trying to toss it. At least for now. "I kept it safe upstairs. You didn't even notice I'd taken it off."

He frowned at that.

It was a difficult thing to explain, but, "I'm trying to save your life, maybe even your soul. And mine." And everyone else's.

His hand dropped. "Wait. Back up. Are you protecting me or are you afraid I won't understand what you're facing?" His expression tightened. "Either way, you're pissing me off. Now, calm down and start from the beginning."

I couldn't. Not unless I knew who was with me. "You have to trust me. I have to trust you." I reached out, taking his hands in mine. He was hard with tension. Rawness burned in his expression, shaking me to the core. "It's the only way." My hands trembled, and my mouth was dry. "I need to see inside you."

He watched me for a long, slow moment. "Lizzie, you're not making any sense."

I snorted, out of pure desperation, or maybe I didn't know what else to do. "Trust me," I told him.

When it came right down to it, I was more in tune with Dimitri than I was with anyone in heaven or on Earth. He was the most important person in my life.

He had a sliver of me inside of him. I was in his soul.

We were connected, ever since I'd saved his life by giving him a part of my demon slayer essence. Now that I had my instincts back, my power, I'd use that bond to look into his heart and soul. If he'd let me.

"Please," I said. I understood his hesitation. Truth be told, I didn't want to see every deep dark corner of his soul any more than I wanted him to see mine. There are some things we should be allowed to keep separate and whole, even from those we love. Now, we had to strip that away and lay us both bare. He'd see my insecurities, my failings, and I'd see if he had any doubt whether or not I was the one he truly wanted for the rest of his life.

Yes, the fight ahead would be brutal. Now, at least, we had what we needed right here.

His eyes shone with frustration, fear, hurt, and love.

"You know I trust you," he said quietly. "With my life."

He gave himself over to me, his emotions naked, his spirit willing. He didn't ask for any other explanation. At that moment, if it was even possible, I loved him more.

I clutched his hands, at the same time, opening up my demon slayer senses. It was all or nothing. If he were possessed, it would enter me as well.

For better or for worse...

I embraced our connection and his true intentions washed over me.

His heart beat raw against his chest. The evil water nymph had escaped. He cursed under his breath, and it came out as a lion's snarl. It had attacked the demon slayer. Its orders were to kill.

Lizzie Brown is mine.

The demon slayer stood in the clearing, her hair damp, her breaths coming hard. She watched him warily, but she didn't back down to a griffin.

Impressive.

She looked so small, so vulnerable, but there was steel underneath. He'd followed her for weeks, but he'd never been this close. And now, as her gaze locked with his, he felt something in him shift.

He wanted to say it was how she'd fought. She was brave. But, no, it was more than that. She inspired loyalty.

The biker witch beside her didn't work well with others. Not since her own daughter had betrayed her. Yet the witch believed in this slayer. Trusted her.

Then there was the annoying little dog. It had bit him without the least bit of provocation. The foul creature had even seemed to enjoy it. Yet it had been willing to die for her.

Who was she to inspire such loyalty?

He'd been playing griffin politics for so long, trying to put together a team to save his sisters, he'd forgotten what it was like to find someone who was so completely genuine, so refreshingly open, even if she wasn't completely aware yet of what she could become.

It was almost a shame to lie to her.

He jerked, then pressed harder against me. These were his memories, not mine. I had no right to them. But I needed to see inside him. I needed to know.

His palms burned and his head felt ready to explode. But she wasn't there yet.

"Try it again, Lizzie." He handed her another switch star, schooling his expression as it singed his fingers.

Her mouth quirked. "You realize I just decapitated the Shoney's Big Boy."

"He was asking for it." A grin tickling his lips, despite the pain, despite everything. She made him feel, in a way he'd never allowed himself. "Let's try again."

She threw, coming closer to the target this time, even though she sighed in frustration.

He reached for another star. Every touch took a year off his life. But damn fool that he was, he knew she was worth it. It wasn't only about his sisters anymore. It was about helping her reach her true potential, even if that meant she would leave him.

"Dimitri," I whispered. He had his eyes closed, as if it could shield him from me knowing. There was nothing so personal as being inside a person's mind. But in his case, it was beautiful.

He held a wedding ring. It was a wrap-style, made to fit around her diamond solitaire engagement ring. The jagged aquamarine-colored stones glinted in the afternoon sun. They were the most rare and precious things he could give her.

They weren't cut by a jeweler, or bought in a store. These were pieces of skye stone, one of the last things he had left of his original clan. They had belonged to his mother and radiated a quiet beauty.

He would give this to her on their wedding day.

It was tradition to have the stones blessed by the head of each of the oldest clans. He'd made it to five of the kingdoms already. He was tired, but happy.

He smiled to himself. She had been asking where he was going, had been a little impatient even. But it would be worth it when she saw. Perhaps she'd be so busy when they met with her mother, she may not even notice him gone.

These stones not only expressed his love for her, but they could absorb it and give it back to her, even when he wasn't there to tell her how much she meant to him.

He'd go to the ends of the earth to make her feel that way.

My breath caught in my throat when I felt the true depth of his love for me. It filled me, drew from my strength and gave it back a thousand fold. He needed me, like no one ever had before. He wasn't corrupted by a demon. Dimitri was with me, body and soul.

Tears stung my eyes as I slowly came back to myself. "It's not you," I said. The words themselves sounded beautiful.

He looked at me with such love it undid me completely. "You did discover my surprise."

"I love it," I said. I couldn't believe he'd go to the ends of the earth for me.

"You're worth all that and more." He tugged me into his arms and kissed me. I gave myself over to him as his arms wrapped around me, safe, like they always did.

Grandma banged on the door. "Are you done in there? Whatever you're doing, this isn't the time.

We've got to talk about what happened in the Cave of Visions."

I understood her frustration, I really did. But, now wasn't the time. I pulled back, gazed up at him, his bottom lip damp from my kiss. "I need to talk to you. Somewhere where we won't be disturbed."

"All right." He twined his fingers in mine. The biker witches started beating on the door. "This should be fun."

My room was certainly out, as was his.

We opened the door on a gaggle of witches shouting questions. It was like the paranormal paparazzi, with Dimitri as my hunky bodyguard.

He pulled me close and cut through them like I never could.

"How'd you do that?" I asked, as we cleared them.

"Extreme focus."

We headed down the stairs, with Grandma and the gang close behind. I didn't know how we were going to shake them.

We were almost to the foyer when the doorbell rang. I didn't know who that could be, considering it was at least eleven o'clock.

My mom rushed from the sitting room to answer.

"What are you—" I managed to utter, before she gave a half-apologetic glance and opened the door to the VanWillens and the Rodgersons, two of her country club couples.

She did not look surprised enough. I wanted to scream. I'd told her no more guests.

The Gucci couples gave exaggerated hugs and sighs and talked about late flights and rude taxi drivers.

I broke away and found Rachmort as he came in from the sitting room.

"They have to go," I told him.

My mentor shook his head. "It's too late. They're a part of it now."

Jumping Jesus on a pogo stick. Everyone was in danger, and I didn't have the one thing I needed that could stop this.

"Keep moving," Dimitri said under his breath, as he drew me straight for the mini-society gathering in the front hall.

I glanced over my shoulder at Grandma. "You follow, and you're out of the loop," I said under my breath.

She looked like she wanted to thwack me over the head with a Truth spell, but she didn't.

Dimitri tensed as we approached the VanWillens.

I put on my best grin. "Hi! So glad you could make it! We ran out of ice. Be back in a jif!"

His grip on me eased as the fight drained out of him. "I don't know what's more frightening," Dimitri said once we'd made it out into the cool night, "the idea of you in the Cave of Visions or what I just saw."

A glimpse of society Lizzie. "Yes, well you're stuck with me now."

"We're not married yet," he mused, as we headed down the steps.

"No." I squeezed his hand. "But you love me."

We let the darkness envelop us as we drew farther and farther toward the front of the house, away from the marks, to where the trees stood tall along the drive. The moon hung low, and the sound of insects and frogs pierced the night.

"Is there any particular place you're taking me?" I asked, fighting to keep up with him.

"Away," he said, as we passed the first gargoyle.

Yes, well, I couldn't wait. Moonlight played of his strong features. He was so determined, brave.

Beautiful. If I needed anyone on my side—for this and in life—it was Dimitri.

I glanced at the darkened path behind him to make sure we were alone, and then the truth poured out of me like water. I explained to him about the three marks, and how the soul of the murdered bride was powering them. I told him about the necklace, and how the grave dirt inside it had been dampening my demon slayer radar. That someone close to us was possessed. At last, I told him what I'd seen in the Cave of Visions, how the most powerful demon I'd ever encountered was powering up to take me on, to hurt everyone I'd ever loved. To kill me.

He didn't hug me, or tell me that everything was going to be all right. Dimitri respected me too much to lie. Instead, he walked beside me, his powerful body alert, no doubt trying think of some detail, some way out that I'd missed.

"You could tell when your uncle was under the influence of a demon," he said, thinking as he spoke, "you said his eyes looked red."

"Believe me, I've been looking for signs." And I certainly would have noticed that. "The only reason I could see through to you, to know you're okay, was because of our bond." And only after I was able to get my demon slayer senses back. "Our connection, what we have, is one of the only things in my life that always comes through."

If my declaration had touched him, he didn't show it. Dimitri was either hearts and flowers or all business. Right now he was trying to figure a way out of this. He stood still, working it through, then his intense brown eyes locked on mine. "Maybe you need more power."

I snorted. "Thanks." I was already doing everything I could.

He shook me off. "Listen to where I'm going." He took a step closer. "When we get married tomorrow—"

I met his calm stare. "If we survive that long."

"—I'll be giving you a part of my power."

I knew that. It was how the magical world worked. But griffin power was all about family ties and protection, not demon slaying.

"Wait." I startled at the realization. "I can gain protective magic to help our families." Combined with my demon slayer powers, it could buy us time. "But we're not married yet."

It was his turn to snort. "That circus in there isn't our wedding. It has nothing to do with us." He drew me close. Kissed me once, twice, his lips lingering over mine. His warm breath caressed my skin. "This is us."

He was right. This was all I needed. I clutched my fingers against his T-shirt, watched them dig in against his firm chest. "What are you saying? You want to get married here and now?"

His mouth tipped into a grin. "I have the ring." He reached into his pocket and withdrew the ring wrap I'd seen when I'd looked into his mind. It was gorgeous. I ran my finger over the two rough-cut skye stones. "Blessed by the seven clans."

"I can't believe you did that for me."

"Come on," he said, taking my hand, "I know a place."

Oh, my God. We were going to get married.

The thrill of it washed over me as we walked down through the trees, away from the gargoyles and the path to the old mansion.

I'd become so used to the dark mass of the house that I hadn't even noticed it anymore until it lifted. "We're off the property."

"Exactly," he said, as we approached a small building among the trees. "I saw this from the air. It's an old Spanish mission chapel."

"It's tiny," I said, drawing near. I ran a hand over the curved, pockmarked roof that was barely taller than I was. It had to be a couple of centuries old.

His broad hand touched the chapel near mine. "Missionaries used places like this to store their religious items. And to sleep."

It was a holy place.

There was a break in the trees here, the sky above us bright with stars.

He leaned closer, drawing me into his arms. "Marry me, Elizabeth Gertrude Brown. Right here, right now. No lion tamer or dancing bears allowed."

I ran my hands up his arms. "I was kind of hoping for a clown car."

He shook his head. "You've got the biker witches for that." He lost all trace of humor as he gazed down at me. "Let's make this about us," he said simply.

He was serious.

I was, too. "Thank you for bringing me here."

"I should have done it when I first saw this place. I love you, Lizzie. You fill an empty part of me that I didn't even know I had until I met you."

I didn't deserve him. "You're the most giving, loyal, brave man I've ever known."

He gave a small smile. "It doesn't mean anything if I can't share it with you." He touched my cheek. "I was afraid to love before I met you. It hurt too much after the way I watched my family destroyed. But you helped me live again. You showed me I don't have to be in control every minute of my life." His fingers traced my skin. "I can trust."

"That's always been so hard for me." I'd never been a big believer in things I couldn't see or control.

Dimitri had changed that. "You make me feel so safe." Loved. He grinned, and I did, too. "Thank you for being the person that makes me believe in happy endings."

Energy prickled along my skin as he opened himself to me. I did the same, showing my love for him with no reservations, no doubt.

"Will you take me, forever and always?" he asked.

"I will." I held out my hand and he slipped the ring onto my finger. It fit perfectly, the stones catching the moonlight.

My throat tightened and my heart beat fast when I asked him in turn, "Will you take me? Forever and always?"

His mouth split into a wide smile. "I will."

The full force of his strength and mine poured from us, merging until we were surrounded by a pure white light. There was never anything more beautiful.

We stood holding each other, complete in the glow of our union. Lovers for life, in control of our destiny. We were the ones who would decide how we lived our lives together.

I felt stronger than I ever had before. Complete. I'd never be alone in this, or in anything else, again. I was home.

CHAPTER TWENTY-ONE

It was hard for us to drag ourselves back to the house. But with Dimitri by my side all night, even the cursed mansion was bearable. I felt the blending of our powers, and it seemed to lift some of the darkness, for now at least.

We'd escaped into his room to celebrate, and after, I slept better than I had since we'd gotten here.

I woke tangled in his arms, my thigh resting on one of his as he ran his hands along my side. He planted an open-mouthed kiss on my neck before moving lower.

My eyes adjusted to the morning light. If this was what it would be like being married, sign me up for an eternity. The sheets tugged and I moaned out loud as a deliciously hot, wet sensation rasped across my breast. He drew harder, his tongue swirling across my sensitive nipple and I arched my hips.

Mmm... I ran my fingers through his hair. I loved waking up this way. It was sweet and invigorating, and I wanted him. Now.

The head of his cock nudged me where I was most sensitive, then retreated.

"Oh, no. Don't tease. Come here," I said, slick and ready. The full, heavy weight of him settled over me as I grasped his shoulders, trying to get him to move up.

He chuckled and rose over me. "My wife is demanding."

"You love it," I murmured as he slid deep inside me.

"I do."

He withdrew and then pushed hard, filling me again.

He made love to me slowly. Perfectly. The things he did to me, the way he knew me, I wouldn't trade it for the world.

I came with a shuddering moan, as bliss tore through me. He followed soon after, stiffening and jerking as he joined me.

We lay together for a long moment, content to simply be with each other. I held out my hand and gazed at my ring, the skye stones twinkling with a life of their own.

His breath was warm against my neck. "Good morning," he murmured.

"Can I stay here forever?" Demons be damned, we had our slice of peace.

He rolled onto his back, taking me with him. "You want my honest opinion?"

My head felt heavy against the rise and fall of his chest. "Always."

"I can't believe nobody's barged in on us yet."

True. I forced myself to sit. We might as well be dressed once they decided to invade. And Dimitri was right. They would.

He planted a kiss on my head as he slid out of bed behind me. "Happy official wedding day."

I tossed a pillow at his fine, naked backside. "I'm glad we did it yesterday," I said, moving to join him in the shower.

He grinned. "Me too."

✝✝✝

By the time we finished a clumsy, yet enthusiastic and ultimately fruitful bout of love in the shower, (I'm telling you now, small spaces and slippery tile do not make it easy), we managed to dress without incident.

"Are you ready to do this?" Dimitri asked as I quickly pulled on a sundress.

"Hey," I said, wondering exactly what we planned to do about a real gown. "As long as I'm with you, I can do anything."

The household was in a tizzy when I wandered out into the hall.

"You're on my shit list," Ant Eater said, stalking past. She wore an honest-to-God dress. Where she'd gotten it, I had no clue. It was a simple green tunic that was actually quite appropriate. "I've got the super glue!" she hollered out.

A door opened down the way, and Frieda's head poked out. "Then what are you doing yelling about it? Get your ass in here."

Dimitri pulled his tux out of the closet. "It'll only take me about five minutes to get dressed."

Showoff. I took a step forward and nearly made mincemeat of Pirate, who was lying in the doorway.

"Whoa, baby dog!" I stumbled to avoid him. "Watch out."

He leapt up, colliding with my ankle before turning in a circle and plopping down in the middle of the traffic way.

"*Now* it's baby dog," he huffed, giving his best doggie glare. "Let's not even talk about last night when I was by myself for an entire night." He cocked his head. "I'm a pack animal. You know what that means? It means I need company."

He'd always been happy snuggling up with Sidecar Bob, or one of the other Red Skulls. Then again, the wedding was an adjustment for him as well. "I'm sorry, bub," I said, lowering my hand to pet him.

He ducked away, and Aunt Ophelia and another woman dodged him, tittering under their breath as they saw me coming out of Dimitri's room.

It didn't even matter. Pirate's mood had instantly lifted because I was paying attention to him, and well, he was a dog. He got off on that.

"You don't even know what's going on." He turned in a circle and sat, "Creely was up exploring the attic where nobody is supposed to go, and she found you a dress!"

Great. "I didn't even know there was an attic."

Whatever they'd found, it better be easier on the eyes than my mom's couture gown. Then again, what did it matter? I was already married in every way that counted. This ceremony, put on for show, was merely a formality—and hopefully, not a disaster.

I still needed to figure out who was possessed and who had stolen my necklace. The protective power I'd gained from Dimitri might have bought us some time, but no telling how much.

Pirate pawed at the floor, his nails clicking against the hardwood. "The dress is in Hillary's room, where she wants you to get ready. She says she doesn't want your hands down Dimitri's pants on your wedding day."

Too late. And heavens to Betsy, "I can't believe she said that."

"I only repeat what I hear." Pirate said proudly, his tail up. "Now she says you have less than an hour, and you need all the time you can get to look good, and do you want to follow me over there or do you want them coming after you?"

I took a few quick steps back to plant a quick kiss on Dimitri's lips. "See you at the wedding, hot stuff."

He smiled as he buttoned his shirt. "Gird your loins."

Pirate showed me across the hall. Because I needed a dog to find my way.

Inside the ready room, I found mom, Creely and Grandma. I was glad they appeared healthy, and so far, untouched, but part of me longed to see a few of my friends from Atlanta. Of course, we'd told everyone to stay away.

I fought back a wave of regret. It's not like I'd taken time out to visit in the past year anyway.

Geez, what was I doing? This was a ceremony, nothing more.

"We have something for you," my mom trilled. She led me over to the bed, with an intricate wedding dress draped over it. "It's antique," she said, lifting it carefully.

"It's a 'beaut," Grandma agreed.

The gown was constructed of ivory silk. It had aged perfectly, saved for a sepia tone to the formerly white gown. The bodice featured a lace overlay, woven into a tiny rose pattern. The floor length cut draped longer in the back, creating a beautiful silk train.

"See?" Grandma nudged Creely. "That was worth breaking into the steamer trunk."

Creely shrugged. "I told you I could have gotten the combination if you'd have given me another minute."

"Here, let me," mom said, taking it from me so I could step back and see the intricately cut sleeves, and touch my fingers to the tapered waist and the boned silk collar.

The realization slammed down on me and I yanked my hands back like the fricking thing was on fire. "That's the dead bride's dress."

"Who?" Everyone said, except for Creely.

She merely nodded. "I thought of that," she said, far too flippantly for my taste. "But you know who probably made it," she reached for the collar of the dress, "the girls' mother, maybe her grandmother as well. If she was still around." She turned the seam out. "Look. Hand stitched. Somebody put a lot of time and love into this."

Great. A family heirloom. It didn't change the fact that she was strangled in it.

Mom moved in close to me, as did Grandma.

"Feel it," Creely said, inviting me to run my fingers over the delicate seams. She coaxed the entire dress into my arms. "It doesn't bite."

It was lighter than I expected, and it resonated with a crystal clear energy that wound up my arms and into my chest. Incredible.

"See?" Creely asked, reading the expression on my face. "It was constructed well. It has power. This was made with love and hope from the family of that poor girl who died."

My mom's hand fluttered at her throat. "Who died?"

Creely explained while I ran my fingers over the intricately woven fabric. Maybe I could go with this. I opened up my demon slayer senses.

The dress was definitely touched by love. And something else. Tragedy. I could sense the faint burn of it. She had definitely died in this dress. But the love was stronger.

It made me wonder. "This could be how the grave dirt powered up the emerald," I said to myself, "It was a place where the family's love and prayers were concentrated." This girl's household may not have been rich, but they had been strong and deeply tied to each other. "Maybe I could use some of that power to release her ghost."

We could certainly use all the help we could get.

"First things first," my mom said, retreating to the bathroom. "You need to dry your hair."

Whoops.

She gave a long-suffering sigh, which was in this case, justified. "Lizzie, I swear, the wedding is in forty-five minutes," she said, expecting me to follow.

Okay. I would. First I had to get one thing straight. "Why are you not downstairs with a clipboard?"

She shrugged. "I let your father take over. Sure, he's quiet, but he's watched me enough times. And the seating instructions were clear enough." She leaned in to me, as if she were sharing a secret. "He has no idea we didn't even rehearse."

That's right. Perhaps my mom really had turned over a new leaf.

I glanced to Grandma and Creely, who were taking turns holding up the antique gown in front of them and looking in the mirror. "Why are you not freaking out over that? Or over the dead bride's wedding dress?"

"I'm starting to learn I can't control everything," Mom said, directing me to lean over as she plugged in her curling iron and started up the blow dryer.

It had taken her less time than it had me.

Then again, maybe not. Precisely forty-four minutes later, I looked like a bride.

"Oh, Lizzie." Mom stood behind me to fluff a curl that I knew would never move because Hillary would never allow it. Her eyes filled with tears. "You look perfect."

I had to admit, she'd done a great job. I even let her plunk a tiara on my head.

The heavy footfalls of guests sounded in the hallway as everyone headed down to the wedding. My stomach fluttered. It was time.

Yes, Dimitri and I had already had our real wedding, but still. This was a moment I may never repeat.

I stripped out of my clothes and held up my hands as mom and Grandma eased the borrowed dress over my head. It smelled faintly of cedar and lavender.

It was hard to stay sentimental, though, knowing that this would be the perfect time for Zatar to attack. I would have all of my loved ones, present and assembled in one spot. If I were a power sucking, soul-destroying demon, this would be my time to strike.

She kissed me on the cheek as I gazed at myself in the stand-up mirror by the door. I looked like a Victorian bride.

"Beautiful," she whispered.

I gave her a small hug. "Thanks, mom."

She handed me an artfully arranged bouquet of peonies and baby roses. Tears welled up in her eyes and she hurriedly wiped them away. "I don't cry," she said, voice wavering.

"I don't either," Grandma said, slapping me on the back. "Are we ready?"

"Sure," I said, trying to get my bearings. "Hold on a minute." I'd left my switch star belt across the hall in Dimitri's room.

Creely, of all people, anticipated where I was going and blocked me. "He can't see you!" she grimaced.

"Truly?" I asked her.

She knocked on Dimitri's door while mom and Grandma shushed me back into the ready room. Less than a minute later, Creely walked in carrying my switch star belt. "Your man looks hot," she grinned.

"Tell me something I don't know," I said, accepting the belt from her and winding it around my waist. The construction of the dress was perfect for weapons carrying. The fit was also tight enough so I could fire easily.

"What are you doing?" My mom asked, her voice clipped.

"This belt holds my weapons," I said, fastening the crystal buckle. "*You* can't see them, but believe me, they work."

Her mouth opened, closed, then opened again. "You are not seriously going to wear a black leather spiked belt with a wedding dress."

"I think it looks nice," Creely said, nudging mom.

The wrinkles on Grandma's forehead deepened. "Your mom could be right on this one. Let us protect you."

"Come on, Gertie, you know she has powers we don't," Creely said, as I modeled my new biker witch bridal look.

My mom opened her mouth to speak, then decided to close it.

"Cheer up," I told her. "At least I'm not sneaking in the back entrance anymore." I'd come full circle.

Her mouth twisted into a wry smile. "Maybe that wasn't such a bad thing after all."

At least she'd stopped crying.

She sighed as we headed out into the hall. "Who knows? Maybe you'll start a new fashion. I can tell my friends it's couture."

"They'll have to admit it's one-of-a-kind," Grandma agreed.

I only wished I still had my emerald.

I was surprised to see my adoptive father, Cliff, waiting at the bottom of the stairs. He could have come up. Most likely, he was scared off by all of the estrogen.

He had classic good looks and thick, flawlessly styled silver hair. He winked at me as we approached. "Nice belt."

"Don't ask," Hillary said, taking her clipboard from him.

"Good to see you, sweetheart," he said to me. Then to Hillary, "The guests are all seated. Dimitri came down a minute ago. He should be out there." He glanced at me. "I strapped a ring pillow to your dog," he said, as if he couldn't quite believe he'd done that.

It had been their only concession to me. A dog laden with fake jewelry. Well, before mom found out I was a demon slayer.

I briefly wondered how she'd break it to dad, or if she'd want me to do it. This was the woman who took two days to tell dad she'd scratched his Mercedes.

"It's your big day," Dad said fondly.

If he only knew.

I opened up my demon slayer senses to detect any sort of irregularity. There were energies bouncing around this place like crazy. I tried to hone in on the worst of them, the most lethal. But nothing was standing out.

Not yet, at least.

Mom and Grandma had gone ahead, leaving Dad and me in the kitchen.

"Pretty day," he mused.

I wasn't sure what kind of conversation to make, so I peeked out the back door. The late morning sun shone warmly over the grounds. Hillary had set up chairs and a pretty archway overlooking the herb garden. It seemed she hadn't quite had the time to make the rose beds as wedding-ready as she would have liked.

Welcome to my world.

Don't let anything eat you.

The thought sobered me immediately because, around here, things would.

"You always were curious," Dad remarked.

Little had I known.

I watched as Mr. Rodgerson walked my mom down the aisle. Strange how I'd never missed the absence of close family until I'd met the biker witches. Then again, my parents had their friends, which I supposed was nice. If this was any other wedding.

The catering staff had set up to the left of the herb garden, far enough back that I could see the roof of the tent on the other side of a small arbor. Pretty.

Dad squeezed my arm. "I'm sorry I couldn't be here sooner. Your mom said you had a busy a week."

"It was something," I agreed.

I admit I got a little misty eyed when Pirate trotted out last. He had a ring pillow on his back and little tux cuffs above each of his four paws. I saw my mom's handiwork all over it, and I loved her for it.

He greeted several of the biker witches he passed, and stopped for a few pets from the Greeks and even one society lady. Bless her.

Everyone was gathered here for me. The emotion of it struck me in a raw, tense sort of way. I'd never liked to be the center of attention. And this?

It felt so surreal. It felt *off*. Maybe it was because I'd never been about to walk down the aisle before.

I realized I *was* nervous. Had some strange, hidden part of me wanted the show? Or was this simply because I knew Zatar could strike at any time? I tugged my right hand out of dad's and let my fingers rest on my switch stars.

"You'll do fine," he said, patting me on the shoulder.

I was a nervous wreck.

Once my mom had been seated, Dimitri emerged from the gardens to the left. He wore a classic black tux that set off his handsome, exotic features and made him look like a Greek James Bond. He was so going to wear that again for me.

The groom's side to the right of the aisle let out whoops and cheers, startling the bride's side. Well, the society part at least. Grandma and the witches joined in the hollering. Aunt Ophelia practically yodeled. When the racket died down, the crowd waited expectantly.

Dad took my arm in his, and I felt the emotion of the moment well up in me.

Before I could let it get too out of hand, I slid out of his grip and moved to his right side.

"Lizzie," he tried to maneuver around me, "you're doing it backward."

Yes, well, I needed my switch star arm free. "It's an old horseback riding injury," I lied, knowing he'd never paid attention enough to know the difference.

"It won't look good," he warned, when I refused to let go of his right arm.

Neither would a raging demon. I didn't have time to argue. I couldn't shake the sense that we were walking into a trap. I still had no idea who the demon was using. There was nothing to do except try to determine where the attack would come from.

"Help me," I murmured to the ghost whose dress I wore.

A form shimmered at the edge of the aisle, between the porch and the back row. It was her! We wore matching wedding gowns. She became more solid, and I saw she was worn and tired. Heavy chains bound her wrists. Another chain wrapped around her neck and wrapped around her body. The chains at her wrists sliced her skin, drawing blood. They tortured her, bent her shoulders.

My mouth went dry. The connection was tangible between us, so much stronger than before. It was as if an invisible cord linked me to her.

"What do I need to see?" I whispered. *Show me the evil.*

Her expression was stark, her face haunted. A trickled of blood ran from the corner of her mouth as she opened it to speak. "I will show you."

Holy frick. She'd spoken.

I hated to do this to her, but, *can you speed it up?* I channeled to her, as my father led me out onto the porch and down the steps toward the white aisle runner.

The dull thud in my stomach turned into a knot.

"Come on, sweetie." Dad nudged me toward her.

I couldn't even look at dad. I was focused on *her*. It almost looked like she wanted to tell me something else, only she couldn't form the words.

Maybe she was trying to warn me.

The deceased Elizabeth acted as the energy behind the demon. She was the key, if I only knew how to use her. She watched me, her fear unmistakable as she held vigil. Behind her, sat rows and rows of my wedding guests, my loved ones.

These people counted on me to keep them safe. It was my duty as a demon slayer to make this right.

My dad led me straight to where she stood. I could have touched her. The air around her sizzled.

Show me what's wrong, I pleaded.

She shook her head. Her fear turning to pleading. *Look and you will see.*

I don't get it. I didn't see anything. I didn't understand.

A small quartet to the side began playing the first notes of *Pachelbel's Canon*.

It was a haunting melody, a beautiful one. Chairs creaked as my guests stood and turned toward me.

See, the ghost urged.

I don't— Holy hell. I gasped and would have taken a step back if my dad hadn't held onto me so firmly. Row upon row of my friends and family stared at me unblinking, the whites of their eyes were huge and glaring, their pupils radiated a bright and deadly scarlet.

They were possessed. Every last one of them.

Chapter Twenty-Two

"Come on, hon," Dad urged. I looked up at him. His eyes were blazing red as well.

Fuck.

His hand gripped my arm tighter. I couldn't switch star him, or any of them. He pulled me forward, toward them. I could sense the demon's fury. The malice of the crowd split the air. They were on a razor thin leash, a bloodthirsty horde, ready to attack.

We passed by the ghost, and made our way slowly up each of the ten rows to the front, every devilish pair of eyes on me. I tried to tell myself that my friends and family were no different than they had been a few minutes ago. I could just see it now.

It didn't help.

I pasted a smile on my face. I couldn't let the demon know I'd seen through his ruse, if it was even possible to fool him at this point.

Dimitri stood waiting for me at the front. His eyes were blessedly normal, from what I could see. We'd go down together.

With each step I took, I was more and more consumed by their possessed stares, those unblinking red eyes. They followed me all the way down the aisle. They waited for me as Pirate stood near the front row, his gaze glowing red as well.

With each step I took toward my groom, they surrounded me.

Slowly, deliberately, I took each horrifying step through the wedding crowd of the damned. If they attacked, I had no shot. I wasn't an exorcist. And there were too many of them.

Even if there had only been one, I had no idea how to toss demons out of a living soul. And I certainly couldn't kill my mom or my Grandma, or even little Pirate.

The demon had trapped me in the worst way possible.

He'd set out to get me at my own wedding. He'd set a similar trap for the first bride. What I'd give for my necklace right now.

I searched for Rachmort, who was officiating this monstrosity. He stood off to the side, wearing a black suit trimmed with gold. His eyes were pink, not as bad. Lord, who was I kidding? I didn't know what pink meant.

Dimitri was the only other one not exposed. Too bad he didn't know what the hell was going on. His expression tightened, and I could see he felt my fear. It could have been from the way our powers had touched together, or simply because he knew me so well.

Despite the fear, he kept stoic, and so did I as I placed one foot in front of the other. There was nothing else we could do.

At last, I reached him at the ceremonial archway. He took my hands, his lips brushing my cheek.

"Which one is possessed?" he asked, tightly, his breath warm against my ear.

"All of them." I said against his skin.

His fingers tightened on my waist and cursed under his breath as we turned toward Rachmort.

Dimitri's expression betrayed nothing. "You need the emerald," he said, low, so that only I could hear.

No kidding. It held the kind of protection I'd need if a battle broke out here. That's why one of these possessed people had stolen it.

Rachmort strode forward, reaching into his pocket, going for God knew what. My hand itched to draw a switch star.

He withdrew a piece of paper, along with a pair of gold reading glasses that he perched on the end of his nose. I let out a breath I didn't even know I was holding.

"Welcome family and friends," his voice boomed over the crowd. "We are here today…"

Maybe I could call for the necklace. I closed my eyes and pictured the teardrop emerald. I imagined the weight of it, the size, like a large grape. It radiated heat when it was about to act. It vibrated with energy and power. Dimitri's palm warmed against mine as I squeezed tight and let his strength merge with mine. I felt our connection like a physical entity. Dimitri and I were one. The stone was linked to both of us. It had been a gift from him, freely accepted, and meant to be mine.

Mine. It hummed, responding to me like nothing else I'd ever owned. It called to me, wanted me. *Come back.* I pictured it whole and alive again, resting against my chest where it belonged.

I could almost, almost feel it. And then, suddenly, I knew where it was.

It was behind me, in the crowd. I turned as Rachmort began waxing poetic about love.

Grandma sat in the front row, her hands folded over her loose orange tunic dress. She didn't fidget or even blink. Next to her, my mom and dad remained equally distant and detached. It hurt to see the people I loved stare at me so coldly.

Something had grabbed hold of them. The longer they sat in the garden, so close to the center marker, the worse it would get.

I tunneled my thoughts, tried to bury my anxiety, quiet the ticking clock as I forced all of my thoughts, hope and energy toward the stone.

Come to me.

Grandma hissed as a lump formed on her shoulder. My first thought was that something was attacking her, hurting her. I rushed for her as she fought. Groaning and straining, fighting the emerald as it emerged from a hidden seam in her sleeve.

"You took it?" I balked.

The second's hesitation cost me.

She clutched the emerald, used her other hand to grab a live spell from her bra. Dimitri reached her before I did. She hurled the twisting silver spell at me. Dimitri blocked it, and it slammed into his shoulder. Screams erupted from the crowd as black smoke shot up. Dimitri gasped. Horrified, I saw the plume bury him in ash and vapor.

"Dimitri!" I reached him too late. His limbs twitched and stiffened, and he froze solid where he was. She got him with a paralyzer. Damn it.

I ran for Grandma, ready to tackle her if I had to. I couldn't shoot her.

Frieda tossed a spell jar that broke behind me as Grandma took off toward the center-most dark mark. Behind me, I heard my mom scream.

"Go!" Rachmort hollered.

Right. So he could attack her? I searched the crowd. Flappy snarled and beat his wings. Pirate was attacking the ring pillow on his back and mom glared at me with murder in her eyes. Cripes. I didn't want to have to hurt her, or anybody I loved.

Gertie was pushing seventy-seven, but the possessed could move fast. Not to mention the fact that she'd had a head start, and I was in heels. Not like I could take them off around here. I watched her disappear behind an overgrown hedge and ran headlong for that spot.

It opened up onto an arched trellis, laden with vines. Dammit. I kept my hand on my switch stars and ran, my wedding gown catching against my legs, my mind racing to think of a way to take her down. I had crystals. Every stinking one of them was for healing only. I had the ghost, who had disappeared as soon as trouble started and was chained down herself. There was the creature that lived in the back of my utility belt, but I didn't know what he could do, and I hadn't even seen him in a month.

The path curved once, twice. My rib cramped. How hard could it be to catch up to an old lady? One with super-human demon strength.

Cripes.

I saw the center clearing straight ahead. Grandma stood waiting for me, smiling. She held a silver paralyzing spell. It wiggled and curled around her thumb.

I nearly tripped over my heels trying to slow down. She had me alone, in the center of the demon's power zone. She wasn't going to kill me. Not by a long shot. It was clear she wanted me for something far worse.

My heart hammered against my chest, and my breath came in short pants. She merely waited. I couldn't screw this up. Everyone was depending on me—Grandma most of all.

Even if she was about to kick my ass.

Birds screeched. A winged beast the size of a Clydesdale flew in from the west. It was a griffin, with the head of an eagle and the body of a lion. I desperately tried to see if its eyes were red, but it was impossible from this angle. It threw its head back and roared. The griffin's tail swishing against the blue sky, it reached for us, claws outstretched, like a hungry bird of prey.

Grandma threw herself to the ground, and I did, too, not sure who was attacking until I saw gold tips at the end of the wings. Dimitri! Grandma drew the same conclusion, rolling on to her back and hurling a red spell at his head. A death spell.

It exploded against his chest.

Ash and fire rained down. Grandma and I scrambled out of the way as Dimitri landed hard, rolling onto his side. His massive lion's body shuddered, his eagle's beak gaped. Death spells killed by strangulation.

My throat itched, my breath came short as I breathed the putrid air. Or maybe because I was so closely tied to his life force. I rushed to him and tried to turn him over, but he was too heavy.

He lowered his head, gasping as his muscles flexed. I felt the pain of it as his body forced a jarring shift. His wings shook and crumbled. The coarse lion's fur retreated, his griffin form collapsed in on itself until I clutched a gasping, choking, naked human being. My beautiful husband.

Grandma stood above us, smirking.

"Reverse it!" I demanded. It came out as more of a desperate plea. This wasn't a jar spell. I couldn't control it with a counter-brew. If I even had one. No, this was a personal, live spell that would do her bidding and kill the man I loved.

She towered above me, her eyes glowing hot. "You will do as I say now," she demanded, in a hollow voice. "It will be quicker if you are moving and acting freely." She raised her hands and I watched as the sky above us darkened. The ground began to tremble.

Sweet Jesus. "Grandma, push through this," I implored. I needed her back. Desperately. If there was some trace of her inside this shell, I needed to see it. I needed to work with it. I had to find some way to save her, and Dimitri, and myself.

Chapter Twenty-Three

The Earth gave a mighty jolt as Dimitri grasped for breath in my arms.

The demon was coming.

Grandma loomed above me, eyes burning, jaw clenched as she ripped away my slayer essence, channeling my power straight to hell. Holy mother. The last time a demon had tried to do this to me, I'd killed him by ripping his heart out. Could I really do the same to my own Grandmother?

Yes. If it was the only way, I would.

She wore my emerald around her neck, suspended by its delicate bronze chain. It pulsed as the demon drained it as well.

My stomach clenched as the power was slashed from me, piece by horrifying piece. Knees weak, I tried to stand.

"Stay with me," I begged Dimitri.

His face was flushed, his lips had turned blue. He was going to pass out, and in a few seconds, I wasn't going to be able to do anything either. I felt my strength rush away from me in another terrifying throb, leaving me light-headed. I stumbled sideways.

The ground jolted, and I pitched forward toward Grandma.

She jerked sideways, smart enough to stay out of my reach. "What? Am I not draining you fast enough?" Her mouth set into a hard line as she upped the voltage. Pain seared through me, and I watched her shake and suffer as it stole her life force as well.

Shit. She wasn't going to draw this out. Unlike the demon I'd bested in hell, Grandma didn't play. She knew me and was intimately aware of what I could do to her given half a chance.

She was utterly ruthless, willing to end herself, implode us both in order to end it quickly.

I had to get the necklace and free Grandma if I even hoped to save Dimitri and beat back the demon. My limbs heavy, my breath came in pants.

Dimitri lay motionless, his face in the dirt.

I tried to crawl to him. "Let me at least be with him," I screamed. I couldn't even say the last part, *as he dies*.

Panic flashed in her eyes. "I ain't falling for that shit," she said, blasting me in the stomach, driving me farther away.

The Earth pitched. I used the tilt along with my last bit of power to drive myself off the ground and launch myself at Grandma. I levitated for a brief, hot moment and went straight for her neck.

My fingers closed against the emerald. It was brutally cold, searing to the touch. I held on like the souls of everyone I loved depended on it.

I ripped the stone from her neck and fell backward, knowing I was in deep shit as I retreated, broken and unable to fight back. My pulse pounded in my ears, and I struggled to even feel my arms and legs. But I had it! I had the emerald, clutched in my hand.

Grandma grabbed me by the hair. She jerked me up painfully and drew a dagger out of her pocket. She unsheathed it with her teeth.

The necklace chain went liquid and wound around my hand. The humming metal streaked up my arm and circled my throat. It attempted to harden, but not fast enough as she exposed my throat and slashed down at my jugular.

The knife sliced straight through the soft metal. I gasped. I was beyond the pain. I waited instead for the blood.

And revenge.

Sure as hell, my Grandma wasn't behind this. The demon was.

He might be strong, but I was, too. I used my last remnant of hope to hit her with a full blast of angel power. It was the only thing I had left, the one edge I had to combat a demon.

I dug deep, past my hurt and anger and fear. I searched for the love I had for Dimitri, who lay dying or possibly even dead on the ground. He was the man who gave me everything of himself, who made my real wedding possible and who would never leave me, come hell or demon spawn. I thought of Hillary, who shocked me by being willing to change for me, a demon slayer, a girl who wore a switch star belt to walk down the aisle. Pirate, who only wanted to be with me, no matter where I was or what I was doing. And who was going to have to tolerate a lot more nights locked outside my bedroom if I had anything to say about it. I also had my biker friends, who were willing to ride hard, live on the run, and then go to a society tea party for me. Because they loved me.

I shoved all of that power, all of that love at the demon inside Grandma. And I redoubled it when I thought of Grandma herself, how hard she must have fought before she succumbed, how she was the one who always stood up for me, and accepted me, and challenged me to be something more than I ever imagined I could be.

She staggered back under the force of pure energy and love. It drove me to the ground as blinding light blazed from my hands. I kept pushing it out, even as I emptied myself of power, and energy, and life.

"Enough!" Grandma screamed, covering her eyes, her hair whipping behind her. "I'm back! I'm back!"

I poured everything I had into blasting her even harder.

She jolted back, fighting me, clawing at it like it was a swarm of angry bees. "You always gotta overdo every fucking thing."

The power flowed from me. My nose ran. My teeth rattled. I clenched them harder.

"Stop it!" she screamed. She fisted her hands at her sides. "Give me a God damned break!" she glared at me. That's when I saw her eyes were sky blue. Normal.

I gasped and let my own hands drop to my side, immediately feeling the weight of them. A chill ripped through me. If I wasn't careful, I was going to pass out. "You have to help Dimitri."

Grandma staggered over to where he lay. I had to crawl.

"Shit, shit, shit," she muttered under her breath. She dug in her bra until she drew out a wriggling white spell. She swayed on her feet, yanking off the top of the silver snake ring on her left hand. She tossed the severed cobra head onto the ground. Protruding from the ring, which was now basically a snake neck, was a lethal looking needle. Grandma plunged it into her chest.

I stumbled to my knees, ready to blast her again if I had to. I didn't know if I had the strength.

The needle pierced the flesh above her heart. She breathed like she'd run a marathon, winding the spell around and around the bloody snake head.

It was the counter spell. I'd used one last year, on Ant Eater. From a jar.

She drew back and launched it at Dimitri.

It sizzled over him, piercing the skin at his neck as I struggled to reach my husband. The top of the ring lay on the ground, untouched.

"Did it work?" I asked. I didn't know what was still wrong with her, or how long I'd freed her, and the scary thing was, I didn't care. Right now, we needed to save Dimitri. The rest of it, I could handle if I just had him.

Grandma looked like she was about to faint. Bright red blood stained her tunic. "Turn him over."

Hands shaking, I did as she asked. Dirt clung to his cheek. He wasn't breathing. Oh my God. I couldn't lose him now. We'd come too far for this.

The spell glowed at his throat. I shoved hard at his chest, forcing the air out. He gasped hard and took one glorious, shallow, unsteady breath, then another. The relief of it staggered me.

I watched him for a moment, soaking it in.

I held his head in my lap, murmuring against his cheek, as Grandma sat down hard next to me, her hair tangled around her eyes, her skin pale and slicked with sweat. "Christ. I feel like I got plastered by a semi."

"Try a demon," I said. Dimitri's breathing evened out. He still hadn't opened his eyes. By all that was holy, it made me sick to think how close we'd come to losing him.

The ground rumbled beneath us. We weren't out of this yet. Not by a long shot.

Grandma clenched her teeth and closed her eyes.

Her entire body trembled.

Pure dread settled in my stomach as I tried to recover. "The demon's coming back." She wasn't free.

She grit her teeth. "Not yet."

No, but soon. I brought my hand up to my neck where she'd tried to knife me, shocked I hadn't bled out all over the ground. The emerald lay over my jugular. I hadn't even felt it move. To be fair, I could still barely feel my own hands and arms. My finger caught in a groove, and I realized the knife had cut a deep gash in the stone.

Dimitri's eyes opened and he coughed.

"Don't speak," I told him. The skin on his neck was bright red and I didn't know if he had a crushed windpipe or larynx or what.

Grandma shook her head. "Look Lizzie, there's not much time. The demon still has his hooks in me, and he's pushing back hard. Kill me if you have to, but another will come, and another, and not even you can fight off an entire clan of possessed griffins."

I didn't get it. "Why did he possess everyone?"

"Because his first two attacks on you failed, and it frustrated him. When you took off the emerald, he saw an opening, and decided the wedding was the best moment to overwhelm you with force, so he wouldn't fail again."

I looked down at Dimitri. "Well, it's working!"

"No shit, but it's stringing out his power. Break one chain and the whole web unravels—" She clutched at her middle.

"Grandma?!"

Her eyes met mine in horror. "We're too late…"

Dimitri choked. I didn't even know if he'd been well enough to listen. "Go," he waved me off, "I'll catch up."

I hesitated. Hades. He'd nearly died, and I was about to leave him lying here.

"Lizzie," Grandma said, working her way to her feet. "He's right," she said, planting her hands on her knees for support. "Your wedding over there is the key. Zatar needs a blast of power. That means a lot of souls in one place. You brought everybody together."

For heaven's sake. I tried to stand. "I didn't even want a big wedding."

She snorted. "Too late." We both flinched as a boom sounded from the herb garden. She shook her head. "He's coming. We gotta get over there."

I glanced one last time at Dimitri, who had one hand braced on the ground.

"I'll be back," I said, in the most optimistic statement of all time, seeing as I could barely stand, much less fight the Earl of Hell.

Grandma and I took off for the arched trellis in a staggering run.

The sky had grown dark. The Earth rumbled.

Grandma braced her hand against the woven wood as we made the first turn. Her eyes were still normal, but I was waiting for them to go pink. I didn't know what I would do if it happened in here. "You okay?" I called out to her.

She shook her head, still guiding herself along the wall with her hand. "Mostly."

We made the second turn, and I smelled sulfur up ahead. "I can't blast everybody."

She didn't argue. Crimeny. What was there to argue about? It had been hard enough to free Grandma.

My head felt hazy, but I tried to think. "Rachmort deals with lost souls. Can he help?"

We both breathed heavy as we made it toward the last turn. "Is he compromised?"

"Pink eyes."

"Don't trust him. Hell, don't trust me." She doubled over and fought another wave of possession. I stopped, gripping her shoulder to steady her and myself. "The dead bride is the key," she said. Grandma shook me off, and we started moving again. "She is the one powering his connection. Free her and you free us all."

CHAPTER TWENTY-FOUR

Sure. Focus on the dead bride. I was going to be a dead bride if I didn't fix this.

The emerald at my neck warmed, and the metal around it softened and began to snake down my chest.

We broke out of the covered trellis and into an overgrown section of the garden bordered by a tall hedge. The ground rumbled. Smoke and shouting erupted from the other side. I couldn't imagine what was happening, but it wasn't good. The acrid stench of sulfur burned my nose.

My poor mom and dad. Cliff and Hillary didn't deserve this. They never asked to be a part of this world. I'd dragged them into it, and now a demon had them.

Zatar held power over everyone I'd ever loved.

Liquid metal wound around my right arm. Well, it had better hurry. We were going into battle. I drew a switch star and prepared to round the hedge wall.

"Hold up." Grandma grabbed my shoulder at the last minute and shoved my back against the prickly, overgrown bush. "They're going to attack." Her mouth set in a grim line.

No kidding. Unless she was talking about something different. "Do you mean Cliff and Hillary?" No way I could hurt them back.

Grandma was desperate, on edge. "Everyone." She gave me a hard shake. "Zatar's orders are for us to rip you apart, keep you breathing only long enough so he can suction your power and use it to break out of hell."

Cripes. Maybe I didn't want to duck around the hedge.

The ground shook, and I nearly tumbled out anyway.

Okay. *Think.* "Can you fend them off long enough for me to try and free the ghost?"

Her grip on my shoulder tightened. "No."

"Why the hell not?"

She clenched her teeth. "I'm going under."

Fuck a duck.

Then I saw it. Her eyes were going pink around the edges. I shoved her away. "Stay with me as long as you can. That's an order!"

She groaned and punched at the air. "God damned mother fucking demon!"

Yeah, well, she could get pissed off later. "Let's go!"

"Me first," she said, surprising me as she darted out in front. Smart. It could buy me an extra second if they saw her first. The emerald necklace had re-formed into a single, iron arm guard with a row of sharp spikes and the locket at the center. It covered my entire left forearm.

Grandma drew up short, and I nearly ran into the back of her. My guests were in a full-scale battle with each other. It was biker witches against Greeks against society mavens against more biker witches. It was as if they had been primed to hate, born to violence.

Frieda had climbed onto Aunt Ophelia's back and had her hands wrapped around her neck. The large Greek woman spun and sat, crushing Frieda against a white folding chair as the biker witch tried to take a bite out of the older woman's ear.

A sharp pain lanced my ankle. "Ow!" Pirate had sunk his teeth into my skin. I yanked him away, careful not to hurt him, losing my shoe in the process.

I had him by the collar. He bared his teeth. "Die, demon slayer!"

"Gimme!" Grandma snatched him, and he tried to take a chunk out of her arm.

Flappy shrieked and I watched him crush the catering tent, blood lust in his eyes. The white dragon's razor-sharp claws ripped through the thick canvas and shot out as he flew straight for me.

Frick! I ran, dodging hockey great Matt Shott, and taking out Mrs. Rodgerson who had lost her blonde wig and was kicking a live spell jar at Antonio and Creely. Luckily, I was going down because Sidecar Bob had tossed a spell jar at my head.

I fell onto my right knee. A Mind Wiper spell headed straight for me, and I deflected it with my bronze-plated arm.

The ghost stood in the center of the horde, shackled, held in place by a demonic force.

Flappy was almost on me, claws out. Grandma's eyes were hot pink.

"Go get her!" she screamed, as I scrambled to my feet. Grandma dove in front of Flappy and took the shot meant for me.

Zatar's power crackled in the air like loose lightning.

I ran for the ghost, and when I glanced back, I saw Grandma rising from the ground, her shoulder bloody, her eyes scarlet, and her stare lethal.

Rachmort came at me from the side. I threw out my arm, ready to block him when he dove past me and took Ant Eater down.

White wedding chairs littered the ground. I shoved them aside as I made my way to the ghost. She clutched at the chains that held her. The manacles were lined with sharp spikes that pierced her skin. Rivulets of blood ran down her body. I didn't know what I was going to do to get them off of her.

How do you break a soul bond?

"Get her!" Creely hollered, and the entire crowd shifted its malice toward me.

Holy hell. I needed a minute. *By all that was holy. Please!*

A cool blue jolt of power seared through me. Clan magic. I hoped to God. It numbed my ring finger as it rose up from my skye stones, encasing both the ghost and me. Creely bounced off the blue energy and fell to the ground, stunned. I couldn't quite believe it myself.

I was shaking. My demon slayer instincts screamed for me to draw a switch star, to kill them all. It took everything I had to turn my back on the mad rush of bikers, in-laws and society mavens set to attack. I had to trust Dimitri's magic, and my own.

I had only one idea on how to free the ghost, and it had better work. I reached for the locket, and this time it, it clicked open at my touch.

The grave dirt had to be the answer. I'd known all along I needed to take it, I just didn't know why. But this dirt was from the place where her family and friends had mourned for her. They'd prayed over her. Used their meager resources to build a monument to remember her. Those people hadn't been able to reach her in the dark place she'd been taken. She was shackled. Cold and alone. But she was loved. I could bring that love to her.

"I have you," I said to the ghost. "I'm here." I touched the rich dirt to her hands, poured the black Earth into her outstretched palms, and the chains fell away.

A look of wonder crossed her face. Her skin began to glow. She reached for me, caressing the dress I wore, then whispered her fingers against my cheek in a silent caress. *Thank you.* She grew more and more radiant. Her words echoed in my mind as she broke free and began to rise up.

I focused on her bravery and her determination. She'd been a prisoner of the demon for more than a century. I couldn't imagine the horror of her wedding night, the betrayal she faced as a human sacrifice. She'd had her very soul chained. She'd been brutally used. They'd taken everything from her. Yet, she never gave up hope.

Amazing.

She must have seen her chance when the demon lured my mom to this place. The dead Elizabeth had called to me, even when I couldn't hear her. She'd asked me to her grave. My necklace had responded. It began to glow, stopping me along the road even when I didn't know why. It had even offered me a vessel when I felt compelled to try and make a difference.

To think, she ended up saving me as well.

I watched her rise and as she slowly ascended, I drew on my angelic strength to try and help her along on her journey. It flowed to me despite the ugliness of today. It was the light in all of us, the light we sometimes have to choose in order to see.

I released it out to her. She glanced back and smiled. For one brief moment, I saw her embrace the joyful spirits waiting for her, before I lost her in the clouds.

The Earth had quieted. The fighting around me ceased. My guests had stopped trying to kill me, and each other.

They looked rather dazed, in fact. Creely sat on the ground, confused as to how she'd gotten there. Mrs. Rodgerson stared at the blonde wig in her hand. Grandma cursed at the blood on her arm, and Pirate made a face, as if he didn't like the taste of what he'd been trying to chomp.

Hillary lowered the folding chair she'd been ready to smash into my head. "What on Earth?"

A middle-aged Greek woman stood next to her, dazed, and handed Hillary the sleeve to her white mother-of-the-bride jacket. "I found this," she said, clearly not quite sure where she'd gotten it.

Frieda wandered over to Grandma. "That was some earthquake." She stopped, holding her stomach where Ophelia had sat on her. "I think my girdle's too tight."

I tried to do a mental headcount, which was hard when none of them were standing still. "Is everybody okay?" I asked. If they were, I wanted to get back to Dimitri and see how he was doing.

"How's my hair?" my mom asked me, tucking a few strands behind her ear, missing the large chunk standing up in the back.

That's when I saw Dimitri stagger out from behind Flappy. He looked a little worse for wear, even though he wore a new tux. The shirt was buttoned only part of the way up, exposing his upper chest and throat. The dragon licked him, and rolled onto his back for a belly scratch, as if he hadn't probably been trying to eat my fiancé a minute or two ago.

"Thank heaven," he headed toward me, and I met him halfway, glad he was still in one piece. It was a miracle we all were.

He hugged me tight, and I savored the feel of him, and the steady rise and fall of his chest.

When I at last drew back, I had to ask, "where'd you get the new tux?"

He shook his head and drew a bow tie out of his pocket. "Antonio had one stashed, in case that date you're supposed to get him with Dyonne goes really, really well."

Mrs. VanWillen moved to stand next to mom. "I've heard of the earthquakes in California," she tsked. "What will you do now?"

I drew back from Dimitri. "We're going to do the wedding anyway. Mom picked out the perfect spot," I said, watching her blush.

"Yes," Dimitri agreed. "And while not even Hillary can plan around earthquakes, everyone we love is here, and this is where we want to be."

Hillary beamed. The society folk clapped politely and the biker witches started clearing chairs. Meanwhile, Dimitri cleaned up and a few of my in-laws managed to put out a few small fires we'd neglected to worry about.

A few minutes later, Pirate had retrieved the ring pillow and our loved ones began gathering with us in the former herb garden.

Dimitri and I stood at the center, holding hands as everyone surrounded us. My father stood at my left. My mother stood at my right. Rachmort eased his way past Aunt Ophelia, digging in his pockets for his glasses. They were broken. He put them on anyway.

He gave us a warm smile. At last, everything was as it should be. "Welcome family and friends," he began, reading with the intact lower part of his bifocals. "We are here today to celebrate the joining of Lizzie and Dimitri. I've watched both of them as they've grown to love each other, and I can't think of a more suitable," he paused, looking over the destruction, "loving place for them to be." He glanced out over the crowd. "You helped make it that way."

A cold nose nudged me under my dress. Pirate gazed up at me. "Psst. Lizzie! I've got the rings!"

He didn't. But I managed to pry the plastic ones off his pillow anyway.

Rachmort cleared his throat. "Elizabeth Gertrude Brown, do you take Dimitri Helios Kallinikos to be your lawfully wedded husband, now and forever?"

"I do," I said. Dimitri was much, much more than that. He was the keeper of my soul.

My father handed me the real ring. I'd chosen a simple gold band, engraved with our names inside. I slipped it onto Dimitri's finger, and his hands closed around mine. Then we both smiled as I added the plastic one onto his pinkie. It had to be good luck if Pirate hadn't lost it.

"Dimitri Helios Kallinikos, do you take Elizabeth Gertrude Brown to be your lawfully wedded wife, now and forever?"

"I do," he said, "with all my heart," as he touched the skye stones on my ring and kissed me.

†††

The catering tent had been destroyed in the mob action at the start of my wedding, but lucky for us, the biker witches still had all of the supplies they'd gathered for the post-wedding kegger.

They'd strung lights up over the back porch, tapped the keg and placed Dimitri and me in the lawn chairs of honor. Mine even had a white and silver bow.

You're My Best Friend by Queen blared out over the speakers. Dimitri's in-laws danced on the lawn, while Diana and Dyonne fended off a couple of suitors who had crashed the wedding, perhaps hoping Rachmort would perform an extra ceremony or two.

"I wonder what happened to Neal," I said. His garage band was supposed to play this gig.

Dimitri shook his head. "Neal's always late. I think the party will survive without him."

The Pabst Blue Ribbon was certainly flowing. Hillary held out her cup while Cliff manned the tap. "I haven't done this since college," she giggled.

The Rodgersons and the VanWillens stood out on the grass by the slip-n-slide, oohing and aahing over the creative entertainment, while Frieda and a bunch of other biker witches got mostly soaked. The rest of the society mavens wondered at a "completely devious and intoxicating" new snack that Ant Eater had dubbed, "pelures de porc."

Meanwhile, I accepted a plastic cup from Grandma and watched her plop down with us. I was truly lucky to have these people in my life. This is all I'd wanted, a place where we could all come together.

I took a sip of beer. "You look beat," I told her.

She swore. "Being possessed does that to a person."

"Do you even know when it started?" Dimitri asked, twining his fingers in mine.

She shook her head. "It had to be right after we got here. I was losing hours, stumbling around. I knew Zatar had done something to me, but he made it impossible to say anything. Then Ant Eater confronted me, and he got her, too. It spread like a disease."

Dimitri squeezed my hand. "The dress was my first clue."

Grandma winced. "It was designed to weaken her." She turned to me. " Zatar wanted to take your power, your soul at the wedding. He needed all of us eventually, but your demon slayer energy was key. He didn't want you fighting back." She took a swig of her drink. "The poison would have blended into the material better. But you tried it on right away."

Ha. Well, "I was angry."

She harrumphed. "Pissed is more like it." She frowned. "The curses were supposed to weaken you, too. Or else they would have killed mister hot stuff over here," she said, glancing at Dimitri.

"It was worth the risk," he said, as if we weren't talking about his life.

Did I know how to pick them or what?

Creely walked over, the bottom of her shirt full of pork rinds. "Have the corn dogs come out yet?"

Grandma shrugged. "Ask Melody. She's manning the kitchen."

Creely cursed. "She's probably in there eating them."

Grandma grinned. "Creely here was one of the last to fall."

"No kidding?" The engineering witch stood a little taller. "I didn't feel it."

Grandma rolled her eyes. "You're too damned logical. Your mind has no cracks." Creely smiled at that. Then frowned when Grandma added, "Zatar got you when you sat down and got all misty eyed in the fourth row."

Aww…Creely cared.

She made a break for the corn dogs.

"Sorry about your emerald," Grandma said.

I ran a finger over the stone. It had healed itself, but there was a soft line running through it where the gash had been. "It gives it personality." And it had survived. We all had.

My mom dragged a half-burned wedding chair over to our little group and sat down. "Are we safe now?"

she asked, doing a butt dance in her seat, "because I have a surprise for you."

The back door opened and Melody the weapons witch came out, holding an artfully stacked tray of Twinkies. They were shaped into an "L" and a "D."

"It was the only thing they had," mom said, quickly, "but if you get closer, you can see I made little doves out of wrapping paper."

"Martha Stewart, eat your heart out," I said, leaning over to hug her.

"This is a nice party," she said, sitting back, content.

"Now it is." We'd freed the ghost. We'd lifted the darkness.

"All you have left is the honeymoon," my mom teased.

That was one secret I didn't see when I'd entered Dimitri's head. I turned to him. "Where are we going?"

"Hyperborea," he answered triumphantly.

"Hypo-what?" Grandma asked. "What about Vegas or something?"

Too many demons. "I thought Hyperborea was mythical," I said.

Dimitri grinned. "I told you it would be some place fun. It's the griffin version of Monaco," he said proudly, "only less crowded."

"And I think the food's better," Pirate said, curling around my feet.

"You've never been there," I told him. He was my dog. I'd have known.

"No, but I licked the brochures," he said happily. "Did you know they talk to dogs there? And they let dragons stay in your hotel room!"

I turned to Dimitri. "We are not taking the dragon on our honeymoon."

"He's family," Dimitri said, drawing me out of my chair. "Besides, they have special activities for the pets. They can run the obstacle courses, and we'll sneak back to the room. It'll be perfect. You'll see."

I looked deep into his eyes and saw the love I'd sought my whole life. I was humbled and touched by his pure acceptance of me as a person, and at that moment I knew. "It will be perfect because I'll be there with you."

ABOUT THE AUTHOR

Angie Fox is the *New York Times* bestselling author of several books about vampires, werewolves and things that go bump in the night. She claims that researching her books can be just as much fun as writing them. In the name of fact-finding, Angie has ridden with Harley biker gangs, explored the tunnels underneath Hoover Dam and found an interesting recipe for Mamma Coalpot's Southern Skunk Surprise. (She's still working up the courage to try it).

Angie earned a Journalism degree from the University of Missouri-Columbia. She worked in television news and then in advertising before beginning her career as an author. Visit Angie at www.angiefox.com

Made in the USA
San Bernardino, CA
22 November 2013